Brooklyn Wars

Books by Triss Stein

The Erica Donato Mysteries
Brooklyn Bones
Brooklyn Graves
Brooklyn Secrets
Brooklyn Wars

Brooklyn Wars

An Erica Donato Mystery

Triss Stein

Poisoned Pen Press

Poisoned Pen Press
4014 N. Goldwater Blvd., Suite 201
Scottsdale, AZ 85251
www.poisonedpenpress.com
info@poisonedpenpress.com

Printed in the United States of America

For Ella Dobbis Finkelman and Simon Finkelman
Always remembered

Acknowledgments

My thanks to Warren Carson for sharing his remarkable memories of growing up in wartime Brooklyn, to Gil Podorson for telling me about the Navy Yard in the 1960s, and to Anne W. Hamburger, Ph.D., for obtaining a vital resource and for much more.

A shout out to the staff in the Brooklyn Collection of the Brooklyn Public Library, who created and maintain comprehensive files on the Navy Yard. Without them this book would not exist.

To Turnstile Tours for fascinating and informative walks around the Navy Yard.

To Bob, as always, for contract, computer, and proofreading expertise.

Chapter One

You would think three hundred acres of undeveloped Brooklyn real estate could not still be up for grabs. Especially when it is adjacent to a thoroughly gentrified neighborhood and has dramatic Manhattan skyline views. But you would be wrong.

This was once the Brooklyn Navy Yard. The long ago decision to close it forever involved the Department of Defense, Congress, the city government, and several unions. It left lasting scars.

Another long conflict raged about what that valuable piece of land could or should or needed to become. Add in real estate moguls and possibly organizations that prefer to be nameless.

It's Brooklyn. Nothing is obvious.

I considered all this while on a bus stuck in traffic, running late, on my way to a public meeting about the future of this grand spread of formerly public land. I was so late that I would not have time to explore the old docks or see that dramatic skyline view across the river. Damn. You might also think that in New York, with the subway, buses, taxis, and my old, unreliable car, I had a lot of choices for getting from here to there. At rush hour, all of them are bad except the subway. And that did not get very close to my destination.

Trapped on a bus, I could fume about my time being wasted, think about my complicated life, or review my information about this meeting. So I reviewed.

It was always called the Brooklyn Navy Yard, though its proper name was the New York Naval Shipyard. Established in

1801, during World War II it was truly an engine of victory, operating 24/7 to build ships and keep the ones already built in fighting condition. Shipshape, literally.

I was stunned when I learned that sixty-three streetcars a minute stopped at its gates to deliver workers. It held five miles of roads and thirty miles of railroad tracks, a radio station, a hospital, several cafeterias, and a post office for the men—and women!—who worked there. Many of the employees never worked anywhere else.

When the Navy decided in 1963 that it was too outdated to keep open, those people didn't just lose their jobs. They lost their whole world.

This was one of New York's never-ending sagas of land use. I was trapped in my own never-ending saga about land use, writing a history PhD dissertation about how neighborhoods in Brooklyn change over time.

That's why the Yard belonged in my dissertation, no matter what my advisor thought. Maybe what I learned tonight would change her mind.

Even hurrying from the bus, I felt the chilly wind from the harbor but I couldn't see it behind the buildings. I went directly from the street to Building 92, a museum and history center, a handsome modern structure wrapped around the 1857 Marine commandant's residence. I didn't have time to be distracted by the building or its enticing exhibits. I had to hustle upstairs to the meeting space, by then standing-room-only, a mix of Brooklyn types. There were neatly dressed older people; younger ones from the neighborhood, loudly dressed but interested enough to be here; a handful of messy, sleeping bodies, perhaps homeless; and some people with the newest Brooklyn look—lumberjack wannabes.

I spotted my reporter friend, Lisa Wang, who motioned to me to share her seat.

"Look at you! They finally took you off the Chinatown beat?"

She hadn't wanted to be the permanent reporter on immigration issues and Chinese restaurants and had fought for a few years to get more varied assignments.

"Now I'm on hipster Brooklyn and the nearby neighbor-hoods." She sighed but she was joking. "Another stereotype but at least it's a change of scene. What brings you here?"

When I explained, she frowned. "Isn't disagreeing with your advisor like me disagreeing with my editor?"

"Exactly. And here you are, so it worked for you."

I spread out the information sheets handed to me at the door and found a sketched map.

Some of the old buildings had been converted to light industry use, including a large film studio. I knew a bit about that. The derelict property was slowly being transformed into a home for all kinds of businesses, yet there was still a big chunk that seemed empty. Then there was where they laid out the adjoining neighborhoods.

Practically next door was Dumbo, once a bustling industrial neighborhood under the Manhattan Bridge—"Dumbo" for DownUndertheManhattanBridge—and then a deserted and scary one, and now home to art galleries in the once-abandoned warehouses. The aged cobblestone streets only added to the charm. Artsy Brooklyn. On another side, though, were several housing projects and not much else.

I was properly oriented when the meeting started. A middle-aged man began, introducing the panel of representatives from the city and the companies investing in the Yard. They would present updated plans. He filled in some history, talking about how the neighborhood in its current form, with the projects, was actually built as housing for Navy Yard workers during World War II.

"In those days, the Yard employed seventy thousand men and women." Just before he drifted into nostalgic storytelling, he stopped and admitted that the justly proud history had trickled away to a neighborhood now characterized by steady deterioration.

Before the panel even had a chance to start, the audience was talking.

An older woman, dressed in a dignified suit with a snazzy hat, stood up and demanded the floor. She spoke passionately, addressing in turn the panel and the audience, about how her even more elderly neighbors needed her to take a taxi to a completely different neighborhood and shop for them.

"I can still do it, but what happens to them when I can't? We are talking hardship here! Don't talk to me about hip Brooklyn. We don't need it. Art galleries!" She made a dismissive gesture.

"We need services we can get to. No one can afford to move out of the projects, but here we are, in the heart of New York and we might as well be in a desert. How are we supposed to do with no services? Tell me that. Without a supermarket? Without a bank or a post office? We can't even buy medications, aging as we are and needing them. How are we supposed to live here? In our longtime—in some cases, lifelong!—homes?"

She certainly hit a nerve. Second speaker in and there was already shouting from the back rows, "You tell it!" and "Amen, sister!" and scattered applause.

This was getting interesting. I straightened up, pulled out my notebook, and got ready.

The next speaker, a community organizer, had scathing words about all the promises made and broken as the Yard was redeveloped. "Very nice, very nice that business is doing so well." His voice dripped with sarcasm. "We are so relieved. But community life is not doing well. It is worse every year. Are we getting more jobs? Why should we believe you now? We can't wait forever."

There was a roar of applause and cheers.

The people at the head table looked flustered and even shocked at the intense reaction. They all seemed to be about twenty-three and I could see note cards shaking in their hands. Their pleas of "People, people, we have much more…" were ignored.

At that point a man in the front row got up, turned to glare at the audience and stepped up to the table. He was average height, but with a mysterious air of authority that commanded attention. He wore a suit that looked expensive even from my distance. Sharply barbered silver hair. He was so erect and poised, it took me a minute to see that he was actually quite old, with a deeply lined face. Amend that: lined face that looked carved from rock. When he glared at the audience, everyone calmed down.

I had only a few seconds to wonder how he did that.

"I am taking charge of this meeting, with the permission of your moderator." He turned to her but he was not asking for permission. She nodded quickly, relieved.

"I am Michael Conti, retired city planner and a consultant on redeveloping the Navy Yard. I've been involved with these issues my whole damn life. If there is anything about the Yard I don't know, it isn't worth knowing. You think you know what's needed here? You want to be heard? Then stop acting like children. You are not in charge. And talking about the great old days is for old people. You want things better? Deal with what is, as it is today. Those tough guys who worked at the Yard in the glory days would laugh themselves silly at this meeting." He paused, seeming to collect himself.

"We'll have time for questions at the end, but first you local people need to inform yourself about where we are now. Hear the news. Then you'll have smarter questions. Got that? So listen up."

And here in Brooklyn, where nobody tells nobody nothing about how to behave? I was astonished to see many audience members nodding and accepting his lecture. The meeting then proceeded smoothly, with speakers and charts and, of course, PowerPoint presentations.

The movie studio would expand, with increased traffic, but also with more jobs for local residents. That was written into the contract. Another large building had added two new tenants doing light manufacturing, with only a small number of jobs to start, but with plans to expand now that they had the space. A tour of the building, a beehive of small businesses, was promised.

And there was going to be a new supermarket, with a pharmacy and other services included. Negotiations were moving forward. An announcement was promised to be forthcoming.

Two people jumped up then at opposite sides of the room, the early older speaker and a younger man.

"Why should we believe any of you? Do you know how many years a supermarket has been promised? Do you have any idea?"

A panelist stood up. "But this time it's different. We are moving ahead…."

The younger man said, "It's always been different, every single damn time, but nothing happens and things get worse here while they get better just a neighborhood over."

There was applause and a lot of murmuring. Lisa showed me her notes. She had written in capital letters: ANGRY ROOM. Yes, indeed.

Conti then stood up again. "Hold your horses. We are in down-to-the-wire negotiations with a major supermarket to move in, right on Navy Yard property on Admirals' Row, where the old houses are now."

"Wait just a minute!" A new voice boomed out before the voice's owner even got to his feet. He had a nineteenth-century beard and a checked wool jacket.

"Admirals' Row? Those are historic houses. Why are they not being preserved?"

Some people booed. The conflict of the meeting seemed to shift to "daily life" versus "historic preservation." And historian, though I am, I had to agree with those on the side of daily life.

"Have you seen Admirals' Row any time in the last decade?" Conti sounded increasingly belligerent.

The questioner shook his head. "Only old photos."

"Then do your damn homework before you ask damn fool questions. Oh, boo-hoo, isn't it too bad the buildings were so neglected for so long? But it's too late. They are beyond saving now. Go look. But be careful." His expression changed to a sly smile. "You might get hit by falling bricks. Or step onto rotting wood and disappear into an old cellar." He shook his head. "Two years out, there will definitely be a giant supermarket on that site."

The applause exploded. This was a room full of happy people. Honestly, some were crying. I knew it wasn't just the store. It was that attention had been paid. I thought about the need to obtain soap and medicine and juice when you are old and ill with no place nearby. Or when you have a pack of children and no transportation.

When I was home with a baby and needed milk and diapers, there was a chain supermarket a short stroller-walk away. Remembering that, I was ashamed of dismissing their concerns as trivial, even in my mind.

I leaned over to Lisa. "You want to sneak off to see Admirals' Row while it's still there?"

"Nope, I've got to hustle and ask these people a few questions before they disperse. See you!" She was gone in a flash, all determination to get a useful quote.

I slipped out and cautiously stuck to the road, hoping there would be enough street lighting to take a look. It was cold, with the harbor breeze adding to the late fall chill. A faint harbor smell—salty, fishy, gasoline—mixed with the wet, weedy odor of overgrown trees in a neglected patch of woods.

As it turned out, Conti's taunting suggestion to go look at the derelict buildings was somewhat dishonest. The road was blocked by traffic cones. Perhaps it was in fact as dangerous as he had said. No one was going to be allowed to get close.

On the other hand, traffic cones could be moved. *Could I?* I probably ought to have asked *Should I?*

I was now some distance from the museum and it was dark and quiet and a bit spooky. Over there somewhere, a ghostly presence, was the former Naval hospital, filled with lives saved and lives lost.

I walked in the footsteps of how many generations of sailors and ship-builders? Quick math. Eight, at least. A strange feeling, since I could also hear the hum of six lanes of traffic from the nearby Brooklyn-Queens Expressway.

Was I being foolish? Perhaps. It wasn't the first time I had been…let's say, a little impulsive. I relished having a small adventure when my teenaged daughter was not there to see me setting a bad example.

Dim light from the street beyond the fence was almost enough. I could not get very close, but close enough to see the five houses, small mansions by modern standards. I, too, had seen photos when they were graceful nineteenth-century homes for the officers assigned to the base. How many families had lived there, laughed and played and grieved and grown up?

Time to go. The low background noises from the meeting were diminishing. I certainly did not want to get locked in overnight. Hurrying back toward the Yard entrance I took a wrong turn in the dark and found myself deeper in the old, empty part of the property.

There were faint sounds coming from beyond the wooded area. Someone walking. A watchman? I did not want to stay to find out. I would have to explain what I was doing there. Did I have any explanation except curiosity? Nope. Before I could trace my way back, I saw a shadow of a man. He was near. Two men. Whispering with a vicious undertone. A shout and a lifted arm.

And then I heard a loud sound. It was a sharp pop and it was close. Someone ran away through the trees. What had just happened?

My phone light showed me a man on the ground. Michael Conti. Bleeding.

It took me a moment to realize the voice I heard screaming was my own.

Chapter Two

People came running. Uniformed officers helped me up from the ground, where I had collapsed, and I slowly stopped sobbing. They had huge, bright flashlights and now I could see the path. I could see the man sprawled on the pavement and a person kneeling next to him, trying to stop his bleeding.

As I told them what happened, I heard an ambulance siren in the background, getting louder. When I told the cops who the victim was, they asked me how I knew and would I identify him? I snapped back, "Everyone here would know." I waved vaguely at the gathering crowd and noted, vaguely, that officers were keeping people back and in order. "He was a speaker at the meeting…most of these people were there…probably…."

By then, a couple of other people were talking to an officer. The ambulance arrived. EMS workers jumped out, swiftly did their job, and moved him to a stretcher. They were gone in minutes, siren screaming again. I suspected it didn't matter. I'd seen him shot point-blank. What were his chances?

They asked me again where the shooter had gone. "It was too dark. I could not see." I wanted to go home. On this cool fall night, wearing a fleece jacket, I was shaking with chills.

Finally an authoritative person in ordinary clothes said to someone else, "She couldn't know where he went. Figure it out from the broken foliage. Get some more lights before you try. And be careful!" He turned to me at last. "You can go home. We have all your information. Would you like a ride?"

"Oh, no, no, I can just hop a bus." Then I started trembling again, and he looked at me with some concern.

"Yes, please. A ride."

Afterward, I could not remember one thing about the ride home, not how I got into the car, not how long it took, not how I got out and up my front steps.

My daughter was waiting there. "Mom, what happened? I heard the police car. You looked wrecked." She had her arms around me, helped me to the sofa, and wrapped an afghan around me.

"What can I do? Should I make a cup of tea for you? Or a glass of wine? Call Grandpa? Or Joe?"

"I don't…" I shook my head. My eyes closed, and I felt tears rolling down my cheeks. Was I in shock?

I forced myself to sit up. "Tea. Lots of sugar. And, no! Don't call anyone." My father would have things to say about my walk in a dark wood tonight. I didn't want to hear them. I didn't know how Joe would react. I didn't want to find out.

Chris went into the kitchen and came back with a box of cookies. They were stale and factory-made, but I appreciated the thought and needed the sugar.

She called from the kitchen, "Tea in a minute," and I heard her voice murmuring on her phone. I did not have the energy or focus to argue with her about who she might call. *How unlike me*, I thought, as if observing myself from a long distance.

Five minutes later I had a mug of scorching hot tea in my hands, syrupy with sugar, and there was a knock on the door. *No, no, no*, I thought as I tried to crawl under the afghan.

It was my friend, Darcy, a stroke of brilliance on the part of my daughter. *She's growing up*, I thought vaguely. A year ago, she would have been mad at me for scaring her. Now, at almost sixteen, she is helping.

Darcy handed me a frosted doughnut from the bag she carried and tucked the afghan around me more firmly before saying, "What happened to you? Tell me all."

"Chris called you?"

"That smart kid? Of course she did. Feeling up to talking now?"

So I did. And when I started shaking again, Chris warmed the tea and Darcy handed me a second doughnut.

They were appropriately shocked. Chris suggested looking online so see if there was any more news, but I could barely glimpse Darcy putting a finger to her lips. Right. I didn't want to hear any more news right now.

"I think a hot bath and maybe a sleeping pill. Or a stiff drink." Chris giggled and Darcy added with severity, "You did not hear me say that. Go start the bath. Plenty of bubbles."

Between them, they got me warm and relaxed and into bed with a spoon of nighttime cold medicine to insure rest. I think I managed to say thank you before I fell into a deep sleep, but maybe I dreamed it.

The morning was much different. I felt fine, though I was mysteriously unclear about what day it was. And what time. School day? Chris home? Did I have work at my part-time job?

It was noon. Chris had left me a note:

> Let you sleep and went to school. Home about
> 3:00. Darcy told me to call—she said it was an
> order!—if you needed any help. Grandpa called. I
> didn't tell. Joe called. I didn't tell. But you need to
> handle them. And look here:"

She had typed in a URL. So I looked. Of course I did.

Conti had died. He was probably already dead when they drove him to the hospital. Deep down I'd known it all along. The NYPD spokesman said they had no leads as yet but it was early days and they expected success.

I only had enough patience to skim the rest, absorbing nothing, but I got that he was a big shot in the regional governance of the harbor.

That could be interesting to read. Some other day.

For today, I was done. I was not, then, ready to admit that last night might haunt me for quite a while. I had given my information and now I could return to my life. In fact, I'd better. I had an appointment with my dissertation advisor this afternoon. That ended my plan to crawl back under the afghan for a long nap. What I needed was respectable clothes, enough time to walk to the nearest subway station and allow a twenty-minute ride—no, thirty, in case of delays—to reach City University's Graduate Center, inconveniently placed in mid-town Manhattan.

Inconveniently for me, anyway. I thought it belonged on the Brooklyn College campus where I'd earned my BA.

I dreaded the meeting, and would have even on a normal day. I had a touchy relationship with my new advisor. I missed Dr. Wallace, the warm woman who inspired me to pursue an academic career, mentored me, and always pointed me in the right direction. This one, Dr. Adams, I couldn't figure out at all. To be honest, she scared me, and I did not scare easily.

She was not a New Yorker, and I didn't know how to read her. I've never lived anywhere but New York. In fact, I've never lived anywhere but Brooklyn. Different parts of Brooklyn, which might as well be different worlds, but hey, they are still New York, not San Diego or Bozeman, or wherever the heck she is from. Actually, from Minnesota. I didn't get her, the outward politeness with a hidden agenda, or so I suspected.

She didn't get me either. She didn't get my sarcastic humor or my upfront comments or my overwhelming life. In fact, she had no interest in my life at all.

I picked up an extravagantly overpriced latte on the way to the subway. I also picked up a trashy tabloid with screaming headlines about the murder last night. For real news I read the august *New York Times*, but for a quick read on the subway? The tabloids, news source of choice in blue-collar Brooklyn, my home turf, did the job. You can take the girl out of Flatbush but…

I ditched it before I entered the halls of academia but I held on to the coffee. I needed the moral support.

The office used to be Dr. Wallace's. I waited in the hall, remembering the day she told me she was leaving. She could not be my dissertation advisor long-distance, but Dr. Adams would take me on.

The office door opened at exactly one minute after the hour. Time to woman up. I sighed, remembering how I used to look forward to meetings in this office.

"Now, Erica, I called you in because I am concerned with how slowly you are progressing. You do know you are scheduled for graduation in May? This year? I finally caught up with all my additional advisees and I saw from your records that you have postponed for two years now."

I started to respond but she held her hand up to say stop.

"Yes, I see you are working steadily, but very slowly. You will end up as an ABD and I do not allow that to happen to my advisees."

The dreaded ABD? All But Dissertation? Someone forever stuck between student and employable historian? She was not kidding. There was not even a glimmer of humor in her face. *But ABD would not be me, lady*, I thought but did not say. *You don't know me at all.*

She rolled right on.

"I know you have the department form that lays out a time-table." She looked at me for confirmation and I nodded. I knew I had received it. I also knew that I had not looked at it lately.

"You should be writing the conclusion and summary chapters now. This month. And you are…?"

"Something has come up. There is one more chapter I should add, about the Brooklyn Navy Yard. It's kind of an example… and changing even as we speak…" I was struggling with my own words. "It's history in the making.…"

"Oh, Erica." She shook her head. "It is so easy to get lost in the research, and the actual moment of saying 'enough' gets pushed back again and again. That is fatal.

"I am giving you a schedule. Weekly meetings with me until the winter break." She turned the computer to I could see the screen. "By then you should be polishing a completed draft. You have to be, if you will meet deadlines for defense in time to graduate."

"But Dr. Adams…"

"Yes, it is unusual to work this way with a mature graduate student, but apparently you need a push." She spoke cordially, smiled faintly.

I was so angry I could barely speak. I need a push? What nerve.

"So now," she went on, oh-so-smoothly, "tell me where you are as of today. Do you really need a Navy Yard chapter? Perhaps it doesn't fit into the overall plan and you can attack the conclusion instead."

How could I tell her I didn't always know how information would fit into the overall plan? How it seems necessary to follow research to see where it would lead? And sometimes I got sidetracked? She said she understood but I didn't believe it for a minute. Plus, after last night? My mind really was scattered all over.

"I saw change in real time last night," I said, grasping for a coherent thought. "I went to a community meeting. It became very heated and I took notes."

She did not seem too impressed, which made me want to chatter on, trying to convince her. I stopped, a full stop, jaw clenched.

"And what will you do with these notes and this meeting?"

"There was a man there." The words tumbled out. The idea followed. "He seems to have spent a long lifetime working in and around the harbor, Navy Yard, and then other things. I thought I could follow his career and see what it says about all the changes." I gulped, then continued as inspiration came. "I'd use it like a narrative thread through the data? How did he sustain a career when his world kept changing?"

"As long as you don't get lost in it. Focus on the changes, not the man." She tapped her pencil on the desk. "Tell you what. One week to get that written and move on." She tapped some more. "You're planning to interview him, I suppose? Get his read on all he did? Did you meet him?" I could feel my heartbeat speed up.

"I can't interview him."

She frowned. "Why? Certainly it's worth a shot."

"I can't interview him." I took a deep breath. "No one can. He died. Last night."

"He isn't that man who was murdered?" She looked shocked. "You should stay completely away from the situation. You'd need to include his death if you write about him, and that won't be solved in time for you." She saw me ready to disagree. "This is not your topic and not your job. Your job is to finish."

She stood up. "One week to get back to me, right? Same time and day."

I nodded and fled but I thought about our meeting all the way home. By then I'd convinced myself Conti's career was the perfect lens to view this topic. If I could do a good enough job researching it I knew I could convince her too. I thought I could.

It wasn't until I was on the train, that I counted up how many years I had been doing this, writing my dissertation. Too many. Well, hell. Unlike most of my classmates, I had other responsibilities. A daughter to raise, alone. An old house to keep standing, alone. A part-time job at the Brooklyn History Museum. Constant money worries. Okay, most of my classmates did share that one.

I assumed I would finish it when it was ready to be finished. It's just that I kept encountering new ideas and developments that should be added to the research. I wasn't prolonging it unnecessarily, no matter what Dr. Adams implied.

It might be time for a letter to my old advisor, asking for, well, for advice. Before I said something extremely inadvisable to my new one.

Chris was home from school and unusually bubbly, once she was sure I was now all right.

"So Grandpa says he will drive us to Buffalo when we go see Grandma."

"What did you say?"

My father and my dead husband's mother in one visit? I could not have heard that right.

"You heard me."

Chris had one of the long weekends her private school seemed to throw around at random and I had promised a trip to Buffalo to see her paternal grandmother. That part checked.

She had a big school project on family history, and wanted to interview the grandmother she had not seen in more than year. That part checked.

"Grandpa?"

My father and my husband's mother never had a thing in common. Not religion. Not ethnic background, which still counts for something in Brooklyn and did even more back then. Not age. My youthful parents. Jeff, my late husband, was the last child in a large family—they were almost a generation apart. And both of them difficult people in all the ways that mattered. Stubborn. All-knowing. Always right. Those ways.

"Grandpa said he would drive." She explained it precisely, as if talking to a child. I could choose to call her out on that, or listen to what she was saying. I somewhat reluctantly made the mature choice. "He said our car wasn't reliable enough for a road trip and he would worry," Chris said. "He knows we can't afford to fly and he had nothing else to do."

"Uh, okay, I'm following so far."

"And wait for this! He said we'd drive at night and have more time there! No traffic to slow us down. You and I sleep in the car. How cool is that?"

There were so many ways none of this was cool I did not have energy to list them all.

"How did it come up?"

"Uh, well." Now she was less bubbly. "We were chatting—well, Mom! Don't look like that. You know we chat!—and I told him about the school break and our plans." She jumped up and hugged me. "It will be fun. Seriously."

She had been close to my parents, but she never described visiting her other grandmother as "fun" before. She was always bored in Buffalo. Her cousins were all much older, Grandma was so old-fashioned. True, kids kept changing all the time, but I was curious about what provoked this particular change.

I could call my mother-in-law and probe a bit. Not gonna happen. I could talk to my dad. Sometime. Joe might know. Chris confides in him, turning him into a substitute uncle. Or a dad?

Or I could ask my sister-in-law, Judy. She was the oldest in her large family, practically a third parent to Jeff. Grandma Donato had lived with her in Buffalo since Grandpa Donato died. If I could manage to stay awake after dinner, I would call then.

"Dinner in ten," I shouted upstairs. Suddenly, exhaustion knocked me into a chair. Last night was hitting me and I didn't know if I needed food, a glass of wine, a nap, a funny movie. A hug. Or all of the above and not in that order.

Chris took her plate to watch some TV before returning to homework, and I called Judy.

"Hi, hon, how are you?" she asked.

I lied and said I was fine, no news, we were looking forward to our visit. Lying on all counts.

"Chrissie told me your father would drive. Now that takes some pressure off you, right? And it will be so nice to see him, too. Now that the kids have moved out, we have room for everyone."

Nice to see Dad? Really? Jeff's family and mine had agreed about only one thing, that we were too young. Underlying that perhaps-reasonable objection was the one they never exactly admitted. Italian Catholic boys shouldn't marry Jewish girls of Eastern European ancestry. And vice versa. If we waited, both sets of parents hoped we'd return to our tribes.

Was that now water under the bridge in the Donato family? My own parents had come to love Jeff and were grief-stricken when a drunk driver ended our brief and happy life together.

All those complicated thoughts raced through my mind in seconds, but I only said, "Chris told you our plans?"

"Yes, and Mom is so excited about this visit. She's been digging into boxes in the attic that have been there since she moved in. She's looking for photo albums, family papers. Of course she shouldn't be up in the dusty attic at all with her COPD, but try to argue? You know Mom. Save your breath!"

So she hadn't changed much. And Judy still sounded like a nice Brooklyn girl after decades in the vast upstate. Suddenly I was looking forward to seeing *her* at least.

I didn't know Chris had been calling, though. I guessed it was a good thing, being fired up about a school project. I guessed.

"And she's cooking of course. I hope you're ready to consume lasagna. And veal parm. And a few Sicilian pies!"

I laughed. "Anything I don't cook sounds good to me!"

"So we'll see you soon? Call from the road to let us know about what time?"

"Certainly. And what can we bring you from New York?"

"Honestly? Your presence will keep Mom entertained and that's a gift in itself."

"I think you mean Chris' presence."

She laughed. "Any new face is helpful. And good bagels would be nice."

An endless day after a shocking night. I was yawning. I would leave the dishes until tomorrow. I could hear my mother's ghostly voice on that subject but I ignored it. My housekeeping standards ("What standards?") were, truthfully, pretty slack, but I remembered what else Mom used to say. "My house, my rules." And this was my house.

I think I fell asleep in my clothes. A ringing phone woke me? I squinted at my clock as the phone kept ringing. It was ten o'clock, not the middle of the night. I finally floated up to consciousness and made a lunge for it. Joe.

"When were you planning to tell me what's going on?"

"Uh. What do you mean?"

"I came by late last night. Thought I'd say good-bye before I headed out to this job on the Island, but before I parked I saw Darcy going in, carrying a bag from Dunkin' Donuts. I know a crisis sign in your life." He was teasing, just a bit, but he also sounded cautious. At least it was clear he didn't know anything.

Could he read my mind over the phone line? Because he went on, "Chris will tell me if you don't. Or I could talk to Darcy herself."

"Darcy is no blabbermouth."

He laughed at my vehement response. "True. But Chris will tell me anything."

That might be true. And besides, I did want to tell him. He had that effect on me, something entirely new in my life.

After my explanation, there was a long silence, so long I wondered if we had been cut off. Then, cautiously, he asked, "And you are okay?"

"I am. I am fine."

"You called Darcy. You didn't call me."

"No, Joe. No." I felt a flutter of—what? worry? guilt? "You have it all wrong. Chris called Darcy on her own." I left out the part about telling her not to call him.

Another long silence and then he broke the tension with a laugh.

"Geez, Erica. Do you think maybe wandering off like that was a bad idea?"

"Yes, as it turned out, but I could not have known, could I?" I sounded calm, mature, not defensive. It took effort. "It was just a little walk, with lots of people nearby."

"Sure it was. Sure. But next time it doesn't work out, would you please call me? I'm here. You know?"

"Are we still on for Thursday?"

"You are changing the subject."

"I can't get anything past you." I giggled. Joe has that effect on me, too, another new thing in my life. It had been a lot of years anyone but Chris made me giggle.

"You bet. Pick you up at seven."

Joe and I had been friends for a long time. Now we were something more, but I wasn't sure what it was, and wasn't sure what I wanted it to be either. I was beginning to have a clue about what he wanted, though.

The truth is, I didn't know how to do this anymore. Date like a grown-up. I married so young, maybe I never knew how. Now I was in the midst of trying to understand something as large as the Navy Yard, but I felt baffled by my own life.

Chapter Three

Conti's murder was on the news in all forms and first thing in the morning. It was not the lead story—he was not a rap star or a football player or a former mayor—but the unlikely time and place and victim made it a story. He had been a player in New York for a long time

I saw it on the local news as I made my coffee. The NYPD spokesman sounded deeply harassed. And who could blame him? It had been less than thirty-six hours.

"Do you have leads?" "Witnesses?" "How is his family reacting?"

I scanned the story in the *Times* as I drank my coffee. They had interesting details about Conti's career and wrote reasonably, if not helpfully, "NYPD is working on the situation, with nothing to report so far." They noted that calls to family members and his office were not returned. I read it on my regular Brooklyn news e-lists. They were all doing a good job of keeping the story alive even though they had nothing new to add.

I didn't want to read every word, but I soon learned I wasn't going to be able to avoid it. When I walked past a news shop, it was screaming at me in headlines from the tabloids on display. All of which I bought.

I felt Conti's murder was following me, when all I wanted to do was forget it. Of course I knew that was absurd. No one was sending me messages, but I felt it even more when Lisa called me.

"I can't believe it. I stayed after the meeting to do my job and I missed the actual big story." She paused, then pushed on. "Did you happen to see anything while you were out looking around?"

What I wanted to say was, no. Definitely no. I wanted to not talk about it. Somehow, though, what left my mouth was, "Sort of."

I could hear the intake of her breath. "Do tell."

I started to describe how I happened on the police cars and the ambulance, but I couldn't do it. I'm a terrible liar. It takes too much energy when all my work is about trying to tell the truth.

"I was there. I saw it."

"You...what?"

"I saw it happen."

A long silence. Then, "Can I interview you? Right now? I need you to tell me everything."

"No, no. No! I don't want my name in your paper. I want to forget about it."

"No problem." She sounded unreasonably cheerful about all this. "Reporters have a wonderful friend called 'anonymous sources.' No one will connect you. Tell me all about it."

So I did. She asked a few questions. I said, "That's it. Not much to tell, after all."

Her response was, "Are you kidding? I have more than anyone else. My editor will love me. And I love you." Her jubilant voice changed. "Seriously, thank you. I owe you big-time."

"I might even remind you of that one day. Go write your story."

Back to work, I entered the dates my advisor had forced on me into several calendars, paper and digital. I'll admit that it looked scary. That was certainly her intention.

When I needed a break, I did not head to online news sites. I checked the predicted weather in Buffalo. I jotted a list of things to bring, including bagels. I jotted a reminder to Chris, "Cold at night there. Pack a robe and warm pj's."

And I finally talked to my dad.

"What's this I heard about you coming to Buffalo with us?"

"And good morning to you, too. Did you have a good night's sleep? How was your breakfast?"

"Come on. I have a busy day."

"Well, my breakfast was at a diner, and I had the All American, with eggs, ham, home fries, and rye toast. Thanks for asking."

"Da-ad!" I sounded like a teen-ager. I moderated my voice. "Ok, Dad, I get the point. But I do have a busy day."

"And I got your point. Yeah, Chris and I cooked up that plan. Makes sense, doesn't it? I am certainly the better driver and I have the better car, with a bigger trunk and more legroom."

Plenty of room in that old gas guzzler, it was true, and he kept it in perfect condition. I could not say the same about my ancient Corolla.

"But listen, Dad? You and Jeff's mom were never the best of friends." To say the least. "I'm not so sure this will work out. All of us under the same roof and all."

"I offered to stay at a motel, but Judy wouldn't hear of it. Worse comes to worse, I will stay with an old friend. She couldn't object to that."

"How do you have an old friend in Buffalo?"

"His name is Western. Best Western."

"Ah. Okay. But that doesn't do anything about Jeff's mom."

"Phyllis? You worry too much. Her and me, we talked some after Jeff died. And she sent me a nice card when your mom left us. There was a saint on it but the thought was kind. I think she's mellowed."

That was a stretch but I could see I was never going to talk him out of this. Not with Chris ganging up on his side. Plus, it's true, his car is much more reliable.

"So your plan is?"

"Pick you up after dinner Friday. Less traffic at night, you and Chris sleep in the car. Get there maybe midnight."

"But did you talk to…?"

"Yes, talked to Judy. She said any time is fine, she'll have the coffee and cake waiting. She was always a nice girl."

"Speaking of food, I hear Phyllis has been cooking up a storm."

He laughed.

So there we were with a plan.

I did my other chores. Packed haphazardly. As long as I had clean underwear and warm pj's I would be fine wearing sweat pants and a warm sweater around the house. Then I spell-checked the report for work and sent it in.

I hustled out to finish my errands and picked up a pizza for Chris.

I took a deep breath then. Now to get ready to go out. On a date. I guessed it was a date. I still had to do some mental gymnastics to think I was dating Joe.

Joe knows me very well, too well maybe, and has seen me with dried glue in my hair scraping old wallpaper, sweaty after a long bike ride in the summer heat, with eyes swollen with tears when a family friend died. But now that things were different, or moving that way, I thought I should make a little effort. Shower and shiny blow-dried hair. Check. But what to wear to a local restaurant? Much nicer than pizza or the abundant fancy hamburger places? Clean jeans? Steal a cute top from Chris? And some makeup? Was that the right amount of effort? Or was that trying too hard?

It was a long, contemplative shower

In spite of my confusion about what to do, how to dress, and then the underlying question of what we were doing, the idea of seeing him put a smile on my face.

Oh, yes, I was in some real trouble here. And to think we used to just be friends.

● ● ● ● ●

I did date occasionally, after I had crawled out of the shock of becoming a widow with a three-year-old, but it took me years to get there. It always seemed a little pointless, though. No one was Jeff, so why bother? Recently I'd been seeing the older brother of a high school friend, but in the end, it was too much like dating a cousin. Too familiar. We stopped with no hard feelings.

And then there was one intense fling, when Chris was away at camp. With an impressive man who turned out to have ulterior motives. It left me with a bruised heart and ego.

This was different. Whatever "this" was.

Dad likes him. But then, Dad's judgment in this area is questionable, to say the least. That Woman, his girlfriend after mom died, was a disaster.

Chris likes the idea. Loves the idea. Campaigned for it long before it was even a possibility. I have told her I don't take romantic advice from someone too young to have a driver's license. Her recent retort has been that in most of the state, she'd be driving right after her fast-approaching sixteenth birthday.

Darcy makes fun of me. She says I am over-thinking. Just go with it, she says. He's a good guy and he likes you, in spite of knowing you so well.

Of course her judgment is suspect too. She introduced me to the last disaster. And she has been married since the week she graduated from college, so what does she really know? She pointed out that with four grown children, there was no form of romantic dilemma she had not heard about, from the married man to the girlfriend who liked women better than men after all.

Chris gave me a passing grade on my outfit, fluffed my hair, and told me, shaking her head, "Nicer shoes, mom! I keep telling you! Try the black sandals." She called to my exiting back, "The ones with heels!" I was not taking love life advice from her, but for fashion? Well, I am that desperate sometimes.

We were going slow, Joe and me. He's made it clear that his skirt-chasing days are on hold indefinitely, but maybe not forever. And yet, every time I am tempted to speed things up, I pull back. Fear? Of him? Not likely. Of losing what we do have. Maybe.

And yet, I was all smiles waiting for him. Chris gently turned me to the mirror. "See?" Then she retreated to her room.

"What? Don't you want to say hi? Catch up?"

There is no sarcasm on earth like a teen's simple, "Sure thing."

When he came in, I was tempted to walk right into his arms. And then I didn't. It didn't matter. He walked right into mine. I had no problem with that.

"I missed you, out there alone in the wilderness of Suffolk County." He whispered it into my ear, while hugging me.

I leaned back to make it possible to look at him. "The wilderness? Easthampton? Home of the rich and chic?"

"Not my kind of place. I'm glad to be back home. Ready? I'll tell you about it over dinner."

"Chris! We're going," I shouted in an upstairs direction.

She shouted down, "Yeah, yeah. Have fun." A giggle, then, "Don't stay out too late."

"My kid is a wiseass."

"Yes, she is. It's one of her most endearing qualities."

"You don't live with it full time." I wasn't truly complaining, though. I was in too good a mood for that.

We walked over to a surprisingly elegant neighborhood steak restaurant. I'd never been there before; I couldn't possibly afford it. It was a lovely room, quiet and pretty; promising menu, without a doubt the best meal I'd had all week; service that made me sink in my comfortable chair, ready to be pampered. I leaned back and sighed.

Joe raised an eyebrow at me.

"Tough week? Are you planning to tell me more about it?"

So I did. And ended with, "And you can't say I did something foolish. There was no reason that little walk should have been dangerous. None! There was a whole meeting room full of people just a shout away."

He smiled. "Dark and empty path? Trees hiding you from the meeting area? Everyone still indoors when you went exploring? How could there possibly any danger?"

"That's why I didn't want to tell you. That attitude, right there."

"I'm just glad you didn't feel compelled to intervene."

"It happened too fast. And you still think I am an idiot." I wanted to be angry. I hate being told what to do. But the way he was looking at me made it hard to sustain. Then he laughed, and I had to, too.

"Things just seem to happen to you. It's amazing."

Our appetizers came, fancy little things I couldn't pronounce but looked yummy. I was starved and could not remember last time I'd had a real sit-down meal. We didn't need to talk for a while.

Then he looked at me. "There is something else. I can tell. Give."

"How can you tell?"

He just smiled back.

"I met with my advisor today." I needed a gulp of wine to continue. "She put me on a schedule. Me! As if I am in a freshman writing class! She seems to think I am malingering and will never finish." I reached for more wine.

"I have wondered about that." He quickly added, "No, not the malingering. I know you aren't. But are you going to be a student forever?"

"That's ridiculous. And insulting, too. You know I am working hard at it."

"Of course I do. No insult intended. But don't you need to leave the cocoon sometime? What comes next?"

Our dinners came just in time to stop the conversation. After a few delicious bites, Joe clinked his glass at mine. "I'm not pushing you. Not my job. So here's to getting the job done, whenever you do."

I could certainly agree to that.

After we'd made happy inroads into our meal, Joe said, "I've been thinking. I'm told that the big step in a modern relationship—hey, don't look so scared!—is exchanging keys." He wasn't looking at me.

"What?" I dropped the chunk of asparagus flan I had speared. "You've always had keys to my house, since right after I met you." He's my contractor. Of course he has keys. I even call him when I can't find mine.

"But you don't have mine." His expression was brimming with anticipation as he dangled a small key chain from his index finger.

"Well. Should I faint and say 'Why sir, this is so sudden'?"

"You can't faint and talk at the same time."

I gave him that 'don't try my patience' look I usually reserve for Chris.

"So what do you think?"

"Ah, yes. Umm, are there other sets out there in the universe, in other purses?"

"Nope. Not in a long time."

So I knew this was not nothing. I took a deep breath and put them in my own purse. With a smile.

He held my hand under the table. "Eat up but save dessert room." Afterwards, I didn't remember what I had for dessert. That has never happened before.

As we walked home, content and slightly buzzed, he said, "Tell me about this trip to Buffalo."

"Oh, my Lord. What do you know?"

"A lot. Chris told me. You and Chris and your dad and your mother-in-law?"

"That's it. With three of the above stuck in a car together for about seven hours."

"Sounds fun."

I lightly punched his arm before snuggling back in. "Not at all. As you know very well."

"You going to be a crazy woman when you get home?"

"Very possibly."

"Something to look forward to."

"If I am, will you hate it?"

"Don't be ridiculous." He held me a little tighter. "I have big shoulders. Use 'em to lean on."

We said good-bye at my house, in the dark corner where the high stoop meets the wall. It took quite a while and included some heavy breathing.

We stopped for a break. "Is this too much like being teenagers?"

"Oh, yeah. Only now we're hiding from your kid instead of your parents."

"Sure have made a lot of progress in our lives." I giggled. "But no, we're not going into my house with Chris at home."

"I know. Those keys I gave you?" He looked at me seriously, smoothing my hair. "We should start using them. No pressure, but give it some thought." A quick final peck. "Come back from your trip with everyone in one piece, okay? No arrests. No felonies. And if it gets completely crazy, remember I'm only a phone call away."

"I got it. That helps."

Another kiss and we said good night.

I had a phone message when I went in, a shaky woman's voice I didn't recognize.

"They say you were the last person to see Michael Conti alive. Could I talk to you? I want…" A deep breath. "I need to know…I'd like to talk to you."

No name. No identifying information. Not a business call. Not a reporter. And how the hell did she know I was there?

No, I thought. *Absolutely not.* I didn't want to talk about this anymore and certainly not with a total stranger. Not tonight and maybe not ever. I hit the Reply button, and harder than needed.

"I am going to be unavailable for three days. Call again next week if you still want to talk to me." So I guess I had a moment of weakness. Either that or irresistible curiosity.

Should I give her my cell phone number? I decided emphatically No. This was a family trip and already had enough complications. I didn't see that I owed her anything.

Chapter Four

I woke up happy and energized. We had a road trip today, always a small adventure. Later in the weekend, I could think about what Joe had said.

I had packing to finish and time for a little rewriting for my advisor since I did not have pre-trip gassing up, tire-checking, GPS-loading. I had to admit to myself that it was a huge relief.

Chris swore she was packed. Then revised that to say it was nothing she couldn't finish after school. I reminded her that it was a family visit, no special occasion, and that she'd need just everyday clothes. To my offer to help her pack, she replied, "No. I can do it myself." Two-year-old Chris used to say that too.

I knew better then, and I knew better now. She had not seen this part of the family, including her older cousins, in almost two years. Her everyday clothes would be her best. They needed to be outfits that proclaimed, loud and clear, "I am all grown up now. And I live in New York." There was much noise from her room after school, including some swearing, tactfully ignored by me.

The first time she went to camp, last summer, she was up all night packing, so this was progress.

Dad arrived, we got all the luggage in the trunk, not without some discussion of trunk-packing philosophy. Pillows and blankets and snacks in the backseat of his vintage Buick, a roomy, king of the road, American car. Chris and I tumbled in.

"A little traveling music, maestro," he proclaimed, and the Beach Boys filled the car.

"You're dating yourself, Grandpa."

"Nonsense. They're classic for a road trip."

I think we were all a little giddy. It had been a long time since we'd made a trip like this.

Chris and I annoyed each other during the excruciatingly boring time of getting out of Brooklyn and into New Jersey. We couldn't figure out how we could both stretch out on the backseat in comfort and she whined until I snapped, "Then go sit in front and be even more uncomfortable."

And just like that, we accommodated each other, a pillow at each end of the seat, a blanket over both of us. And just like that, we were past lit-up urban Newark, past suburban New Jersey traffic. A rest stop somewhere deep in the country, filling the car with cheap gas. We stumbled half awake to use the restrooms, buy doughnuts and healthy drinks. Then we were in Pennsylvania, rolling north on I-81.

I dozed. Chris dozed. Dad hummed along with the geezer rock station. The music was a flashback to Mom and Dad singing along on childhood trips. Mamas and the Papas. Dion and the Belmonts. The Four Tops.

Suddenly we were in front of Judy's roomy, clapboard house with an old-fashioned porch. I must have expressed my surprise out loud, because Dad, unloading suitcases, chuckled. "The geezer is bound to be right sometimes. You both slept all the way."

Judy hurried out in her quilted robe, shushing everyone. Her youngest, tallest son followed, taking the two biggest bags.

"Billy's in bed, and Mom, of course." She hugged all around. "You must be beat. Come in. Allan, bags upstairs, please. Are you hungry? Did you have dinner before you left?" She took a deep breath. "Listen to me chatter! You get inside." She hugged Chris again. "My grown-up niece. So glad to see you."

We staggered straight into an old-fashioned, overheated kitchen where cake, cocoa, and a full coffee pot awaited us.

"Now you help yourselves. Beds are all ready when you are."

Chris blinked. "We slept all the way here. I think I'm awake for a while."

"Well, good. You can tell me all about the trip."

So Chris did. And I did. Dad went off to his well-earned rest. And Judy told us about Allan, stopping at home on the way to a music festival, and Grandma Donato, who sounded more ornery than ever. We laughed a lot.

I tried not to be unnerved by her son's resemblance to Jeff and the way his smile brought him back.

And then, suddenly, we all sagged and it was three in the morning.

"Leave everything and go straight off to bed. Chris, you have the big attic room all to yourself—a choice of bunk beds! And, Erica, you're right at the top of the stairs. There are fresh towels in the bathroom across the hall. Now you sleep tight and for as long as you feel like it. Breakfast can be anytime." She muttered softly, "No matter what Mom says."

She caught me looking at her and turned red. "Well, you know Mom."

• • ● • •

In the morning I dug out my robe and headed downstairs to the welcome smell of coffee brewing.

There were scrambled eggs and bacon, and also biscotti and several other kinds of pastry I could not name. Brioche? Sponge cake? Something filled with cream. And plenty of high-test coffee. All the men were diving into the eggs and bacon; Judy was gulping down coffee. And Phyllis, Jeff's mother, was daintily dipping biscotti into her coffee cup. Everyone except Judy's men were talking. It was loud. It had been a long time since I'd eaten breakfast with a family.

Grandma Phyllis gave me a smile of sorts. "Good morning, Erica. It's nice to see you for breakfast at last. Have a biscotti. I made them, of course."

"Good morning. Thank you. I would never pass up your biscotti." Actually I think biscotti are a dry waste of calories but I stopped myself from saying it.

"That's right. Now come give me a kiss. Chrissie gave me a big hug when she came down." She pinched Chris' cheek. "I adore my little American *cara mia*."

Chris accepted "little," even though she'd hit five-foot six inches, and Judy ignored that "American," which applied to her children too.

"So, my darling, we have work to do. I have very much to show you, so put on your clothes, and we sit down in the living room and begin."

Everyone got up and cleared the table before Judy shooed us out of the room. I realized suddenly that I had nothing to do. Not having any immediate responsibilities happened in my life… well, never. I could go back to bed, a tempting idea. I could go for a walk. I could join Chris and my mother-in-law and learn some of my husband's family history.

Phyllis politely but indifferently made room for me in the living room, crowded as it was with scrapbooks, photo albums, and cartons full of, as she explained, "this and that. They help my memories rise up to the top of my mind."

They were deeply into collaborating on a family tree. "Now see, Chrissie, these are the ones who came to America, and then these were born here. There are baptismal records at Sacred Heart in the old neighborhood. Donato was my husband's name, of course. This is my own family, the Palmas and their connections."

"So no keeping your name after you got married in those days?" Chris shot me a sly smile.

Her grandmother made a sound like a snort. "What nonsense that is!" She went on, "And they were your father's grandparents, that generation. Francis? He was my father and your father's granddad. I can tell you plenty of stories. And write down that he married Carmela Rossi in…oh, I'm forgetting the year."

Though it was Jeff's family, he had never cared much about all that history, so this was not bringing up any of my memories, sad or happy. I started looking at the boxes.

Each box was neatly labeled: Family Holidays. Christmas and Weddings. Funerals. *What in the world could be in that one?* I gave it a tiny pat and moved on. Aunt Philomena / Navy Yard. *What?* The label was on some cartons and also a small metal chest, brightly painted in a lush design of fruits that reminded me of Italian dinnerware. A tiny padlock held it closed.

"Phyllis, did your family have some connection to the Navy Yard?'

Phyllis looked up, annoyed at being interrupted. "Some? Not some. Lots. Half of my family, and it was a big one, worked there one time or another, some right up until the dark day it closed."

"You never told me that."

"So? You never asked." From her it was an accusation. "Don't distract. We will get to that later." She turned back to Chris. "Now, honey, I have some stories about these brothers." She placed a finger firmly on the sketched out family tree.

I went to see if Judy would like to go out for a coffee she did not make. Two coffees and plate of pastry later, we finally had a chance to talk.

"It's been…how long has it been?"

"Must be ten years. You have never been here since we moved Mom, so…when? When we came home to get her?"

"I think so. Boy, was she mad that weekend."

"Oh, yeah, and for a long time, too. There was no life for her anywhere except the old neighborhood. Never mind the fainting spells she was having. Or the aides she fought with. Or… well, you know."

"She looks awfully well now."

"She found a church, a bakery, someone who grows vegetables in his garden and gives them to her. She'll never, never admit it but I think she likes it here after all." She smiled, wryly. "Did you notice how she sounds more Italian than she used to?"

"I thought so! Wasn't she a Brooklyn girl?"

"You bet. She was born in Kings County Hospital and so were her parents! No, she's establishing her identity here in the boonies. And get this? You know her legal name is Phyllis?"

"Sure."

"My dad made her change it when he came home from the Navy. She was named after her aunt and he said he wasn't marrying anyone with an off-the-boat name like Philomena!"

"No! Philomena? It's pretty but…"

"Well, she's back to Philomena now!"

We cracked up together.

"She's making sure these hicks from upstate New York know who she is!"

"I don't know how you live with her."

Judy shrugged. "I'm used to her. The real hero is my Billy. But he grew up himself with his grandma living in their house." She shook her head, smiling fondly.

"Has it been good to have Chris more in her life?"

"Oh, you bet. She's talked about nothing but this visit for two weeks. Talking and cooking and tearing the attic apart for albums."

We went silent, sipping and nibbling. I wanted to ask how Phyllis felt about me these days, all these years later. Should I? Shouldn't I? Seeing Phyllis again stirred up so many memories of that emotional time when we seriously considered eloping. She had softened somewhat when Chris was born but still, I wondered if I could assume anything like good will.

Judy checked her watch. "Look at me, frittering away the morning having fun! I have to get home to make lunch. Come on. We can pick up rolls on the way."

I was astonished at the speed with which she had a meal on the table: rolls, platters of cheese and cold cuts, olive salad, pickled vegetables, macaroni salad, various dressings, sweet peppers. And Dad and Billy walked in the door just as we sat down. Had they been carrying a timer?

Overwhelmed with what was on the table, I settled for cheese and vegetables. Chris, the occasional vegetarian, piled on the cold cuts.

"I keep telling you, Judy dear, that mayonnaise does not belong on an Italian sandwich. Not mustard, either. But do you listen?"

Judy flushed but her voice was even. "Mom, you know you used to put them out on our table. Dad liked it, and sometimes my children did too. And still do." She didn't say "So there," but the toss of her head got it across.

"Humph. It was wrong when your dad wanted it too. He learned to do it when he was stationed out there in America."

"Hey, hey, Mama Phyllis." My dad was jumping in. "You know sometimes we have to give in to these young ones, even if it seems weird. 'Cause why fight?" He winked at her. She merely tossed her head.

What was my dad up to? By her standards, he was one of the young ones himself. And he'd always been the guy who never ducked out on an argument.

"Erica." She snapped it out and I sat right up. "We start on the Navy Yard box after lunch. You may join us if that interests you."

"Well, yes, I am just starting a chapter of my dissertation about it."

"Chapter? With the stories I'm gonna tell you could write a book. You should, too. You young people clean up and then we three go get to work."

"Ma and everyone else, out, out, out. With an empty kitchen I'll get it done in half the time. Billy, you got the supplies at Home Depot? You and Cal going to fix the pipe in the bath upstairs?"

"Count on us," my father promised. "Billy is going be the boss, and I'm gonna hand him the tools."

Chris and I looked at each other with wide eyes. I knew my dad didn't even own a toolbox.

We followed Phyllis back to the living room.

"Now let me explain." She had her finger in the air. This was a lecture. "The Navy Yard had lots of Italians working there. Beside the different unions, there was even an Italian fraternal organization. The Columbian Association. My dad, before he was drafted, my granddad, some uncles and great-uncles. So, Chrissie, you ever been there to see it?"

"No, but Mom has."

"Ah." She gave me a long look. "I was there many, many times when I was little, 'cause my dad came back from the war and got his old job back. They built ships and repaired them there. They tell me I went to the launching of the battleship *Missouri*, and saw Vice President Truman, as he was then, but honestly, I was too little to remember. My grandpa said that battleship he helped build was where the war ended. Wait, I have a picture."

She immediately put her hands on the album and there it was, a photo of men in work clothes, standing in front of the almost-complete battleship holding up tools and smiling for the camera. On the next page, a photo of General MacArthur and Emperor Hirohito on the *Missouri*, signing the treaty that ended the war. I'd be lying if I said it didn't give me chills.

I added, "The battleship where the war started—the *Arizona*, which sank in the Pearl Harbor bombing—was built at the Navy Yard too. Like bookends."

Phyllis looked at me with surprise. "I didn't know that. Or I've forgotten it." She nodded. "They were proud to work there. Now Chris, you need to know it was a huge place. Miles of roads and rail tracks and places to eat and bank. The first time Dad took me that I can remember, I saw the train chugging right through the whole property. I couldn't believe my eyes! And my little brother kept saying choo-choo all the way home.

"Okay, so here's a special piece of family history." She opened another page to four women in a row, dressed in coveralls, their hair bundled up in flowered kerchiefs, carrying lunch pails. And they all had dark red lipstick in place, too. They were striding out of the Yard main gate, smiling, but the men on the side looked shell-shocked.

"Ha. That right there is my Aunt Philomena, the tall blonde, her first week of work. I was named for her; she was my godmother."

"Wow. Mom, did you know about this? There were real Rosie the Riveters? In real life?"

"Chris! What exactly to you think I do for a living? And I've seen that photo before, in the museum."

"You've seen it in a museum? I thought this was the only one. Well, anyway, Chris, she was my heroine when I was little." She stopped. "Of course this...this photo...was taken when I was a baby, but she still worked there when I was growing up."

"Tell about the picture, please. I'm going to take notes."

"It was taken soon after the first women started learning the heavy jobs at the yard. Before, they only did office work, maybe, and sewed in the flag shop."

"For a lot less money, I'm betting?" I already knew the answer, but wondered if Phyllis did.

She nodded. "What I heard—this was from her and my dad too—was that she fought her parents hard about taking that job. There was shouting.

"See, Chrissie, it was a patriotic thing. Some of her brothers and cousins were already in the service and there were calls out to women to take a man's job and free the men up to win the war."

Chris was keyboarding away, paused, looked up expectantly. "And?"

"Well, the way I heard it, she was all fired up to go sign on. But her parents said no way, not ever."

"Why? I mean, wasn't it the right thing to do? Why weren't they proud?"

"Not at first." Phyllis looked back at me. "Erica, how do we explain to this modern young lady? Bring in your history learning, why don't you?"

That might have been the first time she ever acknowledged I had a profession. Or would have, someday.

"Well, I suppose they thought it was unsuitable work for a woman. Lots of people did, at least at first. It was dirty and physical, definitely not dainty."

"Also it meant working with men all day," Phyllis added. "Anything could happen."

"They worried about all that? Come on!" Chris shook her head. "I mean, it wasn't the Dark Ages. You knew them, and I know you. So it's like..." She counted off on her fingers. "Four generations. Not long ago. We could almost touch them." I was so proud. A historian's child. She got it. "So what finally happened?"

"My pop, her favorite brother, Francis, came home from basic training, all decked out in his uniform and the whole family was so proud. They had a flag with another blue star up already."

"Okay, I'm lost. What is all that?"

Phyllis looked at me with a challenge. "Erica?" She thought I didn't know.

"Your story, you can tell."

"Chrissie, families with active duty servicemen got a flag and could add one blue star for each one. The gold stars were for the ones who were killed, so you prayed never to have any."

"Okay, I get it. But back to Philomena...?"

"My pop came home, like I said, and he convinced them."

"How did he?"

"I don't know exactly. I suppose there was yelling."

"That's a great story, Grandma. So she was part of history, doing a whole new thing."

"Oh, yeah. And I can just, just remember that from later in the war. She showed me her ID card one day, proud as proud. And you know, in the end, my grandparents were proud too. They always denied they had ever objected. And there was an evil eye for anyone from the neighborhood who said a critical word. You know people will always try to be...you know, say the mean thing...."

"Malicious?"

She nodded. "That's it. And that's enough for now. A coffee all around, yes? And a slice of cake? Or Chris, do you want gelato?"

"You can get gelato here?" I couldn't resist. "You always said this was a wilderness."

"I never did. Never."

I just looked at her. For a long time.

"Well, maybe. In the beginning. Go. Cut the cake."

"But wait!" Chris hadn't closed her computer. "What happened to Philomena after she went to work? I want to know the rest of the story. Maybe I'll write my whole assignment about her."

"Later. I'm all talked out now. And after we snack, *Cara*, I am going to teach you to make Italian roast chicken, very easy. *Delizioso*. Erica, please take a tray in to Billy and your father. They're watching TV. Two biscotti and two cups of black coffee. I'll fix it."

They were not watching TV. They were napping with the TV as their lullaby. The overheated house, with tightly weatherproofed windows keeping the cold upstate air out, was very conducive to an afternoon nap. They did look like a couple of very large babies. Had they had a hard trip to Home Depot? All that walking up and down the aisles in a store the size of an airplane hangar?

I carefully placed the tray on a table, wondering how the coffee would taste when they woke up. As I turned to leave, I heard the voice on the TV. "Stay tuned to statewide news. Is there a break in the murder of a prominent New York political advisor?"

I turned right back, perched on an easy chair that matched the sofa and munched on a biscotti.

Chapter Five

The voice went on and on, talking about the state legislature's failure to act. What else was new?

Finally, they showed a photo of Michael Conti, and then a man in uniform, speaking authoritatively for the NYPD. The newsman's smooth voice picked up again. "As the police department is looking into Conti's life, they are finding many questions. He had a checkered career that included feuds with prominent people and accusations of graft, unproven, over the years. In his personal life, his divorce took place without much scandal, though his speedy marriage to a much younger woman caused gossip at the time."

As he spoke, photos flashed on the screen. A younger woman in a ball gown at some gala, escorted by Michael Conti. A photo of him escorting a bride. Nothing recent.

If I was going to use him and his career as a plot line for looking at the changes around the harbor, I should start taking notes and so I wrote until dinner time.

The meal was delicious, as promised—roast chicken and lemon potatoes, accompanied by broccoli salad, at Judy's insistence. "Billy and I both need to watch our weight these days. We do *not* need pasta at every dinner." She smiled cheerfully, but muttered to me, "No matter what my mother thinks."

Over dinner, Phyllis asked Judy, "Do you remember Aunt Philomena? "

"A little. I was old enough to go to her funeral. I remember the crying."

"What happened to her?" Chris wanted to know.

"She got sick and died young, right, Ma?"

"Yes, but I always thought there was more to it." Her mother frowned. "She was such an exciting person to be around when I was little, and then she was sad later. It was after the war…"

Chris, very romantic these days, jumped in. "She loved someone who didn't come back from the war!"

"But she never said. And we were close. If it was that, why keep it a secret? Most people who lost someone, they were heartbroken but proud."

Cynical me wondered if he'd come back but not to her. That was a wartime story too.

"Well, did you ask her? Maybe she would have told you when you were a grown-up too."

"No, I did not. In those days I was too busy raising children to go poking into old stories. And then she was gone." She shook her head. "So, Chrissie, tomorrow when we go to Mass, we say a prayer for her, too, along with for your dad and your grandma and my dear husband."

"Mass tomorrow?" That was a shocker.

"Of course Mass. We can go at noon. I know this little one doesn't like to get up too early."

Then my dad said, "Phyllis, it would be an honor to escort you lovely ladies to church, if you would allow me?"

Dad? My dad? Who I knew for a fact had not been in any house of worship except for funerals in twenty years. He met my furious expression with a bland smile that meant "We'll talk later." For sure we would.

Chris gave me a pleading look. "I thought it would be interesting. And we'd be with the family."

Judy winked at me. "I'll go, but Billy sleeps in. He'll find you some breakfast while we're out."

He smiled. "If you like cornflakes, I'm your man."

After dinner, Billy had put an oldies music program on TV and I mean really oldies, not his youth, but his mother-in-law's. Next thing I knew, my dad asked Phyllis to dance and they were doing a creditable Lindy, with careful twists and crossovers.

Chris was open-mouthed. A Jerry Lee Lewis medley inspired Billy to grab Judy and cut a few steps too. Chris and I looked at each other, laughed, and I pulled her off the chair and showed her the basic moves.

We all collapsed, laughing, and…true confession? I did a little singing along and clapping to the rest of the program. Even Chris joined in, torn between her scorn for the boring music and her desire to be part of the fun.

Before bed, Phyllis gave Chris a big hug, saying, "I used to wonder about you as a baby. Where did your blondeness come from? Not your mom or dad. But now I see my Jeff in you. Your height and your smile is him all over."

I often thought that too, always with a pang.

"Actually, now that you're taller, you remind me of Philomena. Put you in a head scarf and red lipstick and you'd see what I mean."

Chris giggled

"She's athletic too, on the girls' basketball team. You know she got that from Jeff, not me, the klutz." I was ignoring the subtext of "Wondered where you came from." Perhaps she had not meant it as a subtle slur. Perhaps.

I cornered Dad when we finally went upstairs to bed.

"Church?" My voice was a fierce whisper. "You are going to church? Have you completely lost your mind?"

"No, no, it's fine. I figure I can throw a little kindness at her."

"Kindness? Come on! You're being charming. To Phyllis!"

"Because being older doesn't mean she's lost all her feelings. She's lonely."

"Lonely? She is surrounded by her nearest and dearest, all of whom she rules with an iron hand."

He shook his head. "She likes to feel young again. That's all it is. Besides you're forgetting something?"

"Yes?"

"Every nice thing I do rebounds to her liking you better." He smiled at my expression. "Yeah, never thought of that, did you?"

The next morning the blessedly silent house seemed to belong to me. I could do some work. Learn more about the deceased Michael Conti.

Diligent searching online produced frustratingly little. And why did I care, anyway? Didn't know him. Didn't like him at the meeting. Did not have a single connection.

Except that I had stood next his dying body and I had not forgotten that. Probably I never would.

That mattered more than the intersection of his career and my dissertation, but still, there was an intersection. I felt sure that if I could get his complete story, it would spark helpful insights. I had to do it, quickly, or abandon this chapter entirely, according to my advisor.

When I picked my head up from the screen two hours later, I had a whole lot of questions. And the harder it got, the more I wanted to dig up some answers.

Being a historian is not entirely different from being a detective, I thought, and not for the first time.

Someone must know more and I knew precisely who that might be. My buddy Leary, a long-retired reporter, crabby, ill, and bored, who would scoff at the word "buddy," but who knew everything there was to know about old Brooklyn. I would have to drop by soon after our return.

Giving up on my search, I responsibly checked my e-mail and my phone messages at home.

There was another voicemail from the annoying mystery caller again. "Can we make a date for Thursday, after you get back? I would be very grateful. Anywhere you want to meet. Happy to take you to lunch or dinner." Long pause. "Please."

What did this woman want from me? As if I don't have enough demands on my time. On my life. I punched the Reply button, harder than necessary and told her I would be at the Brooklyn Public Library, central building, Thursday. She could meet me at four o'clock, in front at the adjoining entrance to Prospect Park.

I'd meet her outdoors, in a well-populated public place, Grand Army Plaza, the splendid, not to say pompous, entrance to Prospect Park. I didn't want to be trapped in a restaurant with someone I'd never met, for a meeting I didn't want, for a reason I didn't even know.

The churchgoers came home, the roast that had been sending its tempting odors through the house was whisked onto the table, and there was a real Sunday dinner. Certainly not a tradition in my own secular but Jewish family. This was Italian-style, with a pasta course and then a meat course. Followed by a nap, I hoped.

Phyllis commanded Chris back to the living room to select what she wanted to take home and I had an inspiration.

"Phyllis, did your family ever know a Michael Conti? Or have dealings with him? Does that ring any bells? It could be a Navy Yard connection?"

"I have no idea. I mean, I do remember Contis, it's not an unusual name, but I don't know if it was that one. Why do you want to know?"

"I'm trying to understand his career for my work."

"Mom, isn't that the guy who was killed?"

"Killed?" Phyllis stepped back. "Killed? So not just curious?"

I was stuck with telling tell the whole story then.

"You need to be more careful," Phyllis scolded. "You're a mother. You have a child who needs you."

Chris caught my eye. She was smothering laughter. "Yes, Mom! You need to be more careful. I am your child, you know." She shook a finger at me and then we both laughed.

Phyllis shot us a look filled with exasperation but when all Chris' material was packed up, Phyllis said to me, "I want you to take that little trunk with the flowers. A loan, not forever." She was pointing to the enameled chest that looked like Italian pottery, bright flowers on a black background.

I must have looked as puzzled as I felt.

"It's Aunt Philomena's Navy Yard trunk." She was impatient with me. "We found it. You take it. Maybe it will be useful. Who knows? You might find that Michael Conti in there!"

"Oh. Thank you. I..." I didn't know what to say. It could be a treasure, or it could be one more item to clutter up my house.

She put a hand on my shoulder and whispered, "All this talk about the old days got me to thinking about Aunt Philomena. I'm so sure there was a story but I was too little to know what it was. I'd hear her name but if I walked into the room the grownups stopped talking." She patted my shoulder. "I had a dream about this trunk last night so I know it's the right thing. I want you to try to find out about her. What really happened."

But, I thought. *But*. I already had work to do. I had Michael Conti's story to track down, and it was a stretching my advisor's patience even to say that was work. Philomena's couldn't be stretched at all. And I had no idea where to start either.

And then I remembered that Dad had said he was trying to create a little goodwill and how it would help me. And Chris. I womaned up.

"Of course I can try. No promises, but I'll try."

"You're a good girl." She patted me again and turned away to Chris.

That was the nicest thing I ever heard her say. That Jeff loved me had never been enough for her. I needed to sit down. I needed some of Billy's high-test espresso. And cookies.

I peeked into the trunk. The inside was enameled too, and painted with flowers, and it was filled to its curved top. I found a stack of clippings in an envelope and below that, some group photos at meetings, with scribbled identification on the back. She didn't always bother with a list of names, just a date, and a fruit salad of letters. I assumed they were abbreviations for organizations. Ah, yes, here was one that said "Work Procurement Committee." And that woman in the front row, the only woman, was Philomena.

Phyllis confirmed it. "See how pretty she was. And how nice she looked in those 1950s suits. And with a stylish hat, of course!

A career gal, that's what they called them then. That man next to her is my granddad, her father. He kept the mustache just to be contrary. Italian men mostly shaved them off by then. No one wanted to be taken for a Mustache Pete." She sighed. "So long ago." Then she snapped back into the here and now. "Erica, so when you look at this, after you go home, you call me if you have questions. You can always mail me a photo if you need me to see it, right?"

"Grandma!" Chris said. "I told you. We can send you a picture through Aunt Judy's e-mail. Try to remember which century we are in!"

"Ha! Ha! I let my grandchildren do that for me, and I'll stay in the twentieth, where I belong."

At last it was time to make sandwiches for the road and pack up. The little trunk was lined up in the front hall along with our suitcases, our car supplies, and our coats. Hugs, good-byes, and promises to be in touch. A firm promise from Phyllis, with a decisive nod. "I'm doing it. Billy will put me on a plane. Easy-peasy. Why not?"

My dad elbowed her. "Why not? I'll take you out and we'll paint the town."

I was pretty sure Dad had not painted the town since his fortieth birthday, and I had never seen Phyllis do it at all. And why had no one discussed this plan with me?

But when Chris replied, "I'm holding you to it, Grandma," it was too late to protest.

Not that I didn't try, once we were in the car.

"You do remember that it is my house and I end up being the hostess?"

"But Mom. We have enough room. She can have the guest bed in my room." She looked shocked that I might protest. "We have it all planned."

"You planning to introduce her to the wonderful Jared?"

"Oh, Mom, please!" She turned away from me, cocooned in a blanket. "I am going to sleep now."

Phyllis in my house? Dear lord.

We drove through the cold, quiet night, past the darkness of empty fields broken up in flashes of brightly lit up rest stops, and passing big green exit signs to small, obscure towns. Painted Post, Horseheads, Bath, Hornell.

Chris and I dozed. Dad's tuneless humming was not loud enough to keep us awake. At one point, I woke up with an idea rattling around my mind. A memory. I remembered something else about the murder I had witnessed. That was a shock. I would I have to talk to someone at NYPD again.

We came home and unloaded quietly on the eerily silent street. Chris mumbled, "Going to bed. I'll take my bags up tomorrow, okay?" In a few minutes, though, I heard her on her phone, catching up. I wondered what could be left to talk about, since she'd been connected part of every day we were away, including this one. I reminded myself how, for a teenager, constant connection, by whatever means, tells your young self you are still here, still you, still known, still wanted.

Being an adult, I could wait. I'd wake up early and talk to Joe in the morning. And my friends. And someone at NYPD.

Chapter Six

It wasn't so early. Pale late-fall sun was streaming into my window. Chris seemed to have risen before me, which never, ever happens, and was out. Or her bags had come upstairs by magic. One or the other.

I wandered around my house in a fog, took my own bags upstairs, unpacked the easy way: everything went into the hamper.

I made a large pot of coffee and drank a large amount of it. Did a few mindless physical chores, waiting for the caffeine to kick in. I started the laundry. I cruised the kitchen, making a list of what to replenish. I plotted how I could get Chris to do the shopping.

I finally found the text message she had sent me.

> B'fast out with Mel + all. Sleep tite.

She'd included a snoring emoticon. Nervy kid. I clumsily replied by text.

> Food shop on way home. Call for list.

After the coffee finally kicked in, I had to sit down at my desk and get serious. Read e-mail. Done. Hmm. HR appointment on my next working day. Put in calendar and wonder what that's about. Done. Re-read outline for next chapter. "Impact of Navy Yard Closing on Surrounding Neighborhood." Done. (Note to self—this was a controversial moment in Brooklyn. Why does it sound so boring?) I would spend the whole next day at the local history collection at the main building of the public library.

Respond to Joe's note, confirming we had all survived the trip. No mayhem, no bodies to bury. Yes, we could talk tonight. I smiled and then made a real effort to set Joe aside. I did not have time to think about him now. And did not know what I thought anyway.

Laundry dried so I went to Chris' room with a full basket.

I was astonished. There were old photos taped all over her wall. They were mostly of Aunt Philomena. She had covered her bulletin board with Post-it notes and on an old whiteboard she had listed "Things to Find Out."

And there was Philomena's little trunk, brought in from my office, now messily ransacked, with photo albums stacked on Chris' bed. What had she done? All that was supposed to be for me to use for research. Not for Chris.

Still, I was proud of her. Before I could take it all in, a random unrelated mom thought crossed my mind. How early did she get up this morning?

This was a family history project in spades. Would she let me be involved? Because I wanted in on this. Something about Philomena in the photos—straight back, clear gaze, tool belt—spoke to me too. Chris seemed to be focusing on her days as a worker, a young woman. Of course. Hard as it was for me to believe, she was only a few years older than Chris was now. Did it seem glamorous to Chris, the bandanna wrapped around the hair, the tools, and the bright red lipstick? The can-do attitude?

There was something else I wanted to know. Why did she look so sad in her later photos? What happened? I admitted to myself that Phyllis had hooked me after all.

I had to dig into that enticing trunk.

There was a stack of photos, large originals of photos from the *Brooklyn Eagle*. There was a time, and within my father's memory, when Brooklyn had its very own newspaper, back when New York had eight dailies. That time lasted for a century and change. I found it hard to imagine.

It would be a job, sorting all this, plus whatever Chris had taken. For now I was only orienting myself, but honestly, I could not resist the clippings. I soon saw I had a complete, if highly biased, history of the Navy Yard closing. Phyllis' father was named under a few of the photos, and a couple of guys who might be cousins. One more with Philomena.

They were meeting with the Brooklyn congressional delegation, discussing the Defense Department's plans for the oldest Navy Yards. Nice and bland, that caption, but clipped to it was a scathing column, also from the *Eagle*, ripping into the possible closing and Defense Secretary McNamara's approach. And well, well, well. It was signed by Michael Conti.

I had no idea what his role was in these groups, or even what the groups were, but I knew I could find out. I wanted to find out. I wrote notes onto Post-its and affixed them to the pages, rearranging the pages of interest to be on top.

I would also have to have a stern discussion with my daughter about taking that trunk from my room and messing with the papers.

A buzz indicated an incoming text.

List?

I called her, and read off the basic groceries needed to sustain our lives.

And now, exactly what had she used from this trunk? The big envelope with clippings about the closing of the Yard was intact. That did not interest her. She was looking for her real-life Rosie the Riveter.

I could leave her with the material she had, but the trunk was going right back to my office. On the way downstairs I met my daughter coming up.

"Mom? What are you doing?"

"Taking back my property." I stopped. "My loan from your grandmother. She gave it to me for a reason, you know. I didn't say you could ransack it. You didn't even ask!"

I was genuinely annoyed and also did not like having to play mom, laying down the law.

"But I thought...I mean...you want me to do good school-work, don't you?" She began with a shocked stammer but her voice got louder with each word. "You always say that I owe it to you! And myself. So I thought...it would be good for my project. It's half our grade for this semester, for crying out loud. You think that's not a little pressure?" She stopped on a gasp. "Oh, just...just...never mind." She stamped upstairs. From the top she threw back, "Be mad at me! But remember I was work-ing while you were still asleep. Now who keeps vampire hours?"

With that, she disappeared into her room. A door was slammed. I didn't know if I should follow her and demand an apology, or cry, or laugh. The remark about hours was funny. None of those choices seemed to go anywhere helpful, so I decided it was time to get to work at the library. I would forget about this fight and leave Chris to calm her own self down.

I met my elderly neighbor, Mrs. Pastore, as I walked up the block. She was dragging garbage cans to the curb for Sanitation Department pickup. I lent a hand.

"Sal hurt his back, pulled a muscle trying to change light bulbs. Silly old man! So I have to do this. Thanks, honey." She looked up into my face. "Everything okay with you? I saw you come home with cops last week." Of course she did. She sees everything on the block. Her twice a day sweeping the sidewalk is merely an obvious excuse.

So I told her.

"Conti? No! That old SOB. You were there? I did hear it on the news."

"You knew him?"

She shook her head vehemently. "I did not. Don't think I ever met him. But I know his wife." She stopped. "His first wife, that is. Before he married that hussy. Some Catholic family they are!"

"You knew his wife? I can hardly believe it."

"Oh, hon, my kids went to Bishop Loughlin, where she worked. And such a nice woman, too. Helpful, kind as the day is long. Now, him. What I heard about the time he gave her? You don't want to know."

That is just a Brooklyn expression. "Of course I want to know."

"Well. Wouldn't you rather forget about him altogether? It's not so good to dwell on bad things."

"True enough, but I am not dwelling on the murder. I am writing a chapter on the Navy Yard and so I got curious about him. It seems like he was a big deal there."

"Ha. Big deal in his own mind, anyway. But Annabelle and I became friendly over the years. Of course it helped that she lived so close."

"*What* did you say?"

"Yeah. She lives a couple of blocks up the street." She winked at me. "Right where the houses go from bricks to stone, and three stories to four." She waved at our modest block. "One of these would not do for the great man. But, yeah, she's still there."

Mrs. Pastore saw the excitement in my face and chuckled.

"You want to meet her? We often meet for a cup of coffee in the morning. Eleven-ish."

"Are you kidding? I'd love to."

"Tomorrow, then, meet me here. Got to get in now. My hands are freezing and have to check up on that silly old fool of a man."

I thanked her again and she left. She adored her old husband and seemed worried.

And I would have a lot of questions for the ex-Mrs. Conti. I wondered if she would be a bitter woman who didn't want to talk about her ex-husband. The guy who went on to a more glamorous life, with a glamorous younger wife, and left her behind. Or she could be so angry that nothing she said would be usable for serious purposes. It would probably be entertaining as gossip, though, I admitted to myself.

On the long walk to the central library, I made a work plan and also stopped for a few chores. I could not evade the homeless men who manned their regular busy corners of this gentrified neighborhood. The man in front of the supermarket who always reminded passing children to read a book. The man in front of a bank, with a paper cup, whose words were so slurred and eyes so glazed I wondered how he managed to get himself dressed and out. The elderly man in a knitted watch cap who occasionally stood near the coffee shop. His outstretched hand was cracked and scarred, and he would not look up to meet anyone's eyes.

I shared my loose change with each of them and gave a smile when the strangely cheerful man near the supermarket said, "God bless."

The library had many files on the Navy Yard, as I knew it would. Newspaper clippings, a few official reports, and—OMG, as the kids would say—an entire dissertation on the topic, a case study in local politics. It was written a lifetime ago, literally. The date was before I was born. But still.

I hit the files, page after page, set aside the items to copy, kept alert for familiar names. It was complex story and I would have to simplify it for my chapter. It was only one chapter, and it had to be less about the maneuvering, which I could already see was prolonged, than about how it affected the community.

Then I got sidetracked by a clipping about a committee meeting because there were two Palma ancestors in the photo. One was Philomena's father, Jeff's grandfather, Chris' great-grandfather, shaking hands with a Brooklyn congressman. They were at a meeting about the fate of the Yard.

It was a connection to the past for Chris. And Phyllis too.

I put my head down on the library table. I was well and truly distracted and I needed to get a grip. I imagined discussing all this with Dr. Adams, shuddered, and that was enough to scare me into focusing. One pile for personal interest. One pile for deep background. One pile for community impact. *See, Dr. Adams?* I thought. *I do know what I am doing.*

I resolved to ignore the voice in my head that asked what my long game was. If I finish in time to graduate, a mighty big *if,* what then? The voice sounded a lot like Dr. Adams and I told it to shut up. First things first. I had a chore right in front of me.

Community impact was the smallest pile of clippings, as most of the material focused on the big story, the process of the closing itself. It would be useful to understanding what happened, while it was actually happening. And then use my distance, now, to see the whole story with some perspective about how the Yard eventually came back to life.

The Secretary of Defense at the time of the closing was a man named McNamara. He came from the corporate world, and—yes, here in the dissertation was a chapter about him and the Yard workers. McNamara thought in numbers. He put his faith in numbers. If the old yards were too expensive to run and not as productive as, say, a Ford assembly line, shut them down. Let private industry do it cheaper and better. I imagined him giving the order and decisively moving on to the next decision without a qualm about the impact on the community.

There was a photo of him. Conservative suit, fussy glasses, perfectly knotted tie, precision part in his gleaming hair.

The Brooklyn workers spoke a different language entirely, not about numbers, but about loyalty and influence and political pressure. They put their faith in politicians who had the president's ear. Who would never let the bureaucrats do this to Brooklyn. Who would save their jobs. And they would never have to deal with the real productivity issues.

I sat back and caught my breath. There it was, the whole story in a few sentences. A gigantic conflict of cultures. I typed furiously, getting this down. It was not exactly my topic but I knew in my bones it was an important point. Conflict of cultures is about the new wave of immigrants affecting the children of the previous wave and the fight for available jobs and paychecks—as I had written about in a few chapters—and about the never-ending conflict over whose neighborhood, city, country this was. Only the details changed from generation to generation.

This clash belonged in there, too—the old Brooklyn ways of doing business being outmoded, outflanked, outdated by the MBAs. That change was still going on today as gentrification spread from old but quaint neighborhoods to former slums. Some people believed the old Brooklyn of the working man was already gone for good.

I triple underlined the sentence that described the Navy workers group approaching the DC authorities—the men who held the fate of the Yard in their hands—with demands instead of requests.

I could see it all, looking like a Frank Capra movie. The plain-speaking Brooklyn working men with big chips on their shoulders. William Bendix is in that scene. The suave, well-dressed Cabinet members with Harvard accents, probably played by Ralph Bellamy.

Except that, unlike a Capra film, the big men won in this one.

When I start dreaming movies in my own mind, it means I've had enough library time and I need to return to the world. I partly blamed Phyllis because while her stories might be helping Chris, they were a real distraction to me. She had made it personal, not actually such a good thing in this academic process—as proven by the movie I was running in my mind.

It was time to meet my mystery caller. I found an empty bench on the edge of Grand Army Plaza and resigned myself to a chilly wait.

A woman in a fur coat with a matching hat came across the plaza, walking slowly, using a gold-painted cane. The fur tipped me off immediately. In this neighborhood, mixed between families who couldn't possibly afford fur coats and liberal activists who wouldn't dream of wearing them, she had to be my mystery visitor.

She stood in front of me, small and chunky, with bright red dyed hair and a face crisscrossed with wrinkles under her heavy makeup.

"You are Erica?"

I nodded and patted the bench next to me.

"I was so nervous, I had the driver leave me over there so he would not see what I was doing." She took a few deep breaths. "It's true then, you saw Mike before…before…"

"Yes, I did." *What did this woman want?*

"Mike." She started to cry. "He's gone. Seeing you, hearing that, it finally seems real."

She pulled herself up straight and patted her wet face with an embroidered handkerchief she pulled from her coat sleeve. "Tell me whatever you saw, please. If you would be so kind."

"First tell me…who the heck are you? How did you find me?"

"Why would you need to know that?" Her gaze was level and hard. "It's such a simple, such an easy request and it would mean so much to me." When I didn't immediately respond, she sighed. "Call me Mary. In those days I went by my middle name to tell me from all my Catholic friends who were Mary too. Mary Pat. Okay? Mary Pat O'Neill." She saw my skeptical look. "All right. Here! Here." It was her driver's license waved under my eyes for just a minute. "Satisfied? So now we are introduced and you can tell me." Her firm voice started to shake. "I need to know. I need that. I need it for my peace of mind."

I doubted it would bring her peace but I told her anyway. She smiled fondly when I described his behavior at the meeting. "That was Mike, all right. Big opinions and a short fuse."

She turned pale under the rouge when I described the shooting. She asked me if he said anything. She asked me if I did. She asked if I got a good look at the shooter.

The answer to all her urgent questions was no. I finally said, "It was a scary experience, and honestly, I don't want to talk about it anymore. And it's a murder investigation. I'm telling you almost nothing, but probably I shouldn't be telling you anything at all."

"I know about investigations." Her face became much less friendly. "How do you suppose I found you? I have friends."

"What are you talking about?"

She shrugged. "I have friends who found you for me. I went to some trouble, but this is very disappointing. You really don't know anything more, do you?"

"Nope. Not a thing. And you still haven't even told me why you want to know."

"Why, my dear, I am—I was—the other woman. The *other*, other woman, I guess you could say. He did have a few, the old rogue. Maybe even a new one now." Her voice shook. "But I was the one who he always came back to somehow, again and again."

"You were…you were romantically involved?"

She gave me a sharp look over the hankie. "We were lovers. Are you having trouble saying that? Or is it having trouble believing it? You do know we used to be young, right? And if I wasn't ever the prettiest, still we connected like magnets." She smacked her two fists together to illustrate her point.

She scrabbled around in her purse, finally pulling out a wallet and then pulling out a cracked and faded photo. It was two teenagers at the beach. The girl was in a modest one-piece suit with a dainty skirt. Chunky body but plump in the right places. Lipstick and eyeliner, and hair rolled into complicated puffs. An impish face and small eyes. Cigarette in her hand. Not a pretty face but with an expression that hinted at something. It was probably sex appeal.

And he was a handsome kid with muscles and Brylcreem-slicked hair. A Brooklyn Romeo.

They stood with their arms around each other, big grins, his hand possessively on her hip. "Coney Island?" I could see the tower of the parachute ride in the background.

"Our place. Quick hop on the subway." She smiled at the photo, with tears sparkling in her eyes. "You'd be surprised what you can get up to under a couple of big beach towels. They used to call it Sodom by the Sea." She surprised me with a wink. "Or maybe not surprised, if you are a Brooklyn girl who ever had a boyfriend."

I shook my head. "He had a car, an old one."

"A different world, then."

"So why didn't you stick together?" I thought of myself and Jeff. "I don't understand."

"He didn't want to get married until we could live nice. No living with the parents for him! Besides, he wasn't done chasing the beauty queens, either. I got tired of waiting, with all my friends walking down the aisle. So I showed him. I married someone else. As it turned out, a couple of someone elses over the years."

She stopped and looked away. "And Annabelle scooped him up. She always had eyes for him." She saw my surprise. "Yes,

I knew her back then, too. She was always a little goody-two-shoes." She smiled sadly. "Mike and me, we ran into each other again one day. At the butcher, if you can believe that. Not too romantic, buying hot Italian sausages."

"So it wasn't over?"

"It was never over. Never. Not through Annabelle, not through Jennifer, not through the other girls. I was the one." She stopped, put her hand over her heart as if it was beating too fast. "That's enough. Since you have nothing else to tell me, I am leaving."

"But I have more questions for you. And you should talk to the detectives and tell them…"

She was already walking away. A car appeared at the curb. She got in and left without turning around again or giving me a chance to ask any of the questions tumbling around in my mind. I didn't even know any way to verify anything she had told me. I punched in her name and found a few listings but none the right age. I punched in her phone number and got "unlisted" back. I hadn't even been able to see the address on her driver's license. So…nothing.

I pulled out my computer and sat in the deepening chill, writing up as much as I could remember. I would have to contact NYPD again when I got home. I was dreading how stupid I would feel, not even being able to identify her.

Home. Chris' coat on the sofa and her book bag on the floor told me she was home. I threw my coat on top of hers and began pulling items out of the refrigerator. Soup and grilled-cheese sandwiches, a nice supper on a cold fall night.

"Chris!" I shouted. "Supper in ten?"

Mumbles from above. I took it as a yes. I would ignore the morning argument.

Chris came in as the smells of vegetable soup and grilled-cheese sandwiches were warming up the kitchen and announced, "I am still mad about this morning."

Exactly what I did not need to hear at the end of this difficult day. "You're mad? That material was for my work. Which, may

I remind you, does provide a little income and is for our future. You should have at least asked." I took a deep breath. "That would be only common courtesy."

She made the same grumpy face she has been making since she was two. I almost melted then and there. Almost. Moms of teens have to be tough.

"Well, my schoolwork is my future. As you tell me and tell me and tell me. College. Scholarships. Remember saying that? So why isn't that just as important?"

I turned around, back to the frying pan, and by exercising enormous self-control did not say a word. By the time I was slapping the crispy sandwiches onto plates, she muttered, "All right. All right. I should have asked. Satisfied? And you know you would have said yes."

Good thing I was facing the stove, because that made me smile. Of course I would have.

Chris went on, carefully, "Anyways I talked to Grandma today and she sent a message for you."

"Yes? Eat up." Soup bowl and melty sandwiches were on her plate.

"She said, look out for stuff about some meetings with politicians? And a big rally? Can that be right? She said she remembers being at a rally, and would remember more, she's sure, if you had pictures."

"Now that's weird. I was actually looking at some of those photos this morning. That's all she said?"

"Yup. For you, anyway." She grinned provocatively. "We had quite a talk."

"Oh? Anything I need to know?"

Chris smiled and shook her head.

"When are you going out with Joe?"

"What?"

She repeated with exaggerated patience, "Joe? When are you going out?"

"Later."

"'Cause he left a message on the phone. Said to text him with the time."

"That's it?"

She nodded and slid me her phone. "Here. You can tell him right now." She smiled a bit smugly. "Don't want him to think you didn't get his message."

"You are way too involved in this."

"That would be a matter of opinion. And what are you wearing?"

"Chris, it's only a neighborhood place with a friend. Not the White House."

"And I repeat, what are you wearing?"

"Good jeans, nice top. What I always wear."

"Not bad. I'll pick earrings for you."

I was about to protest when I remembered her earring collection far surpasses mine.

By then Chris was on her way back to her cave. I called to her, "You know, you can ask me for any help you need on that project. It *is* what I do for a living, more or less."

Words floated back. "Thanks but I've got it. No help needed."

That put me in my place.

I couldn't put off the NYPD call anymore. I had the card of the cop who talked to me that night. Somewhere. I had it somewhere.

Detective Ramos. I didn't remember the name. I hoped for a message system, but he answered himself. I didn't remember anything about those cops, but he remembered me.

"Ms. Donato, what can I do for you?"

I took a deep breath. "It might be that I can do something for you. I maybe learned something useful. It was strange…"

"I'm listening."

He sounded patient but not thrilled.

As I explained about who I had met, he quickly became more interested. "You have nothing except her name? Nothing at all? Come on!"

"She was trying to be mysterious! I think she liked it."

"Great."

"But she called me twice and I have the number she was using. That's worth something, isn't it? Even though it comes up as unlisted."

"You tried it, did you?"

"Well. Yes."

"We can trace it back and probably pull her driver's license, too. And you made notes, you said? Can you send them to me?"

I gave him Mary Pat's phone number and he gave me his e-mail.

"And she said she knew the first Mrs. Conti from when they were kids? Looks like I need to have another talk with Mrs. Conti then."

"So it is a little useful?"

"Could be."

"And will you tell me if you learn more from her? I would like to…I mean, it would be helpful…"

"I can't promise that! Or anything. It's a murder investigation, not a game of *Clue*. I'll be doing my job. That I can definitely promise." He stopped, then went on. "We appreciate your information, though, and thanks for that. Is that everything?"

"No. Not exactly." I took a deep breath. "I remembered something. At least I think I did. And you said to call if I did."

Suddenly his voice sounded very alert. "Ah. I hoped you might. And what would that be?"

I told him what I could, fumbling for words. The shooter was white. Something made me think, not young. Dark clothes.

"And that's it?"

"I'm afraid so. It was only a second of seeing him."

"How about visiting the scene together?"

That was unexpected and extremely unwelcome. What I get for being a good citizen.

"I would, but I don't see the point. It was just that second, in the dark. I don't remember another thing."

"We have ways of making you remember." He was silent for a second and then laughed. "Uh, that didn't come out quite the way I intended. Let's say sometimes we can shake loose a little more from the memory bank. Pick you up tomorrow at eleven?"

Something in his voice told me that if I said no, he'd ask again. I told him eleven was fine.

I was done. Off the hook for tonight. I was sweating but I was done.

Chapter Seven

Joe and I were going out to a quiet neighborhood bar, glass of wine, a chance to talk. He surprised me with a small envelope. "Put it someplace safe."

"Joe?"

"Theater tickets." He grinned. "I am taking you out for a real date night soon."

"Are you trying to sweep me off my feet?" I was laughing, joking, but he didn't exactly laugh with me.

Then he took the envelope back. "On second thought, I'll keep them safe better than you will." As we left, he said, "So how was your trip? It seems no one ended up in custody."

I giggled. "No, no, we were all okay. But my dad? He went to church with Phyllis. Church! My dad! You have no idea what a shock that was. Just being friendly, he said. Just establishing better ties with Phyllis."

"But did it work? Better ties, I mean."

That was Joe, making me think things through again. I found myself saying, "Yes, it probably did."

"And what else did everyone get up to?"

My stories about the personalities involved in the visit, and my reactions, took us until we got to the wine bar. Joe is a good listener and we all need someone, sometimes, who will let us prattle on.

We ordered and then he looked back at me. "So, what I get is, one, Chris got an excellent project going and, two, you may have something useful for your current responsibility and, three, your father and your daughter charmed a woman you've always called a dragon. Sounds like a good weekend's work to me, worth the trip."

"I hate to admit it, but you could be right." I hadn't even put that into words for myself. "She wasn't quite such a dragon this time. Phyllis, I mean. But I'm glad to be home."

He smiled and tilted his glass toward me. It felt good—no, it felt wonderful, to have someone in my life who would let me unload like that and at least pretend that he liked it. How long had it been that I had been going it alone? Certainly I had friends but I did not have a lot of time for socializing and never assumed they wanted to hear every little detail about my life. Joe wanted to.

It took me a while to notice he wasn't saying much about his.

On our second glass, with a plate of mixed Greek appetizers, I asked, "Is something wrong?"

He looked wary.

"I'm prattling on and you are hardly saying a word about yourself. Is it me? Am I being too self-centered?"

"I wasn't sure… ah, hell. I'll tell you. My sister's come back to town."

"Which one? The high school principal? Or your other sister in Connecticut? Oh, wait. You don't mean back, like, moving to Brooklyn?" I'd met the sisters. It seemed unlikely.

"Not those sisters." He wouldn't look at me as he said it.

I sat back. "Okay. What in hell are you talking about?"

He was silent for a very long time. I gulped down almost all my wine before he finally answered, "I have three sisters, not two. Jan in Merrick, nice house, principal, dentist husband, grown kids. Kate in Hartford, college kids, insurance exec, and so is her husband. Not them. I have another one. Alix, the baby." He smiled, but only a little. "She's about your age."

"And she's the baby? Seriously? I am no baby."

"Kidding." He put up placating hands. "I was kidding." Long pause, then he went on. "You don't know Alix, though.

She is…was…ahh…not quite adult." He stopped talking, took a bite and a drink.

"So my two big sisters, they were the good kids. Did well in school, had careers, families. The lives our folks planned for us." He stopped. "I was the one who was off the blueprint. In and out of school, took a few tries to find a career. Married for about five minutes, no kids. Myself, I know my life has turned out fine but they worry about me." He shook his head. "Not too much room for other ideas about life with my parents.

"But Alix? She came along late, when they were, I guess, tired of raising kids." He rubbed his forehead, that classic gesture of weariness. But Joe was never weary. I kept my mouth shut for a change and waited.

"She was the family wild child. Bad boys and alcohol, mostly. Artsy ideas with no focus. First rock guitar, then painting T-shirts. I found her at fifteen, with a six-pack, weed, and a boy old enough to have his own car."

"What did you do?" To a parent like me, it was a scary story. But he wasn't her parent. "How old were you then?"

"Twenty-four, maybe. I dragged her out of the car, told the kid what would happen if he ever came around again. It turned out he was twenty, not a kid, and I marched her home."

"She went, just like that?"

"Hell, no. She yelled and cried, but stopped when I pointed out she was lucky it was me and not our dad."

"Joe? You didn't!"

"I did. Of course I wouldn't handle it that way now."

"I was…I wasn't…"

"Yes, you were. You were wondering if I had lost my mind, right? Well, I was not much more than a kid myself then, but enough older to see she was getting herself into deep trouble."

"How'd that work out?"

"I honestly thought I had scared her into behaving, but she only got smarter about covering it up." He stopped there, ate a bite, sipped the wine. "At seventeen she ran away to Florida with a different boyfriend. To live on a citrus farm! She had a baby that she gave up for adoption, all before she was old enough to vote. Not that she probably ever did vote. Or go back to school or hold a regular job or any of those usual things."

"But, wait. I don't understand. Did you hear from her over the years? You? Or anyone?"

"Me. I did. I was the other confused one, at least for a while, so she thought I understood. She did show up at our grandmother's funeral, surprising all of us. Stood at the back, cried, and disappeared before anyone could talk to her. She sent me a postcard, after, saying only 'Sorry. I couldn't stand to have them all lecture me.' And now I get the occasional phone message about how she will be on the street if I don't send her money right away. Always to be paid back when the next big idea works out."

"Do you? Send the money?" He turned red. "Of course you do. 'Cause you are still her big brother." I jumped up and hugged him, right there in public. He looked pleased and embarrassed in equal parts.

I sat back down, adjusted my clothes and my expression. "Does she? Ever? Pay it back?"

"Never. The plans always hit a bump, never her fault, and then she disappears again for a while." He stopped for a long time, pursued the last of his spinach pie across his plate with a fork, and poured another glass. "She creates chaos whenever she shows up. She's my baby sister and there have been whole years I did not know where she was living."

"And now?"

"She is back. Single. Living at the Y."

"Good grief."

"She left me a message. She's in town, will be here awhile, when can we get together? She sounded…she sounded normal." His voice sounded strangely far away. "No slurred speech or incoherent statements this time. Here." He pulled out his phone. "I'll play it for you."

He was right. She sounded like an ordinary person trying to make a date with her brother. Except for the last sentence in a shaky voice. "I have a goal. It's to clean up the past."

I didn't know what to say. At least I didn't know what to say that would be safe. Joe usually has that quiet assurance that goes with being such a physically capable guy. I had never seen him thrown until tonight.

"So did you? Call her? "

"Tomorrow."

"This call was not…"

"I know. She sounds like a normal person. No way for me to tell you how unlikely that is."

"Is this all on you? I mean, your parents? Your other siblings?"

"Well, I'm not telling anyone, at least until I know what she is up to. My folks don't need the aggravation at this time in their lives." He took a deep breath. "Actually they got that 'tough love' counseling at some point and told her not to show her face until she got her life in order." He saw the uncensored reaction on my face. "Uh, yes, possibly they could have managed that better."

His parents lived in a Florida retirement community and I knew were slipping from active retirees to failing health.

"Truth is, she broke their hearts again and again."

What could I say to that? If it were Chris off the deep end, destroying her life, I didn't know how I would bear it. Or handle it. At that moment, with Chris safe not more than a few blocks away, I was having trouble breathing, merely thinking about it.

Joe finally smiled at me. Almost smiled. "So all that drama between you and Chris?" He waved his hand. "And you and your dad? It's nothing, so much fluff."

"Not fluff. It's completely different. He's the one…" If he wanted to distract me, he was succeeding.

"I know, I know. Just saying, there are problems. And then there are real problems."

"I get it." I wasn't sure I agreed, but I got his point.

It was time to go, drinks done and snacks serving as a meal. He held me tight as we walked home, but he wasn't exactly there, not dependably present, as he always seemed to be with me. His mind was somewhere else. Maybe back in the past with his sister.

Good night was a hug and quick peck.

"I've got to get home and just think out my approach for that call in the morning. I might call in the middle of the night for an edit. Think you can deal with that?"

"Any time." I owed him a few middle of the night calls.

I went in thinking about this surprise, this new look into Joe's life. And I thought I knew all about him.

I almost knocked on Chris' door for a girl-to-girl chat. Then I came to my senses and settled for calling good night.

• • ● • •

The next morning, Mrs. Pastore and I walked over to an old coffee shop, a New York tradition with an enormous menu, friendly waitresses, and low prices. The food was mediocre but with so many choices, it was easy to avoid the leathery eggs and order a safe corn muffin. A pot of coffee was there in front of us before we even asked. It was followed almost immediately by a tiny, white-haired smiling woman in big puffy coat.

When she was done unwrapping scarf, gloves, coat, and hat, Mrs. Pastore did her job. "Annabelle, this is Erica, my neighbor. Erica, say hello to Annabelle Conti."

Mrs. Conti smiled warmly. "Did I know you from Bishop Loughlin? I used to see so many coming in and out, sometimes I miss a few names. No, wait. Your kids would be too young to be there before I retired, and you…are you from the parish?"

"Annabelle, the whole world does not think in parishes. Erica is not from around here and is not even Catholic."

She smiled cheerfully. "This neighborhood is so full of new-comers, and why not?"

This warm woman was not the bitter ex-wife I had expected. I did not know how to raise the touchy subject of her ex-husband's murder in this ever-so-homey setting, where she was ordering pancakes with a side of sausage.

Mrs. Pastore had no such scruples.

"Annabelle, so listen…have you been watching the news?"

"You mean about Mike? Poor man."

"Don't tell me you still have warm place for him!"

"Don't be ridiculous. But he was the father of my child."

I tried to say how sorry I was and she looked at me with a faint smile.

"Any feelings I once had died a long time ago, dear, but still, it was, and it is, a shocking event."

"Young Erica was there when it happened."

Annabelle turned a strange expression on me, curiosity and steel combined.

"I'd like to know what happened."

When I was done, she nodded. "Sounds like his life caught up with him somehow." She looked first at me and then at Mrs. Pastore. "Oh, don't look so shocked." She pointed at me. "You told about that meeting. Well, that was the way he behaved to everyone. Hasn't spoken to his brother in decades, and they were in business together once. And our own daughter? That's a whole story in itself."

Her face and voice were as placid as a pond in June. "To tell the truth, I always figured if anything like that happened to him, Jennifer would be involved." She winked at Mrs. Pastore. Winked, talking about a murder. Had I strayed into *Through the Looking Glass?*

"I knew it." That was Mrs. Pastore, very excited. "I can see it all. She wasn't that cute cupcake anymore and he got restless and they must have had a pre-nup, so she…"

Not a Wonderland story. A soap opera.

Mrs. Conti said it. "Honey, you watch too many soap operas. I wasn't talking about Jennifer for real. Good grief." She turned to me. "I meant it like 'I could kill my husband, he forgot we had dinner plans.' Like, it's an expression. And I know she's said it. She's said it to me."

Mrs. Pastore put her coffee cup down with clattering emphasis. "Now that, I could never get. Not the part about killing him, the other. The two of you talking."

The waitress brought Mrs. Conti's plate, my corn muffin, and Mrs. Pastore's toasted bagel with double butter.

Then Mrs. Conti went on, "I grew better acquainted with

Jennifer over the years. You could almost say we have become friends."

Mrs. Pastore shook a disapproving head.

"Because Mike and I split up so long ago! I admit, I was deeply shocked at the time and then I was angry. I mean, to me, marriage is marriage, a Blessed Sacrament and lasts forever. Being happy?" She made a dismissive gesture. "I knew lots of unhappy marriages. So what? God joined them."

"Well, then...?"

I couldn't wait to hear the rest.

"So when he came to me and announced 'I want more, before I'm too old,' his bags were already packed! It took some time to sink in that I didn't miss him. Not even a little. I like living alone. Who knew? I redecorated my house to my own taste, and played the music I liked, and I lost the complaints, the bossiness, the tantrums."

"She isn't making it up." Mrs. Pastore's face had turned grim. "I saw the tantrums a few times. Everyone at Loughlin did."

"In public? He threw tantrums in public?"

Annabelle nodded slowly. "My daughter used to say, 'Mom, why do you let him?'" She shrugged. "I was brought up to be a good wife. The suits to the cleaner, taken by me, and the cotton underwear, ironed by me. The cooking, oh my God. The porchetta or the sausage and peppers on the table at six on the dot, whether he made it home or not. Every. Single. Night." She shook her head. "It took me a while to learn I could have scrambled eggs for dinner."

"What did you say to her then, to your daughter?" I had to ask.

"Then? I said, you show respect for your father, like I was brought up to do! So she did, except for a few screaming fights of their own over the years. But she married the opposite type of man, someone who thinks she's the cat's meow. She wears the pants in that house and he is fine with it."

She laughed and after a surprised moment, so did we.

"Were they...did they...your ex and your daughter..."

She flung a dismissive hand in the air. "After a while—and

a few heated discussions, I admit—her and me, we agreed not to talk about him."

"And now?"

Mrs. Conti shrugged. "She had kids. He is the grandfather." She paused. "*Was* the grandfather. He wore her down and she let him see them. But she had lots of limits, lots of rules. She didn't like him much and didn't trust him at all but he knew better than to bully her. 'Cause then, you know…" She made a scissors gesture. "She would cut him off the kids. Just like that." She snapped her fingers. "Tough broad, my little girl. And Jennifer helps with that, too."

Mrs. Pastore gave her a shocked stare. I might have too.

"That hussy? Now come on. I remember how you cried and cried when Michael left. She made a fool of you, stealing him like that."

She shrugged, then smiled. "That was then. Now we have a lot in common, it turned out. Because…" She paused dramatically. "Because, she found out her big-shot lover was not such a bargain as a husband. Ha." She shook her head. "And who understood that better than me? Silly girl that she was, she thought he'd always want her, because she was the 'not Annabelle.' Ya know? Not old, not skinny, not Italian, not Brooklyn. Not a housewife. But down the road, the wrinkles outran the Botox." She shook her head. "She was young and, oh, ambitious! I did hate her then. Today? Life is too short.

"Strange, isn't it? And now he's gone. I can't say I even feel anything. Jennifer doesn't either." She caught Mrs. Pastore's sharp look. "Yeah, yeah. I talked to her last night." She threw her hands up. "Ah, enough about that old s.o.b. And you can be sure, I never would have used that phrase in the old days, either, any more than the big D word, divorce."

She summoned the waitress, ordered more coffee and an assortment of Danish pastry for the table. Then she turned to me and asked a barrage of questions about my time in the neighborhood and what brought me here, and where Chris went to school. I explained about the financial aid that kept her in private school and how I had needed the after-school care when she was little.

A change of subject had been processed.

It wasn't until we were leaving, collecting scarves and gloves, that she murmured, "The old bastard had it coming. I'm surprised no one did it sooner."

Before we separated, Annabelle gave me a warm hug, "Call me if you need to know more about his career." She shrugged. "I don't have to watch what I say anymore. And after all those years at Loughlin? It became a habit, helping young people." She patted my arm. "Now you can be one of my youngsters too."

I was a long way from being a youngster, or a Catholic high school student, but I took the offer for what it was, kindly meant.

As soon as she was out of hearing, Mrs. Pastore exploded to me.

"I can never decide if she is a saint or an idiot!"

"What?"

"She could be both. I would find her crying in the staff bathroom sometimes. He had the nerve to show up at his daughter's graduation with that floozy. And they weren't even divorced then. Annabelle had to sit there and smile in front of everyone. They all knew her, of course, because she worked there." She shook her head, then added, "She wore a little tiny skirt and high, high heels."

I gave her an astonished look.

"Not Annabelle! Don't be ridiculous. The second Mrs. Conti. Future second at that time."

His private life made for an interesting story in itself but it would not help my work. I continued to think about it as I walked home, though. The first Mrs. Conti was very different from what I had expected. I wondered what the second Ms. Conti might be like, but that was idle speculation. I had no reason to ever meet her or even to follow up this area of his life. I was writing—trying to write—a scholarly dissertation, not a soap opera, I reminded myself sternly. I might even have ordered myself to get a grip.

Chapter Eight

I kept thinking about that Lieutenant Ramos. His refusal to tell me what he might learn about the mysterious Mary irritated me more each time I thought about it. I had found her for him—all right, she had found me—and he could be a little more generous. I needed to know more. Or wanted to, anyway, and I couldn't do it on my own.

Finally, I imagined telling all of this to Chris and immediately knew what her response would be. Something like "Mom, seriously? What century are you living in?"

I did what should have been obvious from the start. I went on Google and had her unlisted phone number information in perhaps ten minutes. A name: Mary Patricia O'Neill Codman. An address, in a boring stretch of Manhattan's East side with lots of modern, anonymous brick apartment buildings.

I could hardly believe it. And though I had an afternoon with responsibilities, there was nothing that I could not postpone or ignore. I would not let Chris get away with that attitude, but fortunately, I make the rules in our house.

My hands were gathering up my materials and jacket while my brain was still deciding. And on the subway I would write a list of questions, all the things I had been wishing I had said the other day. No more mystery woman. How phony was that? She liked the drama, I thought.

Deep underground, in the tunnels of the subway system, there was no cell phone reception. I didn't get Lisa's calls until

I was out on the street, walking the three long blocks from the station to Mary Patricia's apartment. Two messages, three texts. If she was that excited, it might be worth stopping in a quiet spot to see what was up.

"You'll change your mind about working together, because I found something about Conti I bet you don't know."

"Oh?"

"See. Now you're interested." I was, though I wasn't admitting it yet. "What do you know about his family?"

"Lisa, I am not writing a gossip column! I need to focus on his work and how it played out in the history. Ya know?"

"I also know you, old pal. And you will definitely want to know what I learned. So give. What do you know about his family?"

"An ex-wife." I didn't say I had met her. "A current wife. Maybe a girlfriend or two. One grown daughter."

"Yes, yes, all very public. And there's gossip that the new young girlfriend might be auditioning as wife Number Three. You knew that? But." She paused dramatically. "Did you know about the brother? And their feud? And that they haven't spoken in decades? I dug up that little tidbit, about someone who hated him, from one of the many other people who hated him."

I had to give in and discuss because I wanted to know more. A tidbit? Oh, yes.

"I heard something. It sounds like…I mean, he was a man with lots of enemies. So there is one more. Is that where you're going with this?"

"Sort of. But this brother, he fell out of sight. One of many questions I need to try to answer." I could hear the grin in her voice. "Working on it now. So, was that good enough for a trade?"

She nailed me. It just popped out. "You might have one more person who hated him, but I might have met the only person who will miss him."

"You didn't."

"I most certainly did."

"Tell. Tell now! Wait? Any chance your phone is bugged? I don't want anyone else to pick this up."

"My phone? Don't be ridiculous."

"Then tell. This could be big. I'm recording, okay?"

So I told her about the mysterious Mary, the little that I knew.

"A secret lover in this gossipy day and age? Damn. She's a source no one else knows about! She left out a lot, though, didn't she? How come you didn't pin her down more?"

"It was, let's say, quite unnerving. But I am going to learn more and, yes, I'll trade for whatever you dig up about the brother."

"What are you now? I hear traffic."

"I found this woman's address. I'm on the way to talk to her."

"Again, where are you?"

When I told her, she responded, "I'm coming, too! Where exactly? I'm not far. Don't move! I can be there in twenty minutes. Maybe less."

"Lisa, no, I need to…"

"I'm already out the door." And she was gone.

I waited. It did occur to me that another set of ears and eyes, especially her sharp, trained ones, could be helpful with this evasive woman. And she was there in fifteen minutes.

Wouldn't Lieutenant Ramos be surprised if we learned anything new?

We walked up to exactly what I expected, a mid-twentieth-century white brick apartment building, clean and modern and so very anonymous. Just what you'd want for a love nest, I supposed. There were perfectly trimmed plants in front and a bright lobby with a reception desk and a uniformed attendant. He politely asked for our destination.

"Oh, yes, Mrs. Codman. Lovely lady. Who may I say is calling?"

"Say it's Ms. Donato. She'll definitely want to see us." I thought Lisa's confidence was unwarranted.

He checked on a house phone and told us to take the left elevator to the twelfth floor. We hustled to it before minds could be changed. At her door, I heard the bell ring, footsteps, someone peeking through the security peep hole. Finally, locks turned and she opened the door a crack.

"So it is you. I wasn't convinced. And you have more to tell me? But who is this?"

Introducing Lisa to a woman we could barely see was more than a bit awkward.

Finally she muttered, "I suppose you should come in. You seem harmless enough. I wasn't expecting visitors."

She was in a terrycloth robe, her hair disheveled, a cigarette in her hand. The elaborately furnished apartment had newspapers all over the living room.

"Sit. You can move those papers. I was looking for anything about Mike. Why are you here?"

I started with, "Now I have your name and where you live. It's very nice, by the way."

"It's a few blocks from where Mike had his office. Very convenient for those little visits." Her voice shook. "That was the best part, but he liked his luxury too. He helped me buy it and furnish it. He used to come..." She wrapped her trembling hands tightly around a glass. I was close enough to smell the alcohol.

"You came to tell me more about Mike. So what was it?"

"I, uh, well, I just wanted to know more about him. That's all. I'm writing a scholarly chapter about the Navy Yard and he was there through everything. I thought you probably know all about his career."

She looked at me with disbelief and some hostility. As if, why should she talk to me?

I was about to tell her Annabelle had offered to help—it would either get me thrown out or she would compete with Mike's wife—when Lisa jumped in.

"I'm writing an article about him, about Michael Conti. And I want to get the other side. You must know lots of people didn't like him, but you did. So what is the other side?"

She closed her eyes, shook her head, and looked at us again.

"I didn't always like him, either. Damn straight. But we were true soul mates. It took us too long to figure that out. And he wandered. Me too." She stabbed her cigarette out with a lot of energy, as if she was crushing something. "Believe me, I did my share. But he always, always came back. With flowers. Sometimes fine jewelry. That painting over there. Making up was always great. Thunder and lightning."

"You knew him better than anyone?"

"Damn straight, I did. I knew everything about him." She leaned in. "Lately he'd come to see me, and he wasn't himself. We liked to play cards. It was relaxing, honeymoon bridge or gin rummy. We'd play for silly things. Pennies. M&M's. Strip poker." She looked at us steadily, as if daring us to be shocked at that. For the first time she smiled a little when she said it.

"And he couldn't keep his mind on the game! I won everything, even when I was trying my best to lose. Now I have a jar of pennies and big dish of candy." She started to sob, but stopped herself. "It's right there. Help yourself. I don't need the reminder of him."

"But what was he afraid of? I bet you know." That was Lisa, sounding as cozy as if she was talking to a dear friend. Boy, she was good at this.

"He told me—me! not that WASP cupcake he married—that he was afraid, that someone was threatening him. Trust me." She slammed her hand down on the sofa cushion for emphasis. "My Mike wasn't afraid of anyone, not even mob guys in the unions. Hell, he grew up on the docks. He was a fighter. So this was… it was strange. More than strange. Unheard of for him to say that, and remember, I've been hearing him say things for a lot longer than you girls have been breathing."

"Did he tell this to the police? Did you?" My head was swimming. "They need to know. I mean maybe that threat is what came after him."

"I know. I know that." She whispered it. "But why would I go public now? No one ever knew about me. To tell the truth, it kept things exciting, to be so secret. I'm going to tell someone now?" She grabbed my arm. "Besides, maybe they would come after me too. I know all the good things Mike did for this city, and believe me, he did plenty. And all the bad he did, too. Someone could come after me too, to keep me quiet."

What a drama queen. This little old lady in trouble? But I did try to get her to take her story to the police while Lisa tried to get her to tell us more. That was when she stood up. "We are done. You have nothing for me and I'm not talking about Mike's secrets to anyone."

Lisa tried to ask some more questions but Mary threw open the door to her apartment and stood there, waiting.

"If you are not out right now, I will call the desk. Believe me, this building has security on call."

We looked at each other and knew it was time to go. We didn't say a word until the elevator doors closed, and after the person riding in it got off at nine. Then we couldn't stop.

"She is a character. I love this job! And she shouldn't think she can hide all the secrets, either. I'm on it for real now."

"She said he was afraid. Wow, right? And she feels like she has to keep his secrets, but we don't, right? I'm talking to that police lieutenant tonight, for sure."

"Okay, but can you keep quiet about me?" Lisa grabbed my arm as we reached the lobby but she held the button that kept the door closed. "Please? Because he might give me a hard time about asking questions. Or even, not trust you because you know me? Cops don't like reporters much."

"What? Oh, okay, I don't have to mention it, I guess. But I won't lie if he asks. Deal?"

"Fair enough." She let the button go and the doors slid open to impatiently waiting riders.

"What a day!" She almost bounced, walking down the street. "I've got to get back to the office or I'd say let's have a drink."

"No matter. I've got to get home."

Chapter Nine

Later, Detective Ramos turned out to be fortyish, average height, polite and confident. Good hair. Neat, casual clothes. Nice. I still didn't remember him. He didn't drive a police car but one of those anonymous American models favored by plainclothes cops.

We drove right up to the Navy Yard gate. The guard looked at his badge, made a phone call and waved us through. We parked in the museum driveway. The nice thing about riding with a cop is that he can park anywhere. Perhaps only a New Yorker can truly appreciate that pleasure.

The stop was just a courtesy call, I thought. He could go wherever he wanted. The rest of the property isn't open to the public. It is now a humming beehive of small manufacturing and includes a very private film studio. No casual visitors allowed. I knew that and suspected he did too, but of course now it was also a crime scene.

The young woman at the desk smiled brightly. "Let's get someone to show you around."

A minute later, there she was, a sixty-ish woman with short gray hair and a body that was all muscle. "I am Dr. Randi Hartz, the museum director." She shook our hands firmly. "Call me Randi. What can I do for you?"

After all the explanations, she offered to show us around herself. "It's lucky I have a little time right now." She smiled. "How can I resist a plea to support both scholarship and crime-solving?"

And keep us from going anywhere we didn't belong?

Detective Ramos agreed, with the understanding that she could not listen in or participate in any questioning he did with me. She smiled somewhat coldly. "Do you think I have nothing else to do but play cops and robbers?" She hoisted a large file of papers. "I'll be working when you are."

She set off at a brisk pace and we followed until she stopped. "Now you need to lead the way to where you went that night."

"It was dark so I'm not sure…but I was trying to go toward Admirals' Row."

"You couldn't have gone far. That area is gated and locked. It's too unsafe to have people wandering around there. Our board is afraid of an accident and a lawsuit. Rightly, I suppose." She pointed down the path. "Anyway, come on this way. This is where you must have walked."

I followed, feeling a little sick as I walked back toward the neglected, woodsy area where I had witnessed the murder. I told myself the crime had nothing to do with me. Nothing at all.

We soon came to a dead stop where the crime-scene tape was still up.

When a cop approached us, he called Detective Ramos "Sir" and allowed us in. Detective Ramos indicated that Dr. Hartz should keep back now, and then he turned to me, "Let's start with you standing exactly where you were then."

"Here, I think." I stood where two paths crossed. "I stopped because I was trying to figure out which way to go next."

"And where was the light coming from?"

"Over there." I pointed to the nearest pole that had dimly lit the path. "I guess."

"So you're standing here. Paved path, but woodsy. Yes?" He spoke softly, even gently. "What do you feel on your skin? What's the weather like?"

"Um, getting chilly. Late fall weather and it's nighttime."

"Do you smell anything?"

"No. Wait. Yes. A little moldy smell. Like from fall leaves piling up. I smell it now."

"And what do you hear?"

"Voices. People were talking, coming out of the meeting."

"Where are those sounds coming from?"

"Over there." I waved. "Beyond the trees."

"Can you see any of those people? Take a minute and think about that. Or can you hear what they are saying?"

I shook my head. "No. It was like kids getting out of school. Loud voices all at once. I couldn't make out anything, and I wasn't trying. I did feel safer, hearing them, and knowing I wasn't really alone, even though I was alone right here."

"You were alone here? How did you feel?"

I couldn't see the point of this. He guessed at my impatience. "I'm trying to take you back to that moment."

"I felt a little nervous, and a little, I don't know, disappointed. I wasn't going to see much in this night walk, and I was ready to turn around. Then there was a sound from under the trees. Rustling."

"What did you think about that?"

"An animal, maybe? But it sounded big. It sounded too big for a squirrel or a feral cat."

"Could it be a person?"

I nodded.

"You're doing great." He smiled. "Tell me what happened next."

"I saw a shape in the dark, like a moving shadow. A person-shaped shadow, but I couldn't see more than that. And then he turned a little, like I told you, but it put him in the light. In the split second, I saw a pale face and hands, and I knew, somehow, he was old. Or not young, anyway."

"How old?"

"I have no idea. It was only a second."

"All right. Close your eyes and remember. Now. What did you see that made you think 'old'?"

I tried. I tried hard but there was nothing. And then, to my astonishment, there was. "Gray hair."

"Ah. Very good. Any facial hair? Mustache? Beard?"

"I don't know!" I heard my voice rising. I don't like not having answers.

"You're doing fine." His voice was calm, even soothing. "Fine. Only a few more questions. Take a deep breath."

I did as I was told.

"Now close your eyes again. Very good. Think about this moment. What do you see?"

"Pale face. The hair, gray, peeking out from under something dark. A cap."

"Why are you sure it is a man? What do you see?"

I did see something. "Stubble! Stubble on his face. Or something like that. I'm seeing gray skin."

"What next?"

"He moved and he was back in shadows again. I saw him lift a shadowy arm with something at the end. Then…a loud sound I knew… and then it's all a blur."

I let out a deep, shaky sigh and Detective Ramos smiled. "I can tell you are at the end. You've done great. If anything else comes to you, be sure to contact me immediately, okay?"

"Sure. But there isn't any more."

"Oh? Look at all you remembered today. I went to a hypnotist to quit smoking. Maybe we'll get her in to work on you next time."

He laughed when he saw my horrified look. "Just kidding. But you might have more hidden away in the brain cells, so stay alert to them, okay?"

I was exhausted and sweating, even though we had done nothing but talk and the air was chilly. And when the detective shook my hand, I felt a strange connection, as if we had shared a moment of intimacy. That added confusion to my exhaustion.

"Dr. Hartz? Do you have more to do with Ms. Donato, or should I offer her a ride home?"

"You're done?" She came back toward us checking her watch. "I have some time." She turned to me. "Would you like a little private tour? Something less traumatic? Detective?"

I nodded but Ramos shook his head. "Duty calls. Ms. Donato, thank you. You've been a trooper." He smiled. "Get in touch if you have any more strange phone calls."

"But have you learned anything about the last one?" I saw my chance and took it. I wanted to know if he knew more, now, than I did.

He smiled apologetically, but shook his head. No new information? Or none he would share?

"Does that mean...?"

"Ms. Donato," he interrupted, "thank you." And he was gone. Before I could go after him with my questions, Dr. Hartz said, "Come on." She went off briskly in a new direction. "I have an idea, and I know you'll enjoy this more than your grilling by that cop."

A paved walk ahead, a loop, and then we were at a fence. It was a big fence, tightly padlocked. Through it I could glimpse the ghostly houses of Admirals' Row. I pressed my face against the fence, trying to see it all.

"Let's go." She winked at me and waved a large bunch of keys. "Don't go one step anywhere on your own. Okay? Because if you get hurt, I am in big trouble."

I thought she might have her priorities wrong about me getting hurt, but I was happy to agree.

The houses were lovely. Of course I am biased. I like old houses. I bought my own old house, not a lovely one, against many parental lectures about a bright split-level house on Long Island.

They had simple, classic, early nineteenth-century exteriors but the proportions made them beautiful. They were still beautiful but they were dying. Dr. Hartz moved a large fallen branch that lay across our path. A difficult walk through overgrown vegetation took us to a house covered with vines, like in a fairy tale.

We got close enough to peep in. An elegantly curved staircase but rubble all over the floor, a hole in the ceiling, finely molded plasterwork crumbling and stained.

"Officers stationed at the Yard lived here with families. Once upon a time, there used to be children here, dinner parties, dancing, holidays. Music. They found a rotted piano in one. The strings were all chewed up by animals."

She pointed to the house where half the building had collapsed, and we could see the crumbling rooms within. It was like looking into crazy derelict dollhouses. There was a bathtub upstairs, an old coal range in a kitchen. Delicately stenciled walls and a young tree growing in the dining room.

"You know about Matthew Perry? The admiral who opened up Japan? He was the Yard commander for a while; he lived right over there." She pointed to the largest house.

In another, there was a bathroom piled with rubble and rotting wood. And there were beer bottles, wine bottles, a piled-up nest of now sodden blankets, a makeshift set of table and chairs.

I pointed and Dr. Hartz shook her head. "Oh, yes, there were problems with squatters over the years. And of course teens sneaked in just because the fence challenged them not to. When the buildings were still fairly safe, it must have been a tempting private space. Not now."

She looked sad. "Ten years ago they could have been saved. Some of them, anyway. We have photos at the museum if you'd like to see how they looked then. Now they are too far gone."

Once again I was torn between being a historian, mourning loss of the evidence of the past, and being a social historian, knowing that the new supermarket and the jobs it would bring would change lives in the neighborhood. So, farewell and hail. In the city, the only constant is change.

In the next house, where there was still a roof, we saw a large pile of bottles and cans from hash and spaghetti and soup. The labels were still intact. And a cheap manual can opener and a camp stove. A radio and a sleeping bag rolled up and wedged into a doorless cabinet.

"Damn. I see we still have squatters here." Dr. Hartz whipped out a phone and took pictures. "We should go now. I have to go raise hell with security."

We walked away quickly. "I can't help feeling compassion." Dr. Hartz's voice shook a little. "But they are not safe. It is truly dangerous."

"People are living there? Invisible to everyone? It feels like real ghosts." I shuddered. "Ghosts even while they are still alive, haunting a place that is gone."

"What an admission for a historian! Ghosts, indeed!" Then Dr. Hartz added, "Not to say that we haven't had our ghost stories over the years. But believe me, whoever is eating those cans of hash is no ghost."

A small beep startled us back into the real world. She looked at her watch. "I don't have time to deal with this now. I have a meeting coming up."

We did not stop at the crime scene. In fact, she led me back on a different path entirely. It was a relief to emerge into the bustling working part of the property.

"Thank you for taking me there and giving me a chance to look at this before it's gone."

"I must run. If needed, can someone talk to you about what we saw? That evidence of a squatter?"

I replied that of course they could, but I was sure no one would need to. I was done with the Navy Yard of today, the physical place. I needed to get back to work on the Navy Yard of history, which lived on only in the documents.

Chapter Ten

As it turned out, I was not done. Not even close. Very early the next morning, pink dawn-sky early, there was a pounding my front door, alternating with persistent doorbell-ringing.

"Mrs. Pastore, what in the world?"

"I gotta talk to you right now. I know it's too early. I know. But I have Annabelle at my house and she is raving. You got to come over."

"What? Now? But I don't understand."

"I don't understand neither, but it seems like she's mad at you. Come on! Get your coat on!"

So I left a note for sleeping Chris and got my jacket. Mrs. Pastore was a good neighbor and could also be a force of nature when she needed to be. I knew I had no choice.

The sweet elderly woman I had met was gone. In her place was a raging fury, pacing back and forth in the Pastores' old-fashioned, cluttered kitchen. Her tired old eyes were now bright with anger.

"They came to see me, the cops. Because of you."

"Annabelle. Honey. You know you already talked to them before this."

"Yeah, well, they came back. And they wanted to know about an old love of Michael's. An old, old love, from back when we were kids. Erica told them all about her. They wanted to know who she was and what I know about her."

She sat down suddenly, arms crossed, mouth in a grim little line.

"And? Did you tell? Did you even know?"

"I told them nothing. They have no right to paw over my private life like that."

"But they do." I thought I was being the voice of reason. "They..."

She started to cry. "All those years. All those years. I knew about some of the other women, sure. I didn't like it. What wife would? But I didn't know he was still seeing her. She was some little tramp, even then, young Mary Pat O'Neill as she was then. I can't remember her married names. A real man trap."

Mrs. Pastore handed her a box of tissues.

"I think they were going to Jennifer too. Something one of them said..." She pulled a phone from her pocket and hit one button. "Jennifer, it's me. Call me right away. It's very important."

"I didn't know it mattered, after all these years," Annabelle whispered. "Funny, isn't it?"

The doorbell rang, ripping into her grief.

"At this hour?" Mrs. Pastore grumbled as she went to the front of the house. She returned looking grim followed by a younger woman in a long fur coat. Younger, I thought on second look, but not as young as she wants to seem.

She and Annabelle hugged, and she let the fur coat slip to the floor. In jeans and a glittery sweater, high-heeled boots and makeup at this early hour, even dressed down she looked dressed up.

I was in the yoga pants I had been sleeping in when Mrs. Pastore came to my door.

"What are you doing here? I called you this minute. How did you find me?"

"I called a car right after the cops left. And your housekeeper knew me and told me where you went."

She looked right past Mrs. Pastore's hostile eyes, ignored me, and turned to Annabelle. "We are in some trouble, you and me."

"So they did find you too? Those cops?"

"You do remember I am the actual widow? Of course they found me. They shouldn't even still be coming to you. They should be leaving you alone and dealing with me."

" I suppose they had to question us, once someone with a big mouth told them." She flashed an angry stare at me. "But you? You don't go back far enough to answer questions about Mary Pat."

"Very true. I couldn't tell them more even if I wanted to, which I don't, but they talk to everyone." She ran her hands through her glowing blond hair in a gesture of frustration. Or perhaps, instinctively showing off.

"It doesn't look good to have cops coming to my door. I'll be hearing from my co-op board tomorrow, I'm sure. It's not what they expect on Park Avenue." She almost chuckled and Annabelle almost smiled. "If she was one of Mike's other women, how would I even know which one?" She paused. "You know Michael. He lived his own life."

"How are you doing, honey?"

"Okay. I guess. Did you know he had a pre-planned funeral? So I don't even have to do that. Do you want the information?"

"Hell, no. Only if Nicole wants me to come. But you need to tell her."

"I would, but she hangs up on me. Guess I'll mail it to her."

"It's not right for her not to be there."

"Agreed. The absolutely right thing to do now is show the outside world we are united over his death. I can fake that as well as the next Park Avenue bitch. I don't intend to give them anything extra to gossip about."

Annabelle was nodding her head. "Absolutely right! Nicole will be there, I promise, and I will be too."

"Ha, ha. We can receive together."

"And maybe get some of the girls on the side to stand in line with us." Jennifer smiled at Annabelle, and they giggled.

"That is so ridiculous, it is funny."

The giggling was rising into laughter with an undertone of hysteria. Even Mrs. Pastore joined in, and Annabelle was hitting the table, gasping, "Oh, oh. The very thought of all of us lined up…"

"Together! Graciously accepting condolences!" Jennifer reached for the tissues, laughing so hard she was crying..

I couldn't believe what I was seeing. Then we heard Mr. Pastore bellowing from upstairs.

"What is going on there? Why are you having a hen party at the crack of dawn?"

We all looked at each other, silenced but bursting.

"Crazy broads! I'm going back to bed. Keep it down."

Then we did start giggling again, me included, but very softly.

Jennifer picked up her fur coat. "Come on, Mrs. Conti Number One. I've got a car and driver waiting. I'll take you home."

"Wait." I needed to speak up for myself. "Wait. I have questions. Annabelle, you seem to think being questioned was my fault but I can't keep secrets about it. It's a murder. Don't you both want to have it solved?"

"Actually, I don't know if I care. It is horrible but…"

Jennifer interrupted. "And your other question?" She sounded profoundly uninterested.

"Is it true that there was a brother? And a feud?"

Annabelle sat down so suddenly the chair squeaked. "Another piece of the past. How did you learn about that, anyway?"

I kept my mouth shut.

Now Jennifer looked angry and grim too. "I thought that was long buried."

"You know, Jen, my father-in-law—sorry, *our* father in-law—hated these family feuds. His wife and her sister had a fight over their mother's cameo brooch and never spoke again. He made me promise to keep the family together, but…" She had tears in her eyes. "I felt so guilty that I couldn't."

"I never knew that. But no one could have. It all blew up so long ago. About a boat business."

Annabelle nodded. "They were in a boatworks together, out in Sheepshead Bay. They had a knockdown fight." The two women were talking to each other. I was forgotten but I was listening to every word. "They were punching and rolling around on the rug. The business was going under and he blamed Mike.

"You know he used to come see me for awhile? After Mike left? But then he stopped, and he stopped calling and then he moved out of his little place and no one knew where he was." Annabelle's voice shook. "I don't even know if he is still alive."

"Stupid old men. " Mrs. Pastore said it out loud. "Stupid old men, to let hate poison their family."

"I prayed plenty for them. To St. Jude, for hopeless causes." Annabelle smiled sadly. "And to St. Anthony of Padua."

"For things that are lost?" Mrs. Pastore looked startled and then seemed to realize it was a half-hearted joke.

Mrs. Pastore poured another round of coffee and with a defiant glance at the clock, poured some Sambuca into each cup. She lifted her cup. "*Salut*!" Then we all did.

Annabelle put her coat on and pointed an angry finger at me. "But you. Don't get any more cops in my life. They remind me of all I want to forget. Did forget. Now they make me think about it all over again."

• • ● • •

I went home and curled up under my warm comforter, happy that I had no place to be in the rapidly approaching morning. Only my desk.

I was awake soon, against my will, unable to sleep any more. I found Chris in the kitchen, dressed and ready to go, munching a piece of toast as she zipped her jacket and looked for her gloves.

"So long, Mom." She kissed me before she left. "Have a great day. Got to run."

When I was sufficiently caffeinated, I sat down and tried to think about, well, everything. To unwind some of the tangles. I made a list. My own work—I had to get that chapter on the Navy Yard neighborhood written. And soon. My part-time museum job-I'd had a break at the end of a project, but starting tomorrow, I owed them two or three days a week. Plus that meeting with the HR department. And Chris' family history. How was she doing and did she need my help? Right now it looked like more fun than my dissertation. Joe's suddenly complicated life—how could I help him? Did I want to help him? Yes, I did. I should. Did he want me to? That part was not at all clear. And Phyllis' questions about her aunt.

And I should share my new knowledge with Lisa.

I looked at what I had written and thought there was enough for two lives on that sheet of paper.

Chris came home early and found me in her room, looking at her walls, now even more decorated. Propped up on every surface were boards with pictures

"These are memory boards, Mom." My expression must have been quizzical. "Come on, Mom. You've heard about these. It's a thing. Like, I don't know, scrapbooks. You can buy them all set up but I made mine. You, like, record events or work out ideas or whatever. Put up what you love best to remind yourself." She stared at me again, "Mom! Come on! It's not that hard."

It looked like a big waste of time to me. So does scrapbooking. But Chris was excited, so I tried to pay attention.

"I thought if I was going to write about Philomena, this would be a good way to get organized. See? One for when she worked at the Navy Yard, one for her career after, one for family."

She was so proud of her work, I had to take a good look. Styrofoam boards covered with dainty fabric and crisscrossed ribbons to hold the photos. On one she had reorganized the ribbons to create a family tree, starting with Philomena's parents and ending with Chris herself in a tiny baby picture I recognized. Above it was a photo of Jeff and me in our prom clothes. Where had she found that? And there were Jeff's parents, in their wedding photo. I hadn't seen that one in a long time. Phyllis in her wasp-waisted, bouffant wedding gown and veil with a sparkly crown. So 1950s.

So. A memory board, it seemed, was a tarted-up bulletin board, but with a theme. It still seemed silly, but it did not mean I was not caught up in the oldest set of photos. Arranged for connections, they certainly were more evocative than when I had last seen them, tossed into a shoebox.

Chris took me on a guided tour, pointing out her favorites from the first boards, especially the one of Philomena tightening rivets with a scary-looking tool. And the jokey one, taken with what must have been a simple box camera, of Philomena holding up her first federal paycheck. It was too tiny to read, but it was labeled. Her smile was a yard wide, and the triumphant raised-fist bicep-flexed pose made me laugh.

"This next board isn't so interesting. It's all committee meetings and stuff." She was right about that. No charm and no nostalgia. Nothing but boring people in boring suits. "But here's one…" Philomena in a line with a group of men, arms linked in solidarity, leading a crowd of protesters. They were protesting the closing of the yard.

I looked again. Was that Michael Conti whose arm was linked with Philomena's brother?

"Chris, are there any others like this one? I have a reason."

"I think. Maybe." She dived for the floor and pulled a box out from under her bed.

If only I could get this blown up, or look at it with a magnifying glass.

"You can take this. So what do you think of my plan?"

I came back to the moment with a start.

"I can't tell if it is brilliantly inspiring or a complete waste of time." I smiled after I said it.

"You will know which when I get the best grade possible on my project and you hear how brilliant I am. So there." But she was smiling too.

"Mom?"

"Yes, Chris. I'm right here." I was still looking through the box to see if there were other photos that might include Conti.

"Well, it's about my birthday."

"A long way off."

She removed the box from my hands. "Please pay attention. I'm going to be sixteen."

"Yes, I was there when you were born."

"That is a beyond-lame joke. I am being serious."

"Ok. I'm listening."

"Well, so we need to plan a party."

"We do? I thought you'd want your usual sleepover, movies, games, up all night, waffles and ice cream in the morning."

"You haven't thought about it at all!" She looked very stern. "It's my sweet sixteen. We have to plan something."

Her birthday was many months away. I was not even close to being ready to think about it. But, yes, she had been to some elaborate parties, with catering and a band, and they cost a lot of money I did not have. Was it time to panic?

"Chris, I can't manage a party at a restaurant. I just can't. You have no idea what it would cost."

"But! But, we can't do pizza and a sleepover, like it's nothing. Mom, we just can't." Her voice rose with each word.

"Chris, calm down. It's only a party…."

"Don't tell me to calm down." I should have known better, after fifteen plus years as a parent. "And it's not 'only' a party. How can you say that? It's my sweet sixteen. Everyone talks about them. Everyone! Before and after. I can't embarrass myself in front of my whole class. I can't." She threw herself facedown on her bed. Only being in her own room prevented her from running out and slamming the door.

I must keep calm, I told myself. Two hysterical women in a room is at least one too many. "Chris!" I snapped it out to cut through the drama. "We will think of something, okay? Something affordable that will be fun and do you proud, okay? Not a hotel and a live band, but…"

"Not? Oh, no."

"We can't get into a competition with your wealthy classmates. Not in the plans. That's the way it is, end of story, but we will find something we can do that will make you happy. You have to trust me on this."

She nodded, but her face was still buried in her pillow. And, I thought as I left, that's what I get for sending her to private school. My own sixteenth birthday party was dancing to a boom box in the basement family room, and pizza and sodas for refreshments. Maybe some of the boys sneaked in something stronger. I wasn't telling Chris that part.

• • ● • •

When the call came, it was from a personal phone with caller ID, not the masked number on a work phone. Lieutenant Ramos. I thought, *What now? I don't want to talk to him again. Not now. Not ever. I'm busy. And there is nothing more I can tell them. Not one thing.*

So of course I answered it.

Detective Ramos had something to tell me. "We might've located that woman you met so mysteriously. Not that the first Mrs. Conti was any help in finding her, or the second one either."

"And?"

"We need you to confirm she's the same woman you talked to. I think we can start by sending you a picture. You have a computer?"

"Of course I do."

"Tell me your e-mail and we'll send it. You write back right away, okay?"

This all seemed very strange.

"There were pictures of Michael Conti in her place. That's why they called me. But she lived in Manhattan, near his office.

"I'll need to go over every single thing you told us about your meeting with her and we need to do it today."

I looked at my unfinished page on the screen, my messy office, my calendar reminding me of everything else I needed to do. But I was already dressed. I'd eaten.

"If you must."

He didn't acknowledge my rudeness.

"There's a, um, a thing."

"One more thing?"

"You could say that. She's dead."

"What are you talking about?" I'm sure my voice went up an octave.

"Sorry. I forget not everyone thinks like a cop. Yes, she's dead. Her cleaning lady found her yesterday morning."

"Did she...? Was she...heart...?"

"Only in the sense that people are dead if their heart stops beating." He paused, as if he was thinking. When he went on, it was softer voice. "Hers may have a bullet in it."

I sat down hard. "I don't believe it."

"I'm a cop. Would I lie to you?"

Was he serious? There were lots of ways to answer that question, many of them hostile.

"Let me start again." I had a feeling he had heard his own words. "She was shot, probably..."

"Shot? She was murdered?"

"Looks like it. We're pretty definite it's not a suicide."

Chapter Eleven

"She told me she was afraid." I could barely say the words. "I didn't believe her. I thought she was only being melodramatic."

"And when was this? It's not in what you told us. If she had given you any actionable information, perhaps we could have helped."

"But why are you…? I don't understand…? How did you… My phone number…?"

"Nope, we never found a cell phone. And we did look. But we have her name, partly the same as the one you had. And with the Conti photos it didn't take a genius to guess."

"And you came to me."

"Yes, since we seem to have a relationship now." He stopped. "Just kidding on that. I'm still on the Conti case, of course, so I'm following those connections."

"I am having trouble taking this in. Any of it."

"Give it time. It will sink in eventually, probably while we go over every single word of what you told us. We might need a sworn statement, too, if there is anything that impacts on this. Later today? Will you be home? I'll come by. I'm helping canvass her apartment building this morning. We don't believe no one heard or saw anything."

"Conti helped her buy it, she said." My mouth moved, saying whatever came into my head. My brain was too shocked to be working.

"Hold that thought, and any others you have."

By the time he arrived, it was late afternoon and I had, in fact, forced myself to do some of my own work. I thought I was more relaxed. And more focused. I hoped Chris would not be home before we were done.

I offered him coffee or a soda and sucked up some caffeine myself.

He had the notes of what I had told him.

"I know her full name now," I offered. "Mary Patricia O'Neill Codman. I guess you do too."

"Of course. But how did you get it?"

"I did a little research myself."

"Oh? Same place you learned she was afraid? I'll want to get back to that interesting topic. First, tell me again what she said to you when you met her."

I tried to tell it again, exactly as I remembered it. Then he played a recording he had made the first time I told him. "Not bad. You're saying pretty much the same thing."

And then it was time to tell him about my second conversation with her. He didn't look too happy about what I had done, or Lisa's role, but he listened intently.

"Think. Think very hard. This part about Conti being afraid? Was there anything else at all?"

"No! Honestly, there was nothing. Was she....do you think it was the same gun as the one that killed Michael Conti?"

"You are not asking the questions here. I am." His expression was not as hostile as his words. "Did she say anything else about Conti? Anything else you left out before? Think hard."

"No. No! But Mrs. Conti did. The first Mrs. Conti. She said they went back to when they were kids. They were all from the same neighborhood. Carroll Gardens? They called it South Brooklyn then, I think. Or even Red Hook." I saw no reason to tell him the names Mrs. Conti called her. "Is that a help at all?"

"Maybe. We have to follow up on everything. What else did she say, the first Mrs. Conti? I bet there's more."

How did he know? "She didn't like her at all."

He nodded. "And how did you learn all this?"

"She was over at my neighbor's, very angry about your visit, by the way, and blaming me for it."

"Too bad. We would have come to her anyway. She'll talk to us again, too, like it or not. How'd you meet her?"

I told him about Mrs. Pastore and our two meetings. He listened, not saying a word until I was done.

"Mrs. Conti Number Two was there too?" By then he was almost laughing.

"It was a somewhat, um, let's say, surprising morning."

"I bet it was. And did Mrs. Conti Number Two have anything to say about this mystery woman?"

"No. It seemed like it was before her time in his life. Though it wasn't, as it turned out."

"Okay. Something bothers me, though. It's not clear to me how you have become so involved with the story of the late Mr. Conti."

"What exactly do you mean? You can't think…just what do you think?"

"My thinking follows the facts wherever they lead. That's my job. Right now, they don't lead to you. If I should find out that they do, I'll be back with uncomfortable questions, count on that. But your interest is hard to understand."

I took a deep breath. "It's completely innocent, even boring. I am writing a history dissertation. This will be a chapter. But my advisor is on my back to finish it and she wants me to skip this part altogether."

He listened until I had explained it all. It took the time to have a second cup of coffee.

"I get it now. Your interest is entirely academic?" He smiled. "Pun intended."

Did he mean it, or was he being sarcastic?

There were keys clicking in the front door lock, and I called out, "Chris, I'm in here with a visitor. Okay for you to come in."

Someone came in but it was not Chris. It was Joe.

"Sorry. I didn't know you had company. Everything all right? I did call."

"I turned my phone off for this meeting."

"Would this be Mr. Donato? I did not realize…"

"No, no." I felt absurdly awkward. "This is my friend, Joe. Joe, Lieutenant Ramos."

Joe's expression was wary, barely this side of hostile. "You are talking again about that incident? The other night?"

"More or less." Ramos looked Joe over, and Joe looked right back at him. "We're almost done here."

Joe nodded. "I got it. I'll go into the kitchen and work on that faucet leak, okay?"

"Sure." I stopped myself before I blurted out, "What leak?" There was no leak, but the kitchen is right off the living room. Joe would be able to hear every word we said and he knew it.

"You were saying? Your advisor is on your back?"

"Yes, she is. I wanted to write a chapter about the impact of all the changes at the Navy Yard. She's not even convinced it's a good idea. She thinks I'm totally wasting my time."

In the background I heard the clanking of metal on metal, Joe hammering on a pipe.

"Honking great big piece of real estate, the Navy Yard."

"It's always about the real estate, in a way."

"Tell me about it. Don't I know it. I can't buy a house now where I grew up."

"So my plan is to use Michael Conti's life to illustrate the changes at the Navy Yard. Politics and business and all that. And do it all fast, too. At least that is the plan."

"And you keep asking biographical questions and then stumbling across his murder instead of his life?"

"More or less." I was relieved he understood. "Does that settle your suspicions?"

"My suspicions are never settled until a case is solved. The city pays me to be a suspicious s.o.b." But he smiled as he said it. A nice smile.

He stood up. "It's been a pleasure, Ms. Donato. Call me any time if you think of something else. Can I count on that?" He took out a card and wrote something on the back before giving it to me. "In case you misplaced the first one."

The kitchen was quiet and I could feel Joe's eyes on me before I even turned around. He was leaning against a counter with a few tools still on the floor next to the open door under the sink.

"Are you in some trouble? I saw a police car in front and thought I should stop in."

"You did? What car? He's a detective. He doesn't drive a patrol car."

"I know a detective car when I see one. They aren't hard to spot. And he was parked in a no parking zone."

"How's my leak doing?" I was changing the subject, or at least shifting it.

He finally smiled. "Okay, you got me. That was an excuse to hang around. I wanted to see if you were all right. Are you?"

"If you have time to play games, then put away the tools and come help me make some dinner. Chris will be home in no time."

"I'd like to but I can't. I'd much rather do that than what I am doing." He looked harassed. "I'm having dinner with my sister."

"Oh, gosh. Have you talked at all?"

"Not yet. I have hopes that being in a public place will keep the fireworks down." He smiled with real bitterness. I'd never seen him look like that. "I may be deluding myself, of course. I tend to do that with her."

He was picking up his jacket and walking to the door. Before he left, he stopped and turned back. "I wasn't stalking you, you know. I thought you might need my help."

Was that it? All he would say?

"Go. You need to deal with your sister. Good luck!"

A quick hug and he was gone.

It was the wrong time to respond to his remark about stalking. I wondered, though. Joe, who's been such a friend for so long? Ridiculous. But I never thought our exchanges of keys made it all right for him to hover on my block. Or drop in any time without even a knock on the door. And I didn't know what to call that behavior. Worried about me? Taking care of me? Or checking up on me?

I shoved my questions aside while I threw together tuna and macaroni salad for Chris and me. Hooray for foods that last forever on the shelf. Chris and I caught up on our days. I told her about Lieutenant Ramos but not about Joe's visit. I didn't want to hear what she had to say.

At my desk, I put Lieutenant Ramos' card where I could find it easily, and turned it over to read what he wrote. He'd said to call if I remembered anything at all. On the card, he added, "Or call me anyway."

• • ● • •

In the morning, I woke up thinking about Joe and his sister and wondering how badly it had gone. And still feeling exasperated about his behavior last night. I was more exasperated when I found a text message from him, sent last night right after he left my house.

All truth? Yr dad saw PD car, called me

What? What was going on here? And why was my dad calling Joe? Do they actually call each other? And even more, why was my dad on my block at all?

My dad was checking up on me again? Whatever my uncertainty about Joe, that conclusion was clear. And talking to my boyfriend? My almost, maybe, boyfriend? What am I, sixteen?

It was time for my most reliable way to blow off the tensions in my life. I could have a fight with my father. And he deserved it this time, too.

"When did you and Joe become phone pals?" I was dispensing with social niceties.

"And good morning to you, too." He sounded amused, which was fuel on my flames.

"Come on, Dad! My life is not a joke. Joe let himself into my house last night while I was talking to a detective, and it seems you were behind that. It's not all right."

"Him walking in or me talking to him?" He still sounded calm.

"Both, dammit! Both! Why were you on my block at all? Were you sitting outside, spying?"

My voice rose with each word and my dad sounded a little less calm when he answered.

"No, no, not at all. Ah. Sometimes, but only when I have nothing else to do, I cruise down your street, wondering if I will see you or Chris, and I might, I don't know. Take you for coffee or to do an errand. Not spying. Of course not." Then his own voice rose. "And what if I was? You always were a hothead. What if I found you in trouble and needing my help? What then?"

His growing excitement somehow made me feel better. I'd gotten to him.

"Don't check up on me. Don't. I'm a responsible adult. A homeowner, for crying out loud! So try to remember it, even if your memory is aging. And don't. Do. Not. Ever. Talk to my friends. Ever." I slammed the phone down.

My dad had too much time on his hands. He needed a job.

It was only later that I realized how adolescent I had been. And in my house, I am not the one who gets to be the adolescent. In the moment, though, it felt fine. I'd staked my ground.

For now, I had a meeting at my museum job with human resources. Was there a problem with my time records? A new assignment? Maybe I was finally eligible for benefits? That would be a nice surprise.

When I entered, the coordinator smiled a warm, phony smile. I immediately felt a little chill. This was not about benefits.

"Erica, nice to see you again. And congratulations. We've recently noted that you are due to graduate in the spring. Are you thrilled? You will become Doctor Donato." She almost giggled.

I did not find that reassuring. I felt it even less when her expression swiftly shifted to one of sincere concern.

"I wanted to tell you in person, especially since your supervisors have so enjoyed having you here. All your evaluations praise you to the skies." She sighed.

"Sadly, our budget for next year is not all we had hoped. We would love, truly love, to offer you a professional position when you graduate, but so frustrating, we simply do not have the funds. In fact, we are hoping to avoid layoffs of the staff we already have." The warm smile again. "You do understand that this in no way reflects the quality of your work? That has been excellent and we will hate to lose you. Of course there will be first-class references for any other job."

She looked at me with an encouraging expression, as if she expected me to respond with gratitude. When I didn't, she went on, "So we wanted to give you a long heads-up. To be clear, funding for your job here, sadly, will end in May when you receive your degree. You would be overqualified for your present job, and there is no budget at all for any new fulltime positions." She tilted her head, charmingly, but I was not charmed. I was stunned. "I'm sure you will land on your feet with something wonderful. Are you planning for an academic career?"

Planning? I wasn't planning further ahead than getting through the next dissertation chapter. I suppose I had somehow assumed I would stay on here until…until…I had no idea what would complete that sentence.

"Do you have any questions that I can answer?"

Not one. She could not answer any of my hundreds of questions. I walked out in a daze. I believe I said good-bye, but I could not have sworn to it.

I sat at my desk, not working, not moving, not seeing the computer screen. It was hard to believe I had never thought about what would come next, but I lived my life one step at a time. Early loss had taught me making plans was pointless. Things happened. The museum felt like home by now. I supposed I expected to just stick around until another opportunity presented itself. How dumb was that?

With no idea how long I sat there, I finally forced myself up and out. I had a lunch date with my friend Leary, though date is the wrong word. Appointment, perhaps. And friend might be the wrong word, too. I'm not so sure he would ever use it.

Leary was an aging retired reporter who was grumpy, slovenly, and had lost a leg to diabetes a long time ago. I believed that's when he stopped drinking, but I was not sure. I ran across him while I was looking for some information a few years ago and learned that he knew everything about Brooklyn back in the day. If it happened during his long career, he knew it. And if it happened after, he might be able to hook me up with someone who was there. He was a complete curmudgeon but he still knew a few useful people.

I didn't know if he liked my company or only the food I usually brought, but he always seemed available for a brain-picking meeting. I had thrown together a pan of baked ziti one night, and half was for him. I even sneaked in some broccoli under the pasta and cheese. I had no trouble getting my health-conscious young athlete to eat right. In fact, she lectured me when she was not hitting the potato chips herself. Leary was another story. He had given up his Scotch-and-cigarettes diet a long time ago, but he resisted the very concept of a balanced meal.

He and my father had struck up on odd friendship based on, I thought, being old Brooklyn boys, and that idea made me uncomfortable after my conversation with dad. It's not true that men don't gossip. Had he and my dad been talking about me? They'd better not.

As usual, the outer door to Leary's run-down building was open. I walked right in, noting the further deterioration of the shabby lobby and wondered how safe Leary was here, a subject I could not discuss with him. I tried once and he did not talk to me for weeks.

The smelly old elevator worked that day and in a minute I was pounding on his apartment door.

"I'm coming. Hold your damn horses. I don't move like a race horse, ya know." For Leary, that was a cordial greeting. I know he moves slowly. He uses crutches or a wheelchair.

Four clicks to unlock his heavily fortified door. A little cursing over the tricky third one. I wondered if he had anything as useful as oil spray in his apartment. And if he could find it in the mess.

"I hope you brought lunch." He scowled as he said it.

"Is your blood sugar dropping? Didn't you get meal delivery for today?"

"That crap? And, yeah, what time is it? So let's cut the lecture you're ready to give me and spread out the eats."

A plate of ziti later, with the broccoli stacked on the side, Leary wasn't smiling but the scowl was gone.

"You need something. What could it be this time?"

I was torn between being amused at how predictable he was, and ripping him apart for being such a grouch.

"Are you accusing me of only visiting when I need something? You know you are spinning a story there about the poor, neglected old man." The best defense is hitting back, right?

A tiny smile sneaked in. It was no more than a hint of one, but he helpfully stacked the lunch dishes on a corner of the table.

"Whatcha got on your mind?"

"What do you know about the Navy Yard?"

"A lot. What do you need?"

"Do you know anything about a guy named Michael Conti?"

He smiled. A real smile, full of satisfaction.

"Do I ever."

Chapter Twelve

I snapped my laptop open. "Start talking."

"I heard that he died. What's your interest there? You've got strange tastes for a professor." His expression was so bland I knew he was merely rattling my cage.

"Enough sweet talk from you. One, I am deep in a chapter about the Navy Yard, and, two, I want to use his career as a way of looking at what happened there. And, three, I am a long way from being a professor. Okay."

"Not bad. Not bad at all." He responded to my irritated look with, "No, that's not funning with you. Honest. So, Michael Conti." He almost closed his eyes, as if he was looking at some-place far away.

"He was a real operator. That's what I remember. When I was a mere kid, cub reporters they called us, that was when the Navy Yard closing was big local news. Lots of folks were going to lose their jobs, and lots of them had never worked anywhere else. It was like home to them, a family. So, here's the thing. No one thought the Department of Defense would ever go through with it. Their faith was in political pressure."

"I know about this. And how well it worked out."

"World was changing. They didn't get that. Not that I did, then, either. What did I know? I was about twenty-two, eager but still wet all over. I know now they were never gonna win. I gotta admit, the Navy needed more modern facilities than a

Yard begun when John Adams was president. You know it was that old, right?"

"I had no idea. 'Cause, you know? I'm not exactly up on how to do history."

"Smartass. Did you also know that the new ships they needed were too big to go under the New York bridges? Okay, okay, Conti. I interviewed him one time for the *Eagle*, when the issue was starting to boil. He was working at the Yard then and heading up a committee to prevent the closing. My take on him was that he was a young guy wanting to become a mover. Good talker, as I recall. Real fire-eating union man."

"And?"

"And they failed completely. You already know that. Defense Department won. They had all the power of the budget. They closed their antiquated yards and farmed the work out to private companies."

He had a gleeful look that meant he was getting ready to spring a surprise. Okay, I could play along.

"Something tells me there's a little more."

"Ah, ya know me too well. Conti turned up a few months later working for the company that took over the Yard. An executive, no less. A suit-and-tie guy."

"No!"

"Oh, yes." His smile was smug, but I didn't care. This was too interesting for me to be offended.

"You're saying the union firebrand went to work for the enemy?"

"He did, if that's how you see it. His former union buddies sure saw him as a traitor. And when that shipbuilding company went under, which didn't take long, he went to work on a government commission." He winked. "You can imagine what his union buddies thought of that. Ya know, I haven't thought of him for years. Decades, probably, not until his murder was all over the news. It seems he went on to a long career, though."

He sounded a bit wistful, as if he wished he could get back to digging out the story.

I sat back and thought. Conti's own story was getting more complicated, but it would lead even deeper into the changes of the last half century. It seems he was there for all of it. It was a seriously good idea to write about him.

Leary gave me a hard, suspicious look. "What aren't you telling me?"

I could see why he had been a successful reporter back when. Old and ill as he was, that look pierced right through my brain. I had to tell the truth about my interest in Conti. But I still wasn't telling him about my visit at HR. I wasn't talking about it to anyone.

He shook his head but looked amused. "What are we going to do with you, young lady? The way you get yourself into trouble? What did Len say about it?"

"I didn't get myself into trouble. I was just in the wrong place. And my dad doesn't know. And don't you tell him! I'm serious." He was laughing. "Really. I am really serious. He is too involved in my life already."

"Do tell. I am always interested in these family life stories, as a world unknown to me."

"There's this man. Joe."

"Met him at your house. Your contractor." He looked me over and I felt myself turning red. "I get it. More than a business relationship. How does Len figure in this?"

"I don't know! But they talk to each other. It's too late to say I'll never introduce them—they've known each other for years—but I can say they can't be buddies, can't I?"

"Do I look like Dear Abby?"

"You asked. So I'm going to make you listen. So there." And I told him about Joe dropping in and my dad's role in that.

"So it turns out Joe isn't stalking me," I concluded. "My dad is. I can't live like that."

"Move away."

"What are you talking about?"

"That's the obvious solution. Move someplace strange, like Des Moines. Or Sioux City. No way Len's gonna follow you there. Problem solved."

"And my work? And Chris?" It was so silly, I almost laughed, but I wasn't ready to give Leary the satisfaction. The thought did cross my mind that a college teaching job in someplace far away would solve more than one problem. Of course it would create others. Lots of them.

"Figure this one out on your own. I can't solve all your problems."

That did make me laugh and I caught a fleeting smile from Leary as well.

"You gotta tell Len to butt out. Make it loud and clear. He's a Brooklyn boy like me. We don't do subtle."

"I have told him. I do tell him." I sighed. "He doesn't listen."

"Does it cross you mind...?" He was not looking directly at me but over my shoulder, at an empty spot on his empty walls. "...your very youthful mind that he might be lonely?"

That stopped my racing thoughts. Leary had said the L word. *Lonely*. I think it was the first time since I'd known him.

He was still looking away from me.

"Maybe. I guess. But I don't even hover over Chris like that, and she is still a kid. Almost still a kid." I heard my own words. Possibly she would disagree about the hovering. More than possibly. And I was not about to admit to the occasions I casually walked past her school at dismissal time for the chance of running into her.

I jumped up to clear the table, put the extra food away, wash the dishes.

"I must be heading home. I've left you enough for lunch or dinner tomorrow. No more pasta today!"

"Yeah? Who's hovering now?"

Was it in the genes?

"I'm not answering that, you troublemaker. You know I'm right. Eat up the rest of the broccoli tonight!"

"Hey. About that Conti? You might find an article or two in my file cabinet. Try the third row, maybe bottom drawer."

Leary's apartment is a mess. Unless a home aide was there earlier, I scrub the sink when I do the lunch dishes, scrub both table and chairs before we eat. I've never seen the sofa fabric under the piles of papers and clothes. But the room he uses as an office is immaculate. Every item he ever wrote is available in a file in a drawer in a wall of file cabinets. There was not a stray paper on his desk, where he knocks out men's adventure stories under various pen names.

Ever since I'd discovered this treasure room, I've wanted to ask him if he knew how much this revealed about him and what truly matters to him. I doubt that I will ever have the nerve.

The Conti file was exactly where he said it would be. They always were. A small file but a few very old items Leary wrote and a few more that I had not seen elsewhere, not written by him but here, I assumed, for background.

I would take them to be copied and added to my own background material. Leary objected to that idea, concerned I would not return them, but that's all a game by now. He knows I will take care of the file. I know he will say yes. And he knows I know.

"Yes, my own desk is covered with paper and files. Yes, I will keep your file separate, in a special place, no chance of mixing it up. Fair exchange for the ziti? Satisfied?"

"Guess I have to be. You're not the flaky kid you used to be. I'll trust you."

"You sound like my dad. And that is not a compliment."

"Good man, your dad."

"Oh, yeah? Not feeling it today."

Before I left, I thought of another way to thank Leary.

"How would you like to meet a young reporter?"

"Oh? Who, what, where?"

"She's a friend of mine who's just been assigned to Brooklyn. She is smart and all, but she sure could use some advice."

That was throwing Lisa under a bus, but I knew it would intrigue Leary.

"Yeah? And who is she reporting for?"

I grinned. "Ask her yourself when I bring her around."

I gave him a quick peck on the cheek, moving in too fast for him to duck. On the way home, I stopped to copy his files, and then I would have a few quiet hours of work. Much needed. I hadn't forgotten my advisor put me on a deadline. Ridiculous at my age and academic status. Did she think it would be useful?

And if I was honest, could I say it would not be?

I thought now about how I had no idea how to job hunt in my world. None. I would have to stay in New York until Chris finished high school. And then there was Joe. How to even start? And who could advise me?

When I got home, there was a message from Mrs. Pastore.

"Can you come over after dinner tonight? About eight? The Conti women are getting together and they want to keep it on the down low, so it's at my house. They seem to think you know things."

Well, no wonder I was having trouble getting work done. I was constantly sidetracked by these events. And what Conti women did she mean? Would there be a whole gang of his relatives? And the girls on the side? And a random thought, how in the world did elderly Mrs. Pastore pick up a phrase like "on the down low," anyway?

I gave myself my marching orders. To the desk. Put Leary's originals away in a safe place. Open the copies. Read and learn. Stay focused on work so I could not think about anything else.

The interview with Conti was fascinating. In his twenties, he sounded a lot like he did when I had seen him, every bit as cocky but perhaps less belligerent. Maybe the belligerence had come along with the long career.

And here was a scrawled note in Leary's nearly incomprehensible writing. I deciphered it slowly and painfully: "Cleaned up work force during McCarthy hearings in 1950s. Sen. McC looked at Army at Fort Monmouth, scared other military in area. No Coms now and since then." There was a name, Vito Palma.

This had never made it into a story. It was merely a stray comment Leary kept because it could be useful sometime? Or did he have a purpose? He was such a pack rat, it was hard to guess. I would have to ask him, but first, I wanted to talk to Phyllis. My daughter's grandmother.

All right, "wanted" was an exaggeration. I never actually wanted to talk to her, but now, I needed to. Here was her uncle's name on pages that connected him to Conti, the closing of the Yard, and perhaps to the McCarthy hearings?

I ran a quick search. There was almost nothing about the Yard and the McCarthy hearings but—aha!—definitely some suspicions or fears about Communist infiltration before the start of World War II. And Communist was a legal political party then. I didn't know that. Leary would laugh at me, so I would not tell him.

Now I needed to steel myself for the phone call. I made some notes to keep myself focused.

• • ● ● •

"Erica? Are you going to tell me you discovered something about my Aunt Philomena? I thought I would hear from you before now."

"I know your Uncle Vito and your aunt both worked with Michael Conti on committees. I have pictures."

"Hmm. So I was right about that. I knew I was."

Interesting. That's not what she said when I was there.

"But what does that have to do with Philomena's life?"

"I found something a little odd, too. Let me explain it to you."

She didn't like what she thought she heard.

"No one in my family was ever a Commie. Ever. That is very insulting."

I took a deep breath. "That's not what I said."

I told it to her again.

"There was an investigation at Fort Monmouth, not so far away. Could they have been worried about that?"

"No, no." She stopped. "Well, I don't know if they were or not."

"Do you remember any kind of scandal at the Navy Yard?"

"No scandal! My family was never involved in anything like that. Great patriots, that's what they all were. Wonderful, hard-working people. You need to investigate in some other direction."

"What are you suggesting?"

"I don't know. And I don't want to talk about it anymore. I need to lie down. Good-bye."

And she hung up on me. Just like that. None of this made me anxious to look further into her Aunt Philomena, that's for sure. I had real work to do and a child to feed.

The child came home, anxious for dinner, but also wanting to talk while she shoveled soup and a grilled cheese sandwich into her growing body.

"So, Mom, about my party? Can we discuss it, please? I have good news."

The best news would be that she wants to have a sleepover, with pizza for dinner and waffles for breakfast. Ten girls in nightgowns on the living room floor.

"I talked it over with Grandpa and he wants to pay for it."

"You did what?" I could not believe what I heard. Literally. I thought I had misunderstood.

"Isn't he sweet?" She was too busy reaching for a second cheese sandwich to see my face. I rearranged it quickly into a mask of a reasonable human being.

"Sweet? Grandpa?"

"M-o-m." She stretched it out to three syllables as only a teenager can. "Yes. Yes he is. I explained the whole thing and he said he'd be happy to give me a party for my birthday."

I had lost interest in my own grilled cheese.

"Did you call him and ask?" I stopped before I started telling her how I would feel about that.

"Of course I didn't! I know you would not like that, me asking. He called me. We do talk on the phone. He's too old for any other way to stay in touch, I guess. So we talk." She gave me a sidelong look. "You should try it sometime. He likes to talk on the phone."

"Oh, Chris." I couldn't let my desire to yell at her for lecturing me—what nerve!—sidetrack the main issue. Much as I wanted to. "Tell the truth: did you ask him for help?"

"N-o-o." Another three-syllable response. "We were talking, as people do, and I told him I was going to a party next weekend and he asked what we planned for mine." She looked at me with reproach. "He does remember I have a birthday coming up. And so I told him I didn't know, we had no plans and he came up with this idea." The words "so there" were implied in her tone, but she wisely left them unsaid. They would not have helped her case.

I didn't want my father to do this. I did not want him to encourage her desires for things we could not afford. I did not want him to provide something that I would have liked to give her. I did not want his bossiness on planning a party. Not that he knew how to do it. And not that I did either.

Chris looked at me with so much hope my heart twisted a little.

"Let me think about this. It makes me uncomfortable but I will talk to him and see exactly what he has in mind. It might cost a lot more than he thinks. Okay?"

"Okay. I guess." She was already up, clearing the table while eating the last of her third sandwich. "I have to make it be okay, but Mom? Please, not too long. I hear from my friends that it takes a lot of time to plan a big party."

What big party? I hadn't agreed to that, but she was halfway upstairs while I was still trying to formulate the right response.

There was a time I would have turned to Darcy, my friend with all the answers. Surviving raising four children into adulthood, of course she had answers. I might still call her but I really wanted to talk to Joe. He always had both wise ideas and a shoulder to lean on, but he had his own problems to worry him this week. He'd call me when he was ready to.

Yes, I should make a date with Darcy.

For now, I had to step over to the Pastores' house and meet with the Conti women. There was no way I would turn down that invitation. Just as I was getting ready, there was a call. Chris and I picked it up at the same time, on different phones.

"Chris, darling." Phyllis. Before I had a chance to say a word, I heard "I'm glad it's you. I don't want to talk to your mother." Really? That's when I should have put the phone down. As if.

Was she still mad at me for the very words, "Communist" and "family" in the same sentence? She went on, "I found something about Philomena. I mean, it was hers. A book. I'm going to send it right to you for your project. I was wondering what is the best way to mail it?"

"Uh, Grandma? Mom would know better than me."

I heard Judy in the background. "Mom, I'll take it to UPS tomorrow. I told you."

"That is expensive. So Chrissie keep an eye out for it, okay?"

I put the phone down then. As I was putting my jacket on, I thought this little get together would be family life from a whole different angle than my conversation with Chris. Or my non-conversation with Phyllis.

Chapter Thirteen

Mrs. Pastore hustled me in and downstairs to the kitchen at the back of the house. We would be well hidden from the street.

"Nicole?" someone called. It was Annabelle Conti, visibly disappointed to see it was only me. Jennifer was there too, looking as out of place in the old kitchen as Annabelle looked comfortable. They both had small wineglasses and large slices of cheesecake in front of them.

"Sit, sit," Mrs. Pastore urged. "Dessert wine or a coffee? And biscotti or cheesecake? From the bakery," she added apologetically. "I didn't have time to bake today."

I sat as commanded, still wondering why I was here. Annabelle moved her chair to make room for me and passed the cheesecake, so I guessed she was no longer angry.

When the doorbell rang again, Mrs. Pastore brought in a woman dressed in leggings, boots, and a coat that was a confection of fluffy pink mohair and lavender fake fur trim. Her long blond braid was threaded through with strands of magenta hair. Her clothes were of equally extreme style, the boots expensive soft magenta suede, the velvety tunic adorned with bright appliqué. She flicked Jennifer's overhanging fur coat off the remaining chair.

So that's what Mrs. Pastore meant by the Conti women. Two wives and a daughter.

"Nikki, it's cold tonight. How can you be warm enough in that flimsy jacket?"

"Well, Mom, this flimsy jacket came right from the designer's studio and cost more than you've spent on all coats in the last decade. Believe me, it is quite warm enough."

"Still going for the art student look, I see," Jennifer murmured, but loudly enough so Nicole heard. As intended, I was sure.

"And you are still wearing fur? Animal skins are so last century."

Annabelle slammed her glass on the table.

"This is not what we are here for."

"Mom, you started it. I don't need your comments…."

Maybe this was not so different from my life with Chris after all, except for the better clothes. Annabelle was saying, "You are still my daughter and I still worry."

Jennifer leaned forward and patted Annabelle's hand. "You are right, dear. We are who we are, but bickering is not the reason we are here."

Annabelle sucked in a deep breath. "We are here to share our information about Michael and make a plan to deal with the harassment by the police department."

I started to say, "But he was murdered. The police have a job to do." I was immediately shut down.

"Not your turn to talk."

"We will get to you in good time."

"You be patient."

Only curiosity kept me in my seat at that moment. My desire to walk out in a huff was at war with my desire to know what the hell was going on here.

"Everyone coming to order?" Jennifer looked around the table, resting her eyes in turn on her stepdaughter and her… what do you call a husband's ex-wife? Predecessor?

"Let's get to it. Michael was a first-class bastard. Pardon my language about your father, Nicole."

Nicole muttered, "Not what you used to think."

"Yes, dear." Jennifer's smile was mocking. "I got older and wiser. You will too. Someday."

"We all know what he was." Nicole's pretty face was distorted by her clenched jaw. "Big ego, lots of damage."

Her mother nodded emphatically. "Exactly how he was. Or became. Honestly, when he was young he was so exciting. And he was fun."

"Mom! He took me to meet his girlfriend and told me how to lie to you about where we went."

"I meant before. When we were younger. And now, to learn, all that time, he was involved with Mary Pat? It hurt, to learn he loved her."

Jennifer said in her cultured voice, "Loved? Not Michael. There are cruder ways to put that. We all know he was chasing skirts all along, right? But I have proof."

She slapped an envelope on the table and removed some photos.

"I hired a private eye. An expensive one. And look what he found for me."

I looked. Of course I did. Black-and-white photos of Michael Conti, smooching a young woman at a bar. Leaving an out-of-town hotel with another one. In the backseat of a limo with a woman and his hands where they did not belong.

No one knew what to say, including me. And then I did.

"Why the PI? Were you going to divorce him?"

"What do you think? It's about damn time."

"But New York has no-fault divorce. So the why the photos?"

She smiled, almost pityingly. "Isn't it obvious? He would prefer to avoid a scandal. He would not have wanted these to be all over the papers."

"Get up to date, lady," Nicole mocked. "There's this thing called the Internet. It would be all over every social media."

"Of course! But he was old school. He would have worried about newspapers. Especially that photo." She put her finger on the one in the limo. "She's a state senator. Married." Her eyes sparkled. "Imagine how messy that could be."

We all sat back, imagining. Nicole finally muttered, "I've got to hand it to you, Stepmom. You have learned a lot."

"And then he went and outsmarted your whole plan by getting himself shot." Annabelle sounded regretful.

"Here are some more photos. Does she look familiar?"

A photo shot through a window. Conti wearing a robe, sitting on a messy bed with a woman not young, not beautiful, in a matching robe. It was Mary Pat.

Annabelle named her before I did, adding, "Look how old she got. Not that she was ever pretty. But look how fat and saggy she is."

"You can see it all in that robe." Nicole shuddered.

"I meant her face, you dirty girl. Behave yourself."

"Mom, I hate to break it to you, but you got old too."

"As we all do," Jennifer admitted. "Not that I am not fighting it every day and at great expense." She waved the photo. "I only found out who she was when those annoying detectives came calling." She pulled out another photo. "That visit seems to have been caused by this."

It was Mary Pat and me, sitting on the bench at Grand Army Plaza.

"What? How…?"

"I told you my investigator was good. So, Ms. Donato, how about explaining this? Since it was you that sicced the cops on us?"

"I don't have to explain anything and I'm not sure I should. In fact, I am ready to go home." I stood. "I've told the detective involved and that's all I need to do."

"And that is how we all ended up talking to detectives. We did not like it." Nicole emphasized each word.

"No, we did not. Not our style." Even sitting, Jennifer seemed to be looking down at me. "Not in the lives we live."

"My dear." Annabelle's voice was soft. "I apologize for giving you a hard time the other day. It was all such a shock. Very confusing. But we would all be so grateful if you could tell us about this. Please stay and tell us."

There were murmurs of agreement, cheesecake passed back to me, a pat on the arm. So I stayed and told how Mary Pat had contacted me and what she wanted. They wanted to know how she knew about me and I could not tell them. As she said, she knew people.

Finally Jennifer said, "Sounds like she is the one woman in New York who would have missed him. Was the one woman." She looked around the table. "Would have, right? I told you my detective said she is dead?"

"He said she was killed? Too?" Annabelle turned white.

Jennifer put up her hand. "That's all he could find out, so far, so no questions. Michael is our problem for today. We all know, whoever it was who pulled that trigger, he had it coming. Right? Don't we know it?"

They sat back, lost in thought, or perhaps memories, and then they all nodded together.

It was a moment out of a fairy tale or myth, three women at different ages, sitting together and talking about vengeance. The Fates? The witches in Macbeth?

It was creepy, the silence and their expressions. I had to say something.

Anything. The first thing that came to mind.

"Who else had reasons? Do you know?"

"Ha. Everyone. His first business partner. When they broke up their firm, somehow Michael ended up with most of the money. Oh, the shouting between them! Of course, that man died years ago. I do believe his grown children sued Mike. Jen, do you know?"

"Yes, they did. That went on for years." She was silent for a moment. "Add my parents to the list. Michael Conti, older, married." She stopped and looked at Annabelle, shrugging apologetically. "He was Brooklyn, Italian. A politician. Not what they had in mind for their baby girl. How do you think I learned about detectives?" She smiled bitterly. "I've never told that to either of you. I should have listened to them but no one could tell me anything then."

Nicole chimed in. "He never had a friend he didn't feud with or a family member, either. I mean, I'm his only child and we haven't had a real conversation in years. I haven't missed him, either." She stopped. Her voice shook a little when she added, "At least, I don't think I did."

"Nicole!" Mrs. Pastore spoke up for the first time. "Look at your mother! She is exhausted."

Very true. Annabelle had put her face in her hands, shutting out all of us, including her daughter.

"I'll take her home. Come on, Mom. Time to roll."

"I'll take her," Jennifer said, "and you too, if you want a ride. My driver is outside. But we haven't quite finished here. What do we tell the detectives? In case they get back to us? That's what none of us want. They can't be allowed to rummage around in our mistakes and wrong decisions."

Annabelle put her head up. "We tell them nothing and then they have no reason to come back. It's too much pain to look at it all again. Agreed?"

All three Conti women put their hands together, looking deep into each other's eyes. They were not looking at me. I was not going to be part of their pact.

Nicole helped her mother to her feet and into her ugly puffer coat. Jennifer wrapped her long fur around herself, ignoring Nicole's critical glance, and the three women left, the middle-aged one and the young one supporting the oldest one. Mrs. Pastore looked at me, eyes wide and I looked back. She had a finger to her lips and whispered, "Not a word until we hear the car leave."

I shook my head. "Not a word after, either. I am beat and I have work tomorrow. I'm going home."

"I understand. And I have to get upstairs and see how my Sal is feeling. But tomorrow? You come by to finish the cheesecake and we can talk about this evening?"

I only had to step over to my own house. There was light coming from under Chris' door, so I knocked and went in. She was still up, messaging away. Before I ordered lights out, I said, "Your mythology class last year. Three scary women? Do you remember who they were? "

"That came up in Mrs. Pastore's kitchen? That's pretty random."

"One of those silly things. Too hard to explain. Do you know?" I was certainly not telling her about this evening.

"Of course." She gave me that "Are you kidding?" look. "The three Fates—Past, Present, and Future. In some stories, they spun the threads of life, like create life or cut it off." She made a scissoring gesture. "Sometimes they were girl, mother, and crone. You know, all the ages of a woman's life." She yawned. "Do you need more now?"

"No, you silly girl. I need you to go to sleep now. Right now. Me, too."

"Did you think some more about my party? Grandpa says…"

"Sleep now! This is no time for a discussion."

It wasn't until I woke up suddenly, in the middle of the night, that I wondered why they all agreed to tell the police absolutely nothing. It wasn't likely the detectives would accept that.

Chapter Fourteen

In the morning, I wondered again if the Conti women were hiding anything more than their own sadness and regrets, but I was soon distracted by Chris' attempts to talk about her birthday over breakfast.

"No. Not now." She looked ready to protest. "What part of 'no' do you not understand? Not first thing in the morning, for crying out loud. I said I would think about it and I will." Before I buried my face in my coffee mug, I added, "Go to school before I get seriously angry."

Her face was on the verge of crumpling when she stormed out the door. There was a loud slam too. I had a second's worth of feeling ashamed and then decided she needs to respect my stance on this. Plus, respect my need for no serious drama first thing in the morning.

Instead, I worked. I needed to be at my museum job tomorrow, so today I needed to glue myself to the keyboard. Thoughts of Chris were only allowed to seep in occasionally, but during one of those moments, I e-mailed Darcy for a long overdue girls' night out and some advice.

My new personal, not to say scandalous, material on Michael Conti did not belong in my dissertation. I regretted that. However, I had other, more acceptable information to write up. Add footnotes. Try to link the Navy Yard history to his series of jobs, some of them with mysterious titles such as "Senior Mayoral Liaison to Port Authority." What the heck did that mean? The

Port Authority is the joint New York-New Jersey body for matters affecting regional transportation, including the harbor. Very powerful. Any New Yorker would know that. But what exactly did he do on this job? I had no idea. I needed to dig some more.

And did it matter? Maybe my idea of using Conti's life to explain and even personify all the changes was not so great after all. My advisor's deadline was looming and I could not seem to sort it all out.

Maybe I needed to drop it and start writing my concluding chapter. Soon. I would, soon. But I wasn't quite ready to give up.

Then I thought more about last night and the meeting of these angry women. Annabelle's joke at our first meeting, that she always thought Jennifer might murder him. It was a joke, right?

I was struggling to dismiss that whole weird scene from my mind, and yet I found it fascinating too, that picture of the Three Fates in a Brooklyn kitchen. I finally admitted I was too distracted to write anymore, saved my work, and dug out Detective Ramos' card. Maybe he would be interested in what I had learned. Or maybe I was being silly.

"I'll take my lunch break soon, Ms. Donato. Would you like to join me? Somewhere nearby? We can talk in detail then."

Out of my cave and into the real world? I looked down at my flannel pajamas.

"Uh. I have a little work to do first. Make it in an hour?"

I hustled to shower and find clean jeans and a sweater with no holes. I would have to tell Darcy about this moment. My stylish friend would laugh, but *with* me, not *at* me. I wouldn't tell Chris, who would definitely laugh at me, and criticize my ancient running shoes, too.

An hour later, there I was, ready for a cheeseburger and with notes for Ramos.

We ordered and we exchanged small talk. When I called him Lieutenant Ramos he told me to call him Danny. So of course I told him my name is Erica. We established that Ramos was Puerto Rican and Donato was my Italian-descended husband's name.

He glanced at my empty left hand. I said quickly, "He died," and changed the subject.

After we ordered, he asked to hear about the estranged brother. He wanted to know everything I had learned. When I asked if it was actually useful, he shook his head. "Who the hell knows? A lot of people are happy Conti is dead. We need to look at all of them. It's not confidential that no one is looking like the obvious perp."

"Cops really say perp?"

"Not really." He smiled. "Only TV cops. I can also say, presumed malefactor, but that's a little pretentious, don't you think? Bet you didn't know cops can say long words." He was still smiling. "Just like a scholar?"

"Ha. I'm a long way from being an official scholar. And actually, I've had a few cops in my life, including my late godfather."

We immediately got sidetracked into a game of "Who Do You Know?" It turned out that we had not a single acquaintance in common in more than forty-five-thousand NYPD employees, but it was fun proving it. We were laughing, saying, "How is that possible?" when Joe walked in.

He was with a woman around my age, very thin and sloppily dressed. I had a twinge of jealousy until I realized she was not his usual type. That is, his usual type before I became his only type. Another glance told me she must be his sister. It was something about their body language. And she had a certain look that reminded me of him.

He stared at us from the doorway and I realized Ramos and I looked like two people having fun on a lunch date. That's not what this was. It wasn't. But Joe's frozen expression said he thought otherwise.

He turned away and walked to a table at the other end of the small room. He was behind me, but I could feel his eyes on my back.

I turned my attention back to Ramos, and returned, deliberately, to the subject of Michael Conti and my evening at Mrs. Pastore's. He wanted to hear all about it.

When I had finished, he looked at me appraisingly. I wondered if my lipstick smudged.

"Did you ever consider detective work? You've got the right mind for it. You've got good questions and you pick up the details better than half my supervisees. And there is a certain tenacity."

I almost laughed. "I've thought sometimes that historians are kind of detectives. But you're kidding, right?"

"Only partly. I know you have a career already. Just saying, if this academic thing doesn't work out."

"That's ridiculous. I don't want to begin another career." I thought it was difficult enough to begin the one I had.

"And can you shoot?" He looked serious. All but his eyes. "No? So time on a range. Or you could skip all the rookie years on the job, and become a PI."

Then his sober expression broke up and we both started laughing at the idea of me chasing crooks or firing a weapon. And I could still feel Joe's eyes.

By then we had demolished our burgers and it was time to go. There was no way to leave without passing Joe's table. I sucked in a breath and vowed to be a grownup.

I greeted him with a deliberately friendly voice and a casual smile, also deliberate.

"You remember Lieutenant Ramos, I think?"

He nodded but did not offer a handshake or a polite smile.

"There has been more about the Conti case. I can't seem to get away from it." Ouch. That sounded silly, betraying my discomfort.

"I see."

"Joey! Introduce me? Where are your manners?"

"Yes, of course." His expression did not change, though. "Erica, my sister, Alex. This is Erica Donato, Allie. She is a…a longtime friend and a client, too."

She squinted up at me, then smiled politely. Carefully. "Very pleased to meet you." Like a well-trained little girl. Her eyes looked like a little girl's, too, uncertain about being with the grownups. That gave me a chill.

"And Lieutenant Ramos of the NYPD."

"Pleased to meet you too." She was reciting a script.

Joe looked at me, still not smiling at all.

"Is there another problem for you with this case?"

"Uh, no. Like I said, more involvement fell my way. Tell you later?"

I quickly threw out, "Have a great lunch" before leading the way to the door.

Outside, Danny Ramos gave me a considering look.

"So that guy? He's not only someone who fixes your kitchen sink, right?"

"Right. Somewhat right. I guess."

He seemed to consider that. "Well, does it preclude me from asking you to have dinner sometime?" He quickly added with a grin, "We can discuss your next career in detection."

It made me laugh. "No. No, it does not preclude dinner."

"Good. I'll call you."

I turned down a ride home, planning to do some errands. And I thought the walk would help me sort out…well, everything. It didn't. My mind jumped from angry families to Joe's sullen attitude to the murders of Mary Pat O'Neill Codman and Michael Conti. Nothing made sense, and damn, where had this day gone? Chris would be home all too soon.

I had a package when I got home, left on top of my steps where anyone could have seen it, a small item wrapped in brown paper and lots of tape, addressed in Phyllis' rounded handwriting.

It was a diary, very old, with the leather flaking off the cover. It was faded blush color, perhaps red originally, or a true girlish pink. There was a strap to keep it closed, with a tiny lock. I pressed the brass button and it opened right up. On the first page, in ink turning brown it said: Philomena Palma. My Own Diary.

Tucked inside it was a note: "Darling Chrissie, I found this in the attic, in a box with old furniture doilies. No idea how it got there but I thought you might find it useful for your project. Hugs. Grandma."

Whoops. I checked the wrapping paper and sure enough, it was addressed to Chris, not me. Now I would have to explain the mistake to her and apologize.

And since Phyllis wanted me to look into Philomena's life, why in the world had she not sent it to me? I guess she was still angry at me for asking about Communism at the Navy Yard.

But in the meantime, before Chris got home? I had a lot of fast reading to do.

Philomena wrote in the rounded, schoolgirl hand the nuns used to teach. The diary began on the day she started work at the Navy Yard, and she'd pasted a photo on the page, tiny, black and white, blurry, a girl with big smile, in men's working clothes. I read, and it felt like I heard her voice, breathless with excitement.

The first pages described what it had taken to get there. She wrote how glad she was that the diary had a lock. "*I can tell you everything, dear diary.*" It was the story Phyllis had told us, but with all the living details.

"*My parents! They are so old-fashioned. I had to fight and fight for this. They said it was not nice for their innocent young girl. It was dirty, physical, definitely not dainty. And of course it meant working with men all day, with no supervision, so maybe they were protective about that, too. Anything could happen.*

When I said, 'Like what?' they told me not to be fresh with them! Mama cried and prayed. Papa said, 'I'd rather see you dead.' !!!"

"*I cried and shouted and threatened to go live with relatives. Mama tried to get the priest from Sacred Heart to talk to me!!!*

Finally my favorite older brother, Frankie, came home from basic training, and Mama told everyone, ahead of time, that the fighting had to stop while he was there. He was going to have a good visit before he got on that troop ship! She made threats about the evil eye but she doesn't really believe all that. But I was so mad I didn't care. I told him, and he told them. Boy, did he! He smacked the table and said if they want all the boys like him to come home, everyone had to pitch in and do what was needed. Then he looked at our parents and said, 'What's the matter with you? You think you didn't raise her to be a good girl? You think she would play the puttana?' They gasped when he said it. Dear diary, it's a bad word that he's not supposed to say in front of me.

"Then he said, 'You think she doesn't know how to behave herself? She's not moving far away where you can't supervise her. And besides, I taught her a good uppercut, so she could take of herself if anyone tried anything.'"

And Mama finally said, 'How do you say no to the boy who's going overseas with a gun?"

Then she wrote about the first few days on the job, how stupid she felt with the tools, how she'd made some friends, how the men at the yard stared at them. She wrote, *"Some fool, again, shouted something rude and I had it. I gave it right back. That settled it. I smacked my hands together and got back to work. And one of those guys even gave me a thumbs-up. I hope my brothers would be proud."*

I was proud. *You go, girl,* I thought.

Chris was home. I heard her burst in. She called, "Mom, what is this wrapping paper? Did Grandma send me a present? It's not even my birthday."

She stood at the stairs with the brown paper in her hand.

I came out of my office with the diary.

"She sent you this. There's a note tucked in the front."

"You opened it. I see my name right here. What's up with that?"

"I'm sorry, honey. I didn't look carefully and assumed it was for me." She looked ready for an argument and I redirected it. "But look at what it is. A real find!"

I handed it to her. "Watch out for the leather flaking off the cover."

She looked it over, carelessly ignoring the tiny chips drifting onto her shirt. "She sent it to me for my project."

"Yes, I saw her note. That's when I knew I had goofed."

"Mom, it's a diary. Philomena's. Do you know how great this is? No one will have anything this…this…is…so…so…"

"Personal?"

She nodded. "It's more than history books. You know? This was the real Philomena's. And now it's mine. Wow. Maybe I could do a monologue of it? Or film it? We need to have a part that is using our imaginations. And no one will have anything like this for their project."

"Well, they might. There are other diaries, and letters, too."

"Pfft. I know. Mel has her great-grandparents' wedding photo. And they were married right at Church of the Pilgrims. You know it? Down the street from school?"

"Yes, of course I do. It's a famous old church."

"And one of the guys, Tom Greeley? He actually lives in a house that was his family's for six generations. Naturally he's writing about that. Even though he hates it and wants to live on a farm. But still. This! Philomena's own diary." She jumped up. "I have to go call Grandma."

"Chris!" She stopped. "Let me read it too. Okay?"

"Oh. Yeah, sure. Why not? You could make a copy."

"I would love to but no. Copying is bad for something fragile. Just read fast, okay? Fast! Cause I'm dying to dig into it."

As she walked away, I heard her saying. "Grandma? You are the best. The diary will put my project over the top. Did I tell you there would be an exhibit of the best projects? What? You want to come? And now mine…" And then her voice faded.

I smiled. I was raising a young historian. Even if she didn't know it yet, she had that history geek gene. She'd probably deny it if I told her. She thinks of herself as an artist.

One of these days I should figure out what colleges offered strength in both and nudge her to apply to a bunch of them. Let her figure it out for herself, but don't let her go someplace where she only has one choice. Is it next year we start some college visiting? What do I know? I went to college across the street from where I went to high school.

For now, all I needed to think about was how to get that diary out of Chris' hands. We could share. I'd taught her about sharing toys in her toddlerhood. I hoped she remembered.

Chapter Fifteen

A peaceful evening. It was about time I had one. Chris claimed she had a big after-school snack and wasn't hungry. She stayed in her room, saying she had work to do. I knew there would be a late-night creep into the kitchen for a sandwich or some ice cream, but that was all right. It meant I could have a sandwich for supper myself. I read some documents for my job, lying on the couch, and fell asleep, still on the couch. I was happy not to hear the words "birthday party" tonight.

My mind was full of things I did not want to think about: nice Lieutenant Ramos and his possible dinner invitation. Joe's face at the restaurant. Chris' birthday. My advisor's deadlines, looming like thunderclouds. With the need to begin job hunting following right along after everything else. Or before everything else?

I could not even sort them out in order of importance.

Text from Darcy:

> Early walk in park tomorrow. Pick you up at 7:30

No. Not that early. It was still cold. It was barely dawn. No. But yes, because Darcy doesn't have a lot of free time and I needed to talk.

That was when I fell into my catnap, escaping. Only Chris' rustling around in the refrigerator woke me up.

"You okay?"

"Fine. I'm fine. Exploring a bedtime snack. Do we have any

salami?" She looked up and giggled. "Mom, go to bed. You know sleeping on the couch isn't good for you."

I nodded, wondering where she got that idea. Probably from me saying it to her. I nodded again and sleepwalked up to bed.

At seven in the morning, I was in my sweats from yesterday, drinking my second cup of coffee, when Darcy hammered on the door.

"Come on, lazy bones. I see your light is on."

She was on my stoop, dressed in brilliant blue spandex running gear, cheeks pink, hair covered by a becoming cap. She was running in place, all bouncy and bright-eyed.

"I hate you."

"No, you don't. You only hate mornings, but that's not news. Anyway, I am off to Provo, Utah, tonight, so this was the only time. Lace up your running shoes and let's go."

Who am I to argue with such an impressive figure? I grumbled but I laced, right after one more gulp of coffee.

"I'm sorry." She urged me out into the bright, cold morning. "But you know this is good for you."

"You're not sorry. You sound like Joe. He thinks exercise is the cure for anything that ails me."

"And it often is. How is Joe, by the way?" Her look told me she heard every mixed emotion in my voice.

We covered the two long blocks to the park before I answered with a brilliant, "I don't know."

A single raised eyebrow. How did she do that? "His life is very, umm. Right now, it's very complicated." I could barely explain. "And I don't know how to handle it. I guess."

"Complicated, how? Not another woman? He's more into you than you believe. I can tell."

I wasn't going to touch that. Not now, not for anything.

"Another woman, but not how you mean it." How much could I tell her without revealing Joe's personal issues? Tricky, especially since I wanted so much to spill everything on my mind.

"He has family problems."

"Joe has a family? Tell me all. An ex-wife? A secret child?"

"What? No! Stop kidding. A sister. And he's not acting like himself at all. And I can't even focus on it, because I have too much else on my own mind."

I spilled everything. We walked at a killing pace and it still took us to the lake deep in the park and back out the handsome stone entrance. As always, she had crisp, problem-solving answers. I guess that's what being a vice president in the advertising business teaches you. Or maybe that's what got her the big job and corner office in the first place.

"So, Chris. Local restaurants with party rooms. Not expensive. I'll send you names. Not glamorous but put up a lot of balloons and loud music and no one will notice. A high school friend of my son has a band. I'll put in a word, you'll get a family and friends price. And let your father help! Why not? It makes him happy and Chris happy, too

"You think?"

"Come on. Of course. And this cute cop? If you want to, have dinner. But you don't even seem to know what you want. So figure it out first. It's not rocket science, honey."

"If it was that easy, would I be talking about it here on a freezing November morning? While exercising?"

"Point taken." She stopped me and put her hands on my shoulders. "Joe has been a great friend, but only you know what he means to you. But..."

"I knew there would be a 'but'."

"But, as to his family crisis, how often has he been there for you?"

"Oh. I can't count that high."

"My point exactly. So?"

"I'd be there for him if I knew how. But I don't know and he's. Not. Telling. Me. He's keeping me out. And honestly, I don't have the energy to figure it all out on my own. To be a sweet woman soothing his rumpled feathers."

She patted me on the shoulder. "You're smart. You'll work it out. Why don't you look convinced by my logic?"

"Because there's more."

When I told her about my work, the two-pronged pressure of my dissertation and the looming need to make some actual plans she grew very serious. My other issues might have seemed slightly amusing to her. Not this one.

"So tell me if I have this right. You've put in all these years with no idea about what to do when you finished?"

"No! Of course not." She stared at me. "All right. Yes, maybe. It sounds so dumb when you say it like that!"

She gave me a small hug.

"It was like this." I needed to explain it. "When I started I was only looking for a masters, to upgrade my teaching license. More money. And then I got interested and I got encouragement, and I somehow ended up committing to the PhD program."

"Somehow? It was an accident?"

"That's how it felt at the time. Like, I would go part-time and Chris was so little and I never truly believed I would ever get to the end."

"And now it's here, staring you right in the face?"

"That's what Dr. Adams is saying."

"So what have you concluded? Isn't the usual career path into college teaching?"

"If you're very, very lucky. The academic job market is bad, seriously bad. Or so I hear. Plus, I can't pick up and go to any old place they offer a paycheck. Until Chris finishes high school, I need to be right here."

"And Joe?"

I nodded. Slightly. Yes, he was a factor too. No, I did not want to talk about him.

"Well, honey, you need to start networking. In fact, you are way overdue. Believe me. I don't know about dissertation writing but I do know about job hunting. I hope you know enough to start with your own department? Talk to everyone! Get advice. Get support. And the history museum where they love you but can't hire you? So get to work! I'll send you some good articles." She hugged me again. "It will not be fun, but honest, it will turn out fine in the end."

"Am I babbling on about me, me, me? How are you? Start with Provo, of all places."

"It's a huge tech center. You've heard that?"

"Uh. Maybe."

She sighed. "I forgot you don't live in modern times. Anyway, I am pitching a client. But yes, Provo." She sighed again. "The middle of nowhere. They promise me I can get alcohol in the local restaurants, but I'm not sure. Isn't my job a whirlwind of glamour?"

I laughed.

"My real news is that there is going to be a wedding. And about damn time!" Darcy's children were all grown and in serious relationships. "Luke and Cassie are finally making it legal. Next summer, on a Caribbean beach."

I hugged her. "You must be so excited. Is there a lot for you to do?"

"Nope. Mother of the groom. The old rule is keep your mouth shut and wear beige. Not that I'd wear beige on a beach."

"Or ever."

"Right. Never. I'm thinking very expensive resort wear. Maybe a silk caftan. But yes, finally, dancing at a wedding with my kid."

By then we were back at my house.

"Thank you. You helped straighten me out."

"Glad to do it. Honestly? It's nice to have company on my morning exercise. Let's do it again."

"Oh, ha-ha. But keep me up to date on the wedding plans, okay?" I smiled. "And have a great trip to Utah."

"Ha-ha right back. I must go home and pack now. Boring clothing, believe me."

"But stylish."

"Yes, walking that fine line, stylish enough to impress but not enough to make them hate me. Business suit but Manolo shoes, maybe."

Now back at home, I had a plan firmly in my mind: support Joe as he has supported me. Figure out what he needs. I can do that. At least, I can be kind. Be there. Just be there. Darcy was the source of all wisdom in my life, somewhere between the mother I lost, the big sister I never had, the older cousins I'd outgrown.

My improved mood lasted about thirty minutes. Joe called and thirty minutes is how long it took him to get to my house.

It went downhill before he even stepped through the open door. He stood on the stoop, arms folded, his normally friendly face all storm clouds.

"What is going on with you?"

"Come in and sit down? Do you want coffee? Or something to eat?"

He stepped in then, but did not sit down. He leaned against the now closed door.

"No coffee, just some answers. I'm serious."

I sucked in a breath of air.

"I can see that you are, but I honestly have no idea what you are talking about."

Honestly, I did have an idea, but I was being cautious. No room for misunderstandings today.

"That cop."

"He has a real name and you know it." I did not like his tone of voice. "And a title too."

"I don't care about his name or his rank. I care about who he is to you." He stopped himself but then continued. "Are you dating him?"

"Don't be ridiculous."

"I know what I saw. Twice."

I've known him for ten years. He never acted like this. Advanced jerk. Never. And I sure did not like it. I did not like the way my heart was beating and my hands were sweating.

"And exactly what is it that you think you saw?"

"Don't play games with me, Erica. Laughing, having fun. The way you looked at him."

"Well, he's nice to look at. So there! And we were talking and laughing. So what? And what makes you think you get to interrogate me, anyway?"

He looked stunned.

"I don't get to question you? But he does, that cop?"

"It's his job, but it's not yours."

"Erica." His voice softened. "You're right, a little. But you and me? I haven't been dating anyone else and I do get to ask what the hell you are doing."

"You do? You think you do? No one does, not even you."

He walked out without another word, and my fury turned into angry tears. Even in my self-righteous fog, I knew I was not altogether right. Okay. Mostly, I was not right. I probably should not have said Ramos was nice to look at. Didn't I know it was oil on the flames? So much for my plan to be kind.

But he hadn't made it easy, coming in with that attitude. I was too upset, then, to wonder where that attitude was coming from. Or to consider how childish my own behavior was.

My own child came down, bed hair all wild, rubbing her eyes. "Did I hear you and Joe? Shouting? Or did I dream it?"

"Nice of you to get up and join the world." I was, to say the least, still angry at everyone.

"Well, gee, Mom. It's only…"

"Noon!"

"So?"

"Go have some breakfast. Or lunch. Something. Wait! Why aren't you in school?"

"School-wide testing. And mine are tomorrow." She squinted at me. "You didn't answer my question."

"Yes."

"Yes, it was Joe, or yes, you were shouting, or yes you didn't answer?"

"All. And we're not talking about it."

She looked wary but her eyes opened up. "Are you crying?"

"No!" It was not a lie. I had been crying, but I wasn't now.

She headed back upstairs with a dramatic sigh.

I went into the kitchen to make some lunch, forgot what I was doing after I put bread and mayonnaise on the counter. I went back to my computer, but the words blurred on the screen.

I started for the stairs to get Chris up for real and then thought, "Why bother?"

I finally curled up on the couch under a quilt from Chris' baby days, and fell asleep. I woke to Chris rattling around in the kitchen. She was fully dressed, hair combed, jacket on.

"I'm making a snack to take out. Going for a walk, okay? See you later."

Her cheerfulness made me want to bury my head under the comforter. I was unhappy with myself and unhappy with Joe. My computer pinging did not make feel better. Unless it was Joe. Who usually calls. But still.

It was Dr. Adams. And I realized that minute that I was supposed to check in yesterday, discuss my progress, assure her I had really, truly, finished this chapter and moved on toward conclusions.

The message was crisp and clear. "See me Monday. Two sharp." I was briefly tempted to claim I had to work at the museum, but no. Telling lies would not improve our relationship. And I knew this was a relationship that was important in my life, whether I wanted it or not. I had better respond. I would, as soon as I was ready to explain why there was not much progress. If I was stuck now, I would have to show her how I would get unstuck.

Then I found Ramos' card and called him. It did seem like a good idea in that moment.

"Hey, Erica. Have you had another useful memory flash for me?"

His friendly voice cut through my bleak mood.

"No, sorry, but I'd love to talk about Michael Conti some more."

"Pressure from above?"

"Ah. Yes. Yes for sure."

"You're scared of your advisor? Tough young woman like you?"

Was I scared of her? Oh, yes. That thought was humiliating.

"I might possibly be able to help. How about we discuss over dinner? I'm off tomorrow night. Do you like seafood?"

I said yes to all of the above. I had no reason not to. It was work. He had useful information for me. That's all. Absolutely all.

Chris was back and I went to harass her about that diary. She maintained that she was still reading it herself, but said she had a later date to go running with some of the girls from the basketball team. I could have it then.

She seemed to get great joy from saying sternly, "As long as you are careful and don't harm it!" I'd raised a smart aleck, that was for sure. Dad would say I had no one to blame but myself.

Housework called. What it actually murmured was, "I could be more interesting right now than your dissertation" but I pretended I heard, "Be a real homemaker for a few hours. It will be a treat."

Just as I was pulling the cleaning supplies out from under the sink, I had a call. The number looked vaguely familiar. The voice was not.

"Forget what you think you know. Forget everything. No gossiping. Or you will be sorry."

"What? What? Who is this?"

But the phone had already clicked off.

I sat on there the floor, shocked and annoyed in equal parts. A wrong number? A crank call? A real threat?

I looked again at the calling number and quickly scrolled through my calls of the last few weeks. It was, impossibly, from Mary Pat. Not Mary Pat, not really, but Mary Pat's phone.

Now I was so shocked I dropped my own phone.

Someone had found Mary Pat's missing cell phone. Ramos had told me they never found one but I had seen her using it. That was the only possible explanation. And was using it to do… what? Call people he had found in her calls made list? Or just me? To what purpose? I didn't know anything, just had the bad fortune of being a witness. Or had some idiot randomly found the phone and was pranking? Just because he could?

I would have to call the lieutenant yet again. Even if it was meaningless. I told myself it was meaningless. I decided to deal with the turmoil in my mind by throwing myself into my chores.

By the time Chris headed out again, I had cleaned the bathroom, done a load of laundry praying the ancient washing machine was still functioning, and made a soup where you open several cans of broth and throw in whatever vegetables are around, plus leftover rice and a can of chilies. It's the only kind of soup I know how to make.

Concrete, visible work was done. I felt tired and just a little more in control of my life. With Chris gone, it was time to read more of that diary. And take lots of notes. I wanted to know what it felt like to Philomena to be there then, doing the work she did. It could be no more than a sidebar for my chapter, but maybe we could do something with it at the museum. And I didn't say it to myself, but I knew that it would be interesting enough to crowd my real life out of my mind.

Philomena flourished at her job. *"It's so real. Real metal, real tools. Someday a real blow torch if I can do it. Not like making change all day and saying, Hi, Mrs. So and So, and asking about her son in the Army or promising the tomatoes are ripe."*

She didn't mind the damage to her nails and repaired her manicures every time she went out. She didn't mind the sweat and the dirt. *"That's what the bathtub is for. As long as they don't start rationing Ivory soap!*

She went to dances for servicemen. I could hear the giggles in her words. *"They look so handsome in their uniforms, and they clean up and shave for the dances. Makes my patriotic young heart beat faster. All those boys from the south talk REAL slow. They're so cute when they say 'ma'am.'"* She was only a few years older than Chris, after all.

"We're not supposed to leave the dances but sometimes we sneak out for a cigarette and a little privacy." She drew a heart next to that sentence and then added, *"Dear diary: Mom and Dad don't know I started smoking. It makes me feel like Bette Davis. And about that sneaking out? Nothing but kissing, even when they try. And do they try! And only if they are really, really cute and nice. I'm still a good girl."* She was so young it hurt.

She wrote about other things too, pieces of her life. Handsome Tyrone Power in the pictures, and Frank Sinatra whose voice made every girl all shivery. Francis, actually, the same name as her brother Frankie. Barbara Stanwyck. "*She has so much moxie.*" And she pasted pictures from a movie magazine next to that page. New shoes and how hard they were to get. Using makeup to tint her legs when she had no stockings left.

Philomena became more of a real girl to me with every sentence. Her writing wasn't sophisticated or deep. It was the diary of a girl barely out of her teens whose world was growing her up fast.

I wondered what Chris was making of all this, and soon had a chance to find out. I heard her tramp upstairs, then come hurtling down. She often took the stairs at a controlled free fall

"Where is my diary? I mean, Grandma's diary?"

"You mean Philomena's?"

"Yes, Mom, you know I do." She looked at my desk with narrowed eyes. "I see you snitched it."

"And no harm done. Chris, this is so fascinating. Are you loving it?"

She collapsed on my other office chair, the impulse to complain blown away. "Are you kidding? Yes, most definitely. She is so...so...like, I could know her even now."

"Except she takes you into a different world, right?"

She nodded, soberly. "Did you get to the part about her friend's brother?"

"No. What was that?"

"He got hurt bad. Wait and see." She shook her head. "But the parts about the boys are funny. Dating life was so diffcrent then." She put her hand out. "Now I need to go back to it."

I wanted to protest. I wanted to keep reading it myself. But what responsible, academic mom throws a roadblock in the study plans of a child?

● ● ● ● ●

That night I dreamed about Philomena. She was in her work clothes, looking, looking, looking for something. A phone was ringing but she didn't answer it. It was ringing and ringing. I finally knew it was not her phone. It was mine.

I dragged myself awake, fumbling to pick it up

"Erica, did I wake you? It's Lisa. I heard something."

"What?" I sat up, willing my brain to start working.

"It's Lisa. I told you! And I heard something about the Conti story."

"Okay. Okay. Now I'm awake."

"They have arrested Jennifer Conti."

"What?" *Was I still half-asleep?*

"The widow. Jennifer Conti."

"That's impossible." *I was not accepting that. Not for a minute.*

"I heard it two minutes ago from a source I trust. They have something more but I don't know what. Yet."

Chapter Sixteen

As soon as it was almost morning, I called Lisa to confirm that she had called me in the middle of the night. She had. Her best information was that there was good evidence for the arrest, but she still did not know what. She was working every source she had. She extracted a deal from me: we share anything we find. It didn't hit me until later that I might be one of her sources.

I called Ramos. I called him a few times, but there was no way to reach him except to leave a message. I conceded to myself, bitterly, he must be busy dealing with his arrest of the wrong person. And I still needed to tell him about that recent phone call. Mary Pat's number, still making mysterious calls, just as she had.

I turned on a news channel but when they finally got around to the story, no one knew more than I did. In fact, they seemed to know slightly less.

It was an ordinary morning. Chris was at school. I would be at my part-time museum job and life would be normal if I could forget this disturbing news. Of course I could not but I tried, in between a few more calls to the lieutenant and checking the news online.

And otherwise, so it was, an ordinary day. No lurkers on my block. No emergency calls from Chris, only a text in mid-morning.

Chem test went ok. Prob.

Prob? Oh, probably. Well, good.

I banished my personal life from my mind and hunkered down. I sat in the library doing photo research for an upcoming exhibit and daydreamed about abandoning my dissertation forever. A dumb idea in reality but a pleasant occasional escape. I even took a walk at lunchtime. The museum neighborhood is on a hill, looking out over New York Harbor. The chilly breeze off the water cleared out some cobwebs.

It couldn't last. Ramos got back to me a minute before I left work and said he was too busy to talk now but would I stop by his office on my way home?

He looked like a man who had not been home in the last two days. He confirmed that was true. I plunged right in anyway.

"You arrested Jennifer? That's crazy."

"No, it's not. You're doing police work? You don't know everything we do."

"Yeah? It is not possible that she's the one I saw that night. So tell me."

"No, I'm not telling you. This is just a…call it a courtesy. It goes both ways." He put up a hand to stop my protests. "I know you believe you told me everything, but you never know. I want to go over it one more time and if you do have anything, then we make it official, okay? I'm trying to be nice here."

"Believe me." I put my backpack down. "I've gone over it again and again, and there's nothing. But I can tell you this for sure. She is absolutely not the man—or woman—I saw pull that trigger. She's taller, bigger. That I can swear to."

"Let's do it one more time anyway."

We went over it step by step, what I'd seen, what I might have seen, what was on the periphery. He hadn't asked that before.

"Wait. Do you think she was there also? Hiding somewhere? Can that possibly be what you're asking me?"

"I don't think anything. The possibility that someone else was there is a question to be asked. We know you said no before, but it's worth taking another look."

"No. No, definitely not. If there was anyone else there, I didn't know about it. No matter what you'd like me to say."

He looked carefully neutral, no skin in the game. "I don't want you to say anything but what you are sure you remember. We don't want any random answer, only the right one. Got that?"

I already knew that. Probably, I knew that.

"But Jennifer? That's ridiculous."

"How well do you really know her?"

That stopped me. The answer was, not very. And I wasn't sure I even liked her. Was I taken in by the everyday hominess of meeting in Mrs. Pastore's warm kitchen? And Jennifer's classy aura? Her style? In what alternate reality could the Jennifer I had met even know someone who would shoot a man in cold blood? As impossible to imagine as her pulling the trigger herself.

Ramos looked even more harassed. "Believe me. She was there, nearby, that night. Witnesses put her at a…well, near. Very near where you were."

"What? Sitting in a car? Lurking out on the street? Disguised as a hooker? Come on!"

I saw in his face a second of wanting to say no to what I had suggested. I tried to picture what was there.

"At a bar?"

A glimmer of a yes in his face and a quick, "There's more. Things she said. Things she did. It might not be airtight yet, but we've got her."

"Not even close!"

"Come on, Erica. Who had the best reason to want him dead? You know the gossip about him?"

"Like maybe there was another girlfriend?"

He looked at me, not committing to anything.

"So you think she decided she's better off as widow than divorced?"

"And after Jennifer, who hated him most?" He gave me a hard look. "You know it was his first wife."

"Annabelle? No way! Impossible." That cheerful and kind old woman? Mrs. Pastore's friend? No. Definitely no.

"And she also had reasons to hate Mary Pat Codman." He saw my indignant expression. "You were forgetting about that, weren't you? It's too much of a stretch to think these murders were unrelated. Only thing is, we can't find anything that links it to her. Believe me, we looked."

"Other people hated him. Why not one of them? Harbor history has plenty of crooks. The mob. Labor rackets."

"That doesn't fly. These days it's mostly businessmen and politicians involved there. Even if they are dishonest—yes, maybe—they don't go in for violent crime. You know that. It's a crazy move for a respectable guy."

He saw my skeptical look. "Even a wannabe respectable guy. Besides? Conti had no real power anymore, so why now?" His expression got more set with every word. "We think we've got it figured out. What I don't get is why you care about Jennifer. For me, getting at the truth is my job. For you? Advisor still scaring you?"

"It's my job, too. I have to find out what happened, to make my chapter true." He nodded. Maybe he understood that. "Besides. I don't know. Maybe the bad dreams will stop when it's all solved."

He almost smiled. "I hear you on that. And now I have to get back on the case, anyway." He pointed to his phone. "I got urgent messages while we were talking."

"I have one more thing. It's about phones. I know this is crazy." I played my most recent, and I hoped final, mystery call from Mary Pat's number. When I was done, he had a page of notes, had recorded the message and was shaking his head.

"We can do something with this, you know. Should of called right away.'

"I know. I know. I didn't want to deal with it. Talking about makes it too real."

He nodded.

"Was it a real threat?"

"Who the hell knows? I'll keep in touch when we learn something. If we learn something. In the meantime, be careful?

Doors locked, no late night subway rides, alert on the street. You know."

I had to smile. "What I always do, right?"

He nodded again.

"You look blitzed."

"Sure am."

"I still think you're wrong about Jennifer." I was collecting my jacket and pack.

"Unless something else happens, I am going to be off tomorrow night. Would you want to talk over dinner, somewhere more comfortable than this office?"

I said yes without thinking. It was a chance to ask more questions, nothing more. I thought. And I left, admitting to myself that Jennifer at a crummy bar near the Yard was pretty strange. Now I owed Lisa a call.

I should have known her first response would be, "Did he say what bar?" and her second would be "I'm going to cruise the bars tonight. Got to. Be my wing man?"

"What in the world are you talking about?'

She laughed. "Seriously, it would be great if you come along. You were there that night! You'd be great backup. And think what you would learn." As I hesitated, she threw in, "Come on. It will be fun."

Trudging around to dive bars after a long day? Not my idea of fun. Then again, I'd never done a bar crawl. Life had interfered with what would have been that stage of life. And Chris had plans for this evening.

I asked Lisa where to meet.

Chapter Seventeen

It turned out to be not much of a bar crawl. We started with the one closest to the Yard. It was a run-down dive, all right. Dirty windows, sticky tabletops, and the smell of beer set the tone. The clientele was mixed as to race and similar as to shabby clothes. They were certainly a few beers ahead of us. And they were all male.

I ordered a bottle of Budweiser so I could skip a questionable-looking bar glass. The bartender was indifferent to our presence. I followed Lisa's lead and pretended I was perfectly comfortable. The beer actually was fine.

Jennifer being here seemed even more unlikely than me being here. Yet here I was.

About halfway through her beer, Lisa signaled the bartender. "Two again, and could I ask a question, if you're not too busy?"

He wasn't busy. I wondered if Lisa was softening him up.

"Yeah, okay." He shrugged as if to say, "No big deal."

"I'm trying to see if a woman was here last Tuesday. I have a picture."

"You cops? Your guys were already here."

"Ah, no. I'm a reporter and my friend here has a personal interest."

He crossed his arms and stared at us. "I didn't like talking to cops but they made it pretty damn clear I would have to, one way or another. Why should I talk about a customer to you?"

"'Cause I could mention this place and you would get lots of new customers?"

"More yuppies asking for fancy drinks? Big deal. But, what the hell? It's a slow night. Ask away. Not promising I'll answer."

She'd come prepared with a photo of Jennifer.

"Sure, she was here. Same woman the cops asked about. Hard to miss that fur coat in this place. Last time I saw one here was…never."

"So what did she do?"

"Asked what white wine we have." He snorted. "When I told her vodka's the only white drink, she settled for that. Sat right over there." He pointed to a dark corner table. "Sat for a long time. Kept checking her watch and looked out the window a few times. Like she was nervous. Then she got up and left." He shook his head. "There was some commotion out there. Ambulances. So that's it."

Lisa smiled sweetly and ordered two more again. "Great, but I wonder if there's more. Like, was she alone? Anyone talk to her? Ever been here before?"

"Her? Here in this dump? Naa. She was alone, she looked nervous as far as I could tell, but I'm not one of those pour-your-heart-out bartenders. Know what I mean? And anyway she didn't say a thing after she ordered except to ask for more. She was putting it away pretty good. Left a big tip, too. Not like that other lady.'

"What?" I squeaked it. "What other lady?"

"There was another lady here that night. Pretty unusual, that's why I remember it."

"And? And?" We both said it.

"Yeah, well she was older. Short and chunky. Saw my second fur coat for the night. Alone, like that other one. Drank one light Coors the whole time she was there, taking up a table. I'd have thrown her out if we were busy."

I had an idea. "Did she limp? Do you remember? Or walk with a cane?"

"Hey, are you a mind reader? She had a cane. I forgot about that."

"Who else have you told about her?"

Lisa was all smiles when he answered, "No one."

I was the one who added, "Not even the cops?"

He shrugged. "They never asked me."

Lisa stood up all smiles and shook his hand. "You've been great. This is a big help."

"Put the bar name in the story. Forget what I said, okay? We can use the business."

Outside, the avenue at this hour was lonely and dark. All my street smarts were on alert as I was kept an eye out for anyone else who was out and about.

Lisa grabbed my arm. "It was Mary Pat, wasn't it? It must have been."

"Oh, yeah. Waiting for Conti? They were always a secret so she couldn't meet him at the meeting. But, think about this. Probably Jennifer didn't know her, but seems like she would have recognized Jennifer. Don't you think? From pictures in the papers at least."

I imagined the two women, sitting separately, with so many connections yet completely unconnected. A picture of total bleakness.

"Damn! And here we are, knowing something no one else does and I don't know exactly what to do with it. Yet. But there must be something. Talk tomorrow?"

It was too late and dark for the long walk to a subway or a long wait for a bus. We called Uber cars to get us home. All the way, I couldn't stop thinking about Mary Pat, hiding in a crummy bar because she couldn't be in public with her lover. Was he worth it, Michael Conti?

And how disturbing that we had talked to her just recently and now she was dead. Had someone hated both Conti and her? Or was she a threat to someone? I sighed. Was my imagination spinning out of control?

• • ● • •

When Chris appeared at my bedroom door too early the next morning, I thought she wanted a ride to school. Instead, she handed me the open diary. "There's a love story, I think. How cool is that? And it sounds so real. Like, I get this completely. (Read it!")

> *"Our first date. My secret crush.* (Philomena drew a little heart.) *We went to a movie, Crash Dive with Tyrone Power, my forever favorite, and Dana Andrews, who's awfully good too. They were so brave. Strange to see Power in uniform when he is already in the Marines for real.*
>
> *"After, we talked about it, how it could be any of us with loved ones fighting. I got a little weepy and he was sweet. He didn't laugh when I told him about how I used to have photos of Tyrone on my wall, but now I am too grown-up for silly things like that. Life is not silly now.*
>
> *"It was not like a date with those other boys. We shared popcorn. We took the trolley home and he held me when it took a corner too fast, but otherwise he was a perfect gentleman. But it all felt different. I wanted him to kiss me good night. More than one good-night kiss. Next time if he doesn't, I will! Really, I will make the first move."*

"You see? Doesn't that sound like something special? The beginning of it?"

Her eyes were shining. "It's like reading a wonderful book, only it's true."

I handed the diary back. "It sure is that, a real-life story. Keep me posted. No. On second thought, read very, very fast so I can read it too."

She left, but then came back.

"I want to go see the Navy Yard in person. I need to see the places she was writing about. Take pictures for my project. And she met him there, standing in line to pick up their pay envelopes." She smiled. "That is so quaint, pay envelopes."

"Absolutely not. I hate the idea. Hate the very thought of ever going back there." And I could not forget or ignore that mysterious phone message. I had not told her, but it was in the back of my mind all the time.

"You don't have to come. I can go myself. Why not?"

"Chris! Have you forgotten my last visit?"

"Not at all." She had that mule-like expression. "But I'd go in the daytime. Of course!"

"Chris, I…"

"I'm an experienced bike-rider now. I'll take my bike. There's not a lot of traffic going there, so it's perfectly safe. Perfectly!" She saw my face and went further. "You know what you saw was only a crazy thing that could have happened anywhere."

"They do have tours," I admitted reluctantly. "So you could sign up for a World War II tour. You'd learn a lot." *And be in a supervised group the whole time*, I thought.

"Tomorrow? It's Saturday. Can I do it tomorrow?"

"See if they have a tour and an open spot. Charge it to my card. And plan to dress warm. It's windy down there on the water."

"Mom! Of course I will." She shuddered. "It will be a chilly bike ride."

She popped back in to report she had found a tour at eleven, signed up, and would be out early enough to ride over.

I didn't know what worried me most, a bike ride through city streets on her own, or my own experiences. The time I went back I had a cop for an escort. I try hard not to be a smothering mother. I fell asleep still worrying.

Saturday morning was bright and cold. I sent Chris off with an oatmeal breakfast for fuel, and harassed her about both calling me when she arrived at the Navy Yard and wearing warm clothes. She only reacted to my harassing with a sarcastic "Sure, Mom."

I knew what she did not: the clothes were a proxy for my rational—somewhat rational—worry about her biking off on

her own and my irrational—well, mostly irrational—dislike of
her being in a place where I had seen a shooting. She was right,
though. It was a fluke in a low-crime—no, a no-crime—location. The new manufacturing businesses made sure there was
lots of security. And, after all, she would be with lots of normal
visitors, history-minded folks like me.

I had research results to write up for my real job, the one with
a paycheck, tiny though it was. Dr. Adams would say my real job
was finishing my dissertation and this job was a distraction, but
then she was a full professor with a salary. And tenure.

I spent one minute telling myself not to let Dr. Adams be
in my head so often, and then buried myself in my task. When
I looked up again, it was because I had a call from Chris. And
about bloody time too. She had never called to report her safe
arrival.

When I pointed it out to her, she response was in a strange
voice, "But I texted."

"What's wrong?" Her tone of her voice had me on instant
alert.

"Mommy?" She hasn't called me that in years. "You know how
you always said, if I was out and there was something, anything,
that scared me, to call? Trust my instincts, no matter what? "

I managed to say, "Yes?" while holding my breath. That was
the rule from the time she was first allowed to walk up the street
to the corner grocery.

It came out in a rush. "This is that call."

"What? Where are you? What…?"

"I'm all right, honest I am, but…"

"Chris!

"Okay. Okay. So I came out of the tour and hopped right
on my bike. I was not even out of the gates when I lost control
and hit a wall. And, Mom, I'm so sorry but I bent a tire and I
think the bike will have to be fixed."

"I don't care about the tire, I care about you." I would worry
about what the tire would cost later. "Are you all right?"

She took a deep breath. "Yes."

"You're sure?" She didn't sound sure.

"Yes! Yes, I am."

I thought, what a colossal pain. But then I thought I could get it home on the bus, right? There's a bus stop outside the gates. I'd have to wait but it could be done." She didn't sound sure. She sounded teary. "I really, really did not mean to bother you. But there's no bus for a long time. And there's a man…"

"*What* man?" I was already collecting purse and keys, still holding the phone.

"He's walking, back and forth and back again. And…and looking…"

"I'm on the way out the door. I'll pick you up. Sit tight. Better than that, there's a bar across the street. See it? The bartender is pretty nice."

"You know a bartender?" She sounded shocked but at least she was distracted for a moment.

I pictured the bar. "No, forget that. You walk right back into the Yard and go to the museum. If they ask, tell them why, and that I'm coming for you."

"But I will sound so stupid. And maybe I am being silly, you know?"

"No argument! Go do it. Now! And we stay on the phone together. I have to put it down to lock the door, but I'm here. Got it?"

I made it to the car in record time. Start, I muttered to myself, start, damn it. And it did. I put my phone on the seat next to me, assured myself that Chris was okay and safe and was heading back to the museum.

I cursed every red light I hit on my way down to the harbor.

From her perch in front of the museum right near the entrance, she could see me pull up. She waved and dragged her disabled bike out.

"You're okay? You felt safe in there?"

"You can see I am fine. But my poor bike?"

She stopped wrestling with the bike and finally looked at me.

"Mom, I feel so stupid. I convince you I'm old enough to do this bike ride, and then look what happened. I could have got myself home, and I should have." Her expression was not nearly as confident as her words. She suddenly leaned over and whispered to me, "Only thing is, he's still here." She grabbed me. "Don't look! I'm trying to pretend I never noticed him."

"Right. Let's get the bike in the car, and while we do, I can take a peek. You lift, I'll maneuver."

We succeeded, with some cursing involved. A compact car is not meant to transport a bicycle. And I did see the man. I almost exclaimed to Chris, "You were afraid of that shaky old guy?"

His clothes were shabby, baggy pants and a baggy sweatshirt. A dark cap. He was somewhat stooped. Maybe old, certainly not young. And he walked up and down a short stretch of sidewalk weaving a little. Frail? Drunk? Mental health issues? He was muttering to himself. I could see that, but I could not make out the words.

It used to be that someone talking to himself was a red flag to give the speaker wide berth and never lock eyes. Now, of course it is probably someone talking into a hands-free phone. But this man did not look like a person with an expensive gadget in his pocket.

"Good that you called. Your instincts were dead-on. I mean, probably he is harmless, but what if?"

"So you don't think I was a silly little scaredy-cat?"

"Nope. I would have been nervous around him too."

What made me the most nervous was that he was still looking as we pulled away from the curb.

"*You* should be nervous but I'm stronger and tougher than you are. Bigger too. I should be more confident."

"Oh, ha, ha. Bigger, yes. Tougher, no way. I learned to scrap as a little kid."

"You only think you can still do that."

Going home after parking, turning the corner to our block, I almost missed him. I was busy with my thoughts, relieved to have Chris home, relieved to be safe on our own block.

And there he was again, leaning against a tree, across the street. At least I thought it was the same man. I only had a fleeting glimpse of him in front of the museum.

I forced myself not to look or acknowledge him in any way. I didn't collapse until I get back in the house.

Why was he here? Who was he? How did he find us? He could not have followed my car home without a car of his own.

And the biggest question: what was I going to do about it? If anything? Certainly not tell Chris for now. I did not want to frighten her. Not, not, not call Joe, my usual source of strength and good advice. Dad? No, I did not want his help, which was not always helpful. He'd be just as likely to cause a scene and get hurt himself.

When I peeked out again and he was still there I'd had enough. He had no right to be hanging around, loitering, on our home block. No right at all.

I slammed out of the house and across the street.

"You!"

He turned quietly to squint at me.

"What are you doing here? Why are you hanging around my house?"

He looked confused, then sly.

"I'm trying to meet someone. Someone else I used to know. Not you. Who are you?"

"I saw you at the Navy Yard today."

"The lady with the car and the bike and that girl? That was you?"

"You were loitering there, like you are here. What the hell do you want?"

"Not loitering. I was waiting for a bus. Now I'm trying to meet someone. Like I said."

"Stay away from my daughter!"

"What daughter? I already said I don't know you or your daughter, lady. And don't care about you either." He turned his back to me, and began humming. That made me even more annoyed. I walked around to make him face me again.

"You go away! You can't hang around here like this."

"I can't? Who says?"

"Against the law." I had no idea if that was true but I said it with conviction.

He turned again, and walked away.

"Wait!" Something had just clicked. "Haven't I seen you before? In front of the coffee shop? You…" I realized I almost said "beg" and switched gears at the last moment. "…open the door?" He hesitated, nodded, and walked away. I hadn't learned anything but at least I seemed to have chased him off.

I was glad I had a date with a detective tonight. Not an actual date but at least a meeting. It would be a chance to get some expert advice.

Did I need to tell Chris, just to make sure she stayed alert, kept her eyes open and—oh, yes—didn't do anything dumb? When she first called me, he was only a strangely behaving old man on the street, probably as harmless as most of them were. Telling her he was hanging around turned it into something much scarier.

It was already too late to wonder. She pounced as soon as I walked in.

"Mom! What were you doing? Was that the same guy? What did he say?"

"Yes it was. I chased him away and anyway he's looking for someone else. He said. Now, listen, Chris. This evening…"

Then I wasn't sure what I needed to say. Scare her? Reassure her?

"I'm going over to Mel's."

"Oh?" Her casual statement lit up all my anxieties. "Were you planning to ask me?"

"Eventually." She was surprised. "You don't mind, do you?"

"No, of course not, but you need to tell me how you are getting there."

"What are you talking about? I'm walking the couple of blocks, of course. Like I have been doing since fifth grade. Why?" She looked up then and saw my face.

"Oh? That guy?" She surprised me with a hug. "It's all right. It's all over. He was just some random weird street guy and I overreacted because of my bike."

I appreciated that she was soothing me, but now was not the time.

"I worry if he followed us home somehow. I don't know if he is telling the truth." I considered his shifty expressions and went on, "I don't know if he even knows what's true."

"No. No. That's too crazy." She shook her head. "You are doing that paranoid parent thing. You've got to work on that."

"What paranoid parent thing?"

She gave me a look and I knew we were getting away from the main subject.

"Now listen up. I mean this! I want you to be extra cautious and extra alert. In fact, now that I think of it, I'm glad you will be at Mel's instead of home alone."

"Mom, that is ridiculous."

"I. Don't. Care. Is that clear? So you either walk over to Mel's with me, before I go out, or you go the long way around, on the avenue with a crowd or…"

"Oh, all right. Or Mel comes to get me and we walk back to her house together? How's that?"

"That would be fine. And stay there until I get home, and I'll pick you up."

"Like a little kid? Mom, I will be so…"

"Embarrassed? Too bad. It's that, or I cancel my plans and yours and we both stay home."

"Okay, okay. I'll do it but I am on record as not being happy. "But," she added with a devilish smile, "Joe would be unhappy if I was the reason you cancelled dinner. Tell him I send my love."

And what was I to say to that?

"It's not Joe. Not really a date either."

"Oh, ha. I saw an outfit laid out on your bed. But, why not Joe?" She stopped abruptly. "Oh. So you really were arguing the other night. I thought I dreamed it."

"We weren't arguing. Not exactly. And I can have other friends. I…"

"Your best sweater is not for…" She made air quotes. " 'other friends.' I understand these things now that I am with Jared, you know. What's wrong with you and Joe?"

"Don't you have more important things to do than cross-examine me?"

"No, not really. I have an investment in this topic, but okay, I see I am getting nowhere. And you're not borrowing my earrings, either."

She returned to her room after giving me an angry look.

I showered and checked the street. He was gone. I greeted Mel, invited her in, and checked the street. I dressed and checked the street. And found a note on my bed. "If he's not Joe, I disapprove." I was so torn between laughing and crushing it into a ball that I did both.

I waited downstairs, ready for a nice dinner out with a nice man. Dress shoes on, even a little makeup. And I checked the street again. No signs of our unwanted watcher under the streetlamps.

I still worried that I had made a huge blunder, letting Chris go off today by herself. How do you ever know where to draw the line? I only knew it was somewhere south of escorting a high school student to school and north of "anything goes."

Then Lieutenant Ramos rang the doorbell and I willed myself to set these thorny questions aside for the rest of the evening. For a few hours, I would not be a mom; I would be a concerned citizen, a serious scholar, and a woman in nice shoes.

Besides, I had other questions to ask him.

Chapter Eighteen

We went to a neighborhood place with weather-beaten wood paneling, oars hung on the walls and photos of boats and surf. It didn't smell of salt air but of food frying. The menu was full of things I don't know how to make and could not afford to buy. Lobster things. Crab things. Flounder done up in fancy ways.

Fish and chips with a cold beer suddenly sounded like the solution to all my problems. I randomly chose an ale from the full-page list. I refused to admit that I had no idea what any of them were, even with the poetic descriptions. Light? Dark? Hoppy? Fruity? Who has time to study all this? But that first sip tasted wonderful. Ordering done, I began to relax at last.

I smiled at Ramos. "Did you get any further with Jennifer being innocent?"

He smiled back. "And here I was about to ask if you were making progress on that dissertation?"

"Ouch. It's too stressful to talk about."

He nodded. "Exactly. So let's not talk about work, yours or mine, okay?" He paused. "How about those Knicks?"

I laughed. "The only teams I follow are my daughter's. She plays lacrosse and basketball. Junior varsity this year."

He looked me up and down. "I'm guessing she's taller than you."

"Oh, yeah. Isn't everyone? It's been a shock to me to have an athlete daughter. And both her teams are doing better than the Knicks."

He looked more cheerful. "Baseball was good this summer, though."

His enthusiasm and my good listening abilities took us through the arrival of dinner.

With some crispy cod and salty French fries in my system, I was fortified enough to talk work. I led into it gently, telling him about Philomena's diary and how excited Chris was.

Perhaps I went on too long. He responded with an extremely polite, "I can see how interesting it could be. It's nice when you can get your kid excited about your work. My dad was a cop. So you see how that worked out."

He had no questions about what I had told him. He didn't understand that I was excited, too, or why I was. It made me sad but he never noticed. He turned the conversation to his own son and how they bonded over sports if nothing else. His son insisted his future was in computers not law enforcement.

We agreed, with some relief, not to talk about parenting teenage children.

"Okay, detective, here's a real-life puzzle." It was my chance to ask for his advice.

When I was done he said, "Yeah, that's not good." He sat back, thinking. "I don't like the sound of it, but there's nothing for us—us meaning NYPD—to do right now. He hasn't done anything but scare you, right? Not something I'd be involved with, normally, except for that Navy Yard connection. I'll need to ask a few questions over there. Talk to their security again. We're still pulling on every thread regarding Conti, making our case airtight." He stopped himself. "Ah, don't repeat that anywhere, okay? Official word is that we are right on top of it."

He stopped and looked at the dessert menu. "Would you like something sweet? Local Key lime pie? From Brooklyn? How is that possible?"

I knew a change of subject when it hit me on the head.

"But they also have chocolate blackout cake. Childhood favorite, right?"

Sharing of the desserts was well underway when a cell phone rang.

"Mine or yours?"

"Afraid it's yours. My ring is from *Rocky*."

Chris, of course.

"Sorry, I am so sorry, I know I shouldn't call now but..."

"Are you all right?"

"Yes, yes, sure. I'm home. Mel is here. Don't fuss, her brother walked us back and she is staying the night. I knew you wouldn't mind."

"No, I'm glad. So would you please tell me why you are calling?"

Across the table, Ramos had an amused gleam in his eyes.

"Well, when we got back, that guy was there again."

"You're sure it was him?"

Out of the corner of my eye, I saw Ramos was not smiling now. He was on full cop alert, putting his card in the check holder, motioning to the waitress, getting ready for a quick departure.

"Well, it's so dark. I can't be sure..."

"Chris!"

"Yes. Pretty sure."

Ramos had already guessed what it was. He was putting his jacket on as I explained.

"Doors locked, shutters closed. We'll be there in a few minutes."

Turning the corner to my block, he grabbed my arm. "Look over there, but be quiet." He didn't point. There was just a subtle nod of his head.

I looked. There was a man there, in the dark patch between the streetlights, right across from my house. I guess I hadn't scared him away after all.

Ramos explained how we would go down the street and up my steep steps without ever staring at him.

I slammed the door shut in relief and called the girls.

They clattered down the stairs.

"It was him, wasn't it?"

"Is it that mystery man? This is so exciting." Mel stopped when she saw our horrified faces. "I mean...yes, it's scary but..."

"Mel! Watch less TV! This is for real and I don't like it."

Mel put a concerned arm around Chris.

"Mom, this is becoming creepy."

For sure.

"How long has he been there? And what has he done?"

How long had it been? An hour. What had he done? Precisely nothing. He was sitting and watching. Sometimes he paced.

In the meantime Ramos was looking through the shutters, concealed but keeping his eyes on the man.

"I'm going to talk to him."

"Seriously? What if he's armed…?"

"You're kidding, right?"

"Sorry. This is all very…"

"I know. I'll be back in five."

Now it was our turn to peek through the shutters, watching a pantomime of an encounter. Ramos approached the man, cigarette pack out. He took one, the stranger took one, and Ramos lit them both, casually standing next to him, leaning against a fence. The man sucked on his cigarette as if the smoke was oxygen. Ramos held his casually, waved it to make a point, tapped off the ash. It never went near his mouth.

They talked. The man jumped up, and Ramos reached into his jacket. We all gasped until we saw he held something in his flat hand. His badge? The man looked at it, made a dismissive gesture and tried to turn away. When Ramos grabbed his arm the man twisted, lifted an angry hand, thrust his face close to Ramos with belligerence we could see from across the street, but Ramos did not move.

At last the man seemed to crumple and put his head in his hands. Ramos pulled him up, held him tightly and spoke to him before turning him around and letting him go. He walked away toward the busy avenue, shoulders now hunched, the fight gone.

The girls were breathing hard and I couldn't seem to breathe at all.

Ramos returned, shaking his head.

"What did you say?"

"Who is he?"

"What did HE say?"

He put up his hands to stop us. "He's a confused old man who could not, or would not, tell me why he was there, but I pointed out he is loitering, showed him the badge, and sent him off. I made it clear that we have an eye on him now, so I don't think he's coming back."

"Well, that's disappointing." Chris said it. "And should we be doing anything? You know, official? Report a suspicious person?"

He smiled wearily. "I'm official enough. Could you swear to it, that he's the same guy you saw at the Navy Yard?"

"Yes." I was sure.

"Consider it reported."

He nodded to Chris and Mel. "Pleased to meet you, young ladies." Then he added, "Stay alert, okay? This guy seemed harmless enough but not altogether connected to reality. So be smart and pay attention to what's around you, right?"

"We got it." Chris said it and Mel nodded, adding, "We are smart city kids."

"You're also teenagers. You get distracted."

They looked indignant until I added, "Honestly, don't we all?"

He turned to me. "I have to say thanks for a very unusual first date."

"Wait a minute. You didn't tell me his name. It wasn't Conti, by any chance?"

I'd been doing some serious thinking.

Ramos looked at me with astonishment, and then started laughing. "As in, Michael Conti's long lost brother?"

I admitted that's what crossed my mind.

"So that would tie up everything with a neat bow? You think he was the shooter too?"

I could feel my face turning red. And in front of Chris and Mel.

"It was only a thought. I mean, you said you are pulling on all the threads."

"We did. Angelo Conti died in 1995."

"You didn't tell me?"

"I would have. He was already at Kings County Hospital, mostly sick from a rough life. Diabetes, blood pressure, ulcers. Then he had a heart attack."

"Were they sure?"

"It was in front of a whole medical team, Nancy Drew. No possible questions about it."

"Oh, well. It would have been a good idea."

"Yeah. Real life doesn't work like that, at least not in this case. Nothing is obvious. Not one single thing." He was done laughing at me. "His name is Tom Doyle. He says. And the address he gave me is on Fourth Avenue. 500. Mean anything to you?"

"Sadly, no."

"Me neither, but you can be sure we'll look further."

After I'd locked the door behind him, Mel said, "Pretty cute guy. Are you going to tell us all about your date? Girl talk?"

Chris wasn't smiling. "You said it wasn't a date. So was it or wasn't it?"

"I'm not exactly sure. Go play video games or something. I don't have to explain it to you."

Mel shrugged but Chris muttered softly, "Yes you do."

I wanted to talk to someone. I could not sort out my whirling thoughts about this disturbing incident. About Chris' reaction to my date. About the date itself, the normal part of it, anyway. About the murder that was clouding all my thoughts, even when I tried hard to suppress it.

I did not want to talk any more to Chris. I did not want my dad. I did not want Darcy. Or Lisa.

All in all, I wanted to talk to Joe, the person who always helped me see everything more clearly. He would have understood that conversation about Philomena's diary, too. And when he teased me, he didn't laugh at me.

I didn't know how to do that right now, to talk to him. We had never had a fight before, but then, before, we were only friends. Maybe we should have left it that way.

In the end I called Leary. It was not too late. He kept odd hours anyway. He's a terrible confidante, the worst person for personal advice, but his no-crap attitude might slap me into another mood.

He got the phone on one ring, but he didn't sound friendly. When I asked if he could talk, he responded, "Five minutes. That's all you get. Than I have a date with the TV. Boxing tonight."

"Boxing? Seriously?"

"Yeah, seriously. The sweet science. This is a classic fight. I saw it in person, back when."

"Ah. Nostalgia tripping."

"Oh, hell, no. Cut the crap. You're wasting your five minutes."

"I need your memory. Does the name Tom Doyle ring any bells?'

"Nope. How about coming up with a context for this? So maybe I can make a connection? Sometimes my brain needs a little more juice to get going these days. Alcohol used to be just the thing."

"Sure it was. Try caffeine. Besides I don't think you have forgotten one single minute of your working life."

He did chuckle at that. "You think I've still got that steel-trap mind? So tell more but you're on the clock."

I gave him the very, very short version of today.

He grunted. "Nice to see you are still getting into trouble."

"I don't get into trouble! It follows me."

"Yeah, yeah. Like a puppy. Don't get me wrong. I admire it but I'm still going to watch the match in a few minutes. Your dad too. We've got some beer all ready." He chuckled. "I'm drinking that crappy diet ginger ale, of course."

"And potato chips?"

"Who are you, my nurse? And your dad says he'll call tomorrow to talk, but now it's TV time. And he says...what's that? Chris' party? Maybe makes sense to you, but not to me."

I heard the TV in the background, a loud announcer voice, and said good night.

It wasn't my dad who called early the next morning, it was Leary. He woke me up to say three little sentences.

"I might have remembered something. Might have. Look again at those files I loaned you." And then he hung up.

So I looked. No matter if my eyes were not entirely open. When Leary remembered something it was worth pursuing.

It was a long time, though, before I found it, a note in Leary's all-but-illegible scrawl. Meeting of a committee from the Navy Yard with the very old, long-serving congressman. Not much happened at the meeting, which was probably why Leary only wrote a short paragraph. Concerns were discussed. Promises were made.

And here were the names of the committee members. Tom Doyle was one. Their spokesman was Michael Conti.

There was no photo. It wasn't a very important meeting, even though the livelihoods of thousands of people depended on the results. There was a reference to a parade or demonstration that was planned. The congressman promised he would be there.

Now that, I could track. I had a photo of it in one of my books and there were newspaper stories. I wondered if Leary had written any of them. They described a large crowd, banners, bands playing, speeches. The theme was "We will never let the Yard be shut down."

As far as I could tell, no one suggested that they compromise with the Department of Defense. No one acknowledged that there might be some genuine issues. No one would have wanted to say that out in public.

Less than two years later, every person who marched that day was unemployed. Except the politicians, of course. And Conti.

Chapter Nineteen

I sensed I had something here, but I didn't know what it was. Maybe a walk would help clear my brain. The girls were still sleeping, so I grabbed a mug of coffee and a bowl of dry cereal of some unknown derivation, something healthy and hay-like that Chris had bought. It would do.

I didn't start with a direction, just a plan to get a little air and sun, but soon I had one. Out of curiosity I was going to walk on over to the address Doyle had given Ramos.

It was easy enough to find but it was not Doyle's home, not his living address or even his mailing address. It was a construction site, a shiny new condominium building rising to replace a block of shabby stores and walk-up apartments.

I stopped a young woman in running gear who was going into one of the still-inhabited buildings. She removed her earbuds to talk to me. She didn't know Doyle but explained she had only lived there for a year or so, with a group of roommates. They didn't know many of the old-timers.

That was the story of life in Brooklyn these days. I wondered how she saw me.

I scanned the nearby stores. The sparkling pink nail salon? Not at all likely. The coffee house that promised Fair Trade beans and gluten-free muffins? Not bloody likely. The corner grocery store? Maybe. The shabby laundry that looked as if it had been there forever? With Chinese letters on the sign? Ah ha. A living stereotype that also happened to be true around here.

The well-spoken Asian boy at the front, reading a physics textbook, was obviously weekend help in the family business. He had no idea, and the weary middle-aged woman at the sewing machine—his mother?—had no idea but she called loudly in an Asian language to an old lady in the back. When the older woman slowly came up to the front she spoke in heavily accented English but she knew what I wanted.

"He's an old man, mostly bald, and maybe confused. He says he lives down the block where they are tearing the buildings down now."

"Not so old." She shook her head. "Maybe now old but when we open here, he young. His wife come with work clothes, very dirty. He had hard work." She gave me a tight smile. "Long time ago now. Not seen him lately."

"Grandma! How can you remember that?"

"I'm old, not stupid." She returned to her chair in the back, head held high.

Great. I had learned something new, but it didn't get me any closer to answers. It only confused me more.

By the time I got home, much against my will I was thinking about a return trip to the Navy Yard. Unless I tossed out this whole chapter. I could hit that delete key and move on. It would be so easy, but I could not stand the idea that I had wasted all this time on it, and I was damned if I was going to admit to my advisor that it had been a mistake.

Maybe I could find someone who was there when Chris was. Someone who led the tour. The website had a whole section about tours. Could I call the tour office? Probably would not find staff there today, on a Sunday.

What I found, instead, was an array of photos from the last tour. Chris' tour. Such fun to get a glimpse of Chris, being herself away from me. She was snapping pictures of her surroundings while someone else was snapping pictures of her. In some she was typing away into her phone, taking notes I thought. Hoped.

The rest of the group looked like the usual mix of tourists, war history buffs, and old Brooklyn fans, people of different ages but all dressed for a chilly harbor outing. Lots of real cameras as well as phones.

And there, in one photo was someone who looked completely different. He seemed to be ignoring both the guide and the view. He was looking at his hands. Or at the tourists. He was the man who had frightened Chris. Probably. And probably the man who was lurking on our block in the dark last night.

Well, I thought, *why was he there? And what was he doing?*

In the photo I couldn't tell if he was staring at Chris or not. Maybe. He was on the fringe of the tour, not fully part of it. Maybe not part of it at all. But I could ask my neighbors if anyone else had seen him on our block last night or any other time. Mrs. Pastore wasn't the only older person who was an informal neighborhood block-watcher. You could call them busybodies—the teen-agers certainly did—but I didn't. They had time on their hands and they swept the sidewalk every day, gardened, sat on their stoops smoking. Kept on eye on things.

Mrs. Pastore was the one I knew best, and Mr. Pastore, who touched up his small front garden every day before he headed to the back to tend his grape arbor and fish pond. I took my laptop with me when I knocked on their door.

"Oh, Erica, come on in. I've got a fresh pot of coffee, and my own walnut roll, too. I did a new thing and frosted it. Some days, ya know, you want the sugar. You'll try a slice?"

I know better than to turn down anything Mrs. Pastore baked.

"I'd love to, but I came by to ask you a question. You and Mr. Pastore, too, if he is around?"

"Sure. You sit. I'll get him from the back. I'm trying to make him work less."

The coffee smelled great and the cake was calling my name.

She returned with her husband

"Sal, you gotta rest sometimes, take a break from the bending and have a little snack. You know you're not a kid anymore."

"Who says?"

She smacked him on his arm, and he smiled.

"I used to help my uncle, Sal senior, in that same garden since I was a kid. This was his house back then. Same grape arbor. And she says I can't do it now?" He shook his head.

He started telling me about his uncle and I was into my second slice of cake before I could ask my question.

"A loiterer? On our block? I can't say that I've seen one. And he'd better not come back. I keep a baseball bat beside the door."

Mrs. Pastore frowned. "We don't get out much at night. But let me see that picture."

She looked at the screen with her glasses off and her glasses on, and finally conceded that she did not know him. "But still, there's something about him. I can't get my finger on it. Old brains, you know?"

"I have a name. Assuming he told the truth." I now doubted that. "My friend asked him."

"Ah." She smiled. "Last night. You went out with that cute cop. He did the questioning?"

"Mrs. P, how did you know that?"

She smiled. "You got a name? So give it."

The name meant nothing, and they apologized for not being able to help.

I went home to make pancakes for Chris and Melanie.

I had my lunch while they had breakfast and chattered about last night. I was amused to see the two athletes, whose bodies were temples of fitness, devouring the bacon. I told them what I had learned.

"Mom, you did all that this morning? While we were still asleep? Wow."

"It's amazing how much…"

Their giggling stopped me dead.

"You're going to say it, aren't you, just like my mom?" Mel and Chris continued together in singsong. "'…how much you can get done when you don't sleep half the day away.'"

"What is most amazing is that we moms all have the same operating manual. Any chance we could be right?" My smile was only half mocking. "More syrup, anyone?"

"And I suppose you are going to tell that cop all about it?"

"Chris. Cut the hostility. He was helpful last night." She was silent and sulking. "And what it is this all about anyway?"

She muttered, "You know," as she stood to carry her dishes to the sink.

A sulking teenager, a mystery I could not solve, a chapter I could not finish, my baffling romantic life. This seemed like a good time to escape to the past, where life was simpler. Actually, any historian knows that's a lie. Life was never simpler. It's only a trick of distance.

Whatever. Philomena's diary would take me someplace that was not my life and that was exactly what I wanted.

I picked up where I had left off, with Philomena writing about her growing relationship. She sounded like the very young girl she was, delighted, silly, swoony. He was handsome, sweet, funny, altogether perfect.

I noted the references to ordinary life during the war. She missed sugar in her coffee. She helped her father in their victory garden on a hot, sunny day. She bravely tasted tripe at a Horn & Hardart Automat, trying to make the best of the meat shortages. At home her father complained about dinners and her mother smacked her big cooking spoon down on the table and said, "If the president says meatless Monday, that's what you gonna have."

She missed the exhilarating dazzle of Times Square and wondered if the lights would ever come back on.

But mainly, she was a young girl, falling in love for the first time and she wrote from her heart. A page with worry about the lack of letters from her brother on a ship "*somewhere in the Pacific*" alternated with a page about a "*heavenly*" evening out. He was different from the neighborhood boys. He thought about big things like politics. And love. There were hints that the relationship was moving past the good-night kiss stage.

I suddenly found myself with tears in my eyes. Her words went right to my memories of Jeff. The wonder of it all. The dazzling feelings. My own heavenly nights.

Reading her pages brought home to me that my romantic life was a tangled mess.

After a page decorated with colored pencil hearts and flowers, I slammed the book shut, walked around the room a few times, and used sheer willpower to force the tears in my eyes to stay right there.

I gave myself a little mental slap. My real reason for having and reading the diary was to learn about what happened to Philomena. I could skip the story of her romance and go right to the end. That shortcut would be easier on my confused emotions, as well as more efficient for my research. Maybe.

The last page was dated January 1, 1946. She said "*I don't want to write here anymore. I am a grownup now, living a grownup life. Everything is different. Even in the middle of the war, I was personally happy. Now the war is over, but I am sad. How strange life turns out.*"

What? What happened to her? I flipped back several pages, taking note of the dates. She wrote every few days in the beginning, but as the war went on, the pages were more irregular, the notes shorter. Grownup life was happening. A brother came home wounded. A childhood friend did not come home at all, his body lying in a Normandy cemetery.

Finally, going back far enough, I found it. He was drafted. She didn't understand exactly how he had ended up in the Army, instead of the Navy, where he could have used his shipyard skills. He was going to Germany.

Before he left, he gave her a ring, an Irish design with clasped hands, with a promise of a better one when he came back. She wore it on a chain around her neck, under her clothes. Her family didn't like him, and she wrote, "*Why have an excuse to fight while he is gone? I won the fight about my job and I'll win this one when he comes back for me.*"

So maybe he died in action, and she never got over it. I understood that. But she was so young. Did she mourn him forever? Phyllis described her as always seeming to have an underlying sadness. I began flipping pages again. If only I could find his full name I could search military records.

After more flipping and months later, Philomena herself gave me the answer in one short sentence. *"He came home."* A sketch of fireworks and hearts followed it.

A page or two later, she wrote a few sentences. *"I am so happy but they will not let me be happy. They all disapprove. He's got no family. He's not Catholic. He's not Italian. Who cares? What did we fight the war for? He'll never fit in. And then they started on the politics and went on and on. I don't care. I don't care, I do not care!!!"*

A month later, she wrote, *"Another battle. Vito and Al. Even Frankie. He's getting better with the physical therapy and expects to go back to work soon. Even he said, 'He's not one of us' And they all said, 'Open your eyes, silly girl.' They said that! What nerve, after all I've done. They said 'The war's over. There are cutbacks at the Yard. Any excuse, they said. Any excuse at all and we will lose our jobs. You don't remember what it was like when there was no work.'*

"Vito threw a newspaper at me. 'Read what's going on in Congress! Communist plots everywhere. And you think you love a Commie? What's wrong with you?'

"He said all that, my horrid oldest brother.

"'You think you know things? Let me tell you.' But then he didn't tell me a thing. Just shouted. And I was so mad I said I would join the party too. Why not? It's legal just like the Democrats!

And Mom and Papa didn't say a word until two of them—my own brothers!—grabbed my arms and shook me. Then Papa said 'Basta! You go to your room' to me, as if I'm a little girl—and to them, 'Go home and cool off.'

"I operate dangerous machinery at work and help repair giant warships. I am no little girl. I did not go to my room. I went out to meet my love instead, and I cried and he held me tight and then tighter, and we started to make our plans."

Wow.

Then, the next day, she wrote about a walk with her favorite brother. *"He said, 'I understand, Phillie, I do. It's love, all birds singing all the time.'*

I said, 'Don't you dare make fun of me'. He apologized but only a little. Then he said, 'Look around you. The girls are all being sent home so the soldiers can get their jobs back, right?' True. A lot of my friends have left. Some of them said they were happy, going home to have babies, but some of them cried and cried.

'Don't you wonder why you are still there? We have some influence, your family. You'll get an office job, but you'll stay. But any problems, any scandal? You'd be out and we will be too. Vito is a jerk but he told the truth about how it was when there was no work at all some days and the only food was what Dad grew in the garden. You remember?'

'Maybe.' I said. 'A little. Lots of carrots.'

'Mama made your clothes over and then over again. One winter Dad and me and Vito shared one winter coat. We all worked different shifts. Now we got families of our own to take care of. You getting what I'm saying?'

I got it, all right. They were scared. Seems like Congress scared them more than the Axis. I don't get that. And it has nothing to do with me and my life!!!!!!
!!"

The row of exclamation points after that, written so hard the pen tore the paper. That told me as much as her words. *Good for you, Philomena,* I thought.

Chapter Twenty

I hoped for a quiet, even dull, evening with no shocking surprises. It was not to be.

Over dinner, Chris said, "Almost forgot. I talked to Grandma after school. She's coming for her visit tomorrow."

I dropped my spaghetti and fork on the floor.

"Would you please say that again?"

"Mom! It's not that hard. Grandma. Is. Coming. To Visit."

"When were you planning to share this with me?'

"I just did." She eyed me warily. "Are you upset or something?"

"Well, Chris…" And I listed all the craziness going on in our lives, concluding with, "So you see why this is not the right time for a visit from Phyllis." A more honest response would have been that no time was the right time.

"You're always busy and stressed. And I am always busy and stressed, like any teen. But I want to see her and she is going to help some more with my project. Get this. She will come to school the day I present it in class. Like, living history."

Did I catch a triumphant gleam in her eye? She'd said the magic words, and she knew it. And I knew it too. I hate when that happens

"Okay. Okay. Give me her travel plans. Is she flying? Alone? How will she get here?" One more thing to deal with in my crowded life. *Like I needed this,* I thought. She grinned.

"And here's the good part. Grandpa volunteered to pick her up at the airport and bring her here, and keep her busy while we are out doing our things. So it's all good."

"I don't get this new friendship between them. Do you?"

"I believe he's trying to help me. It's weird not to have more family, so he's stepping up." She looked right at me. "You don't seem convinced."

I could not say what was on my mind, not even part of it. I glanced up at the clock and snapped out, "Look at the time! I still have work to do and your homework can't be done yet?"

"Not even close." She saw my fraying patience and added, "See? Me. Going. Putting dishes in dishwasher. See me going upstairs."

Should I go do my own homework? Not very tempting. Call my dad and pick a fight? Tempting, indeed, but the satisfaction would be momentary. Call Joe, who often appreciated Chris' smart-aleck attitude more than I did? Very tempting. But no. I would not know what to say and could not face the results of saying it wrong. Whatever it was I might say.

I checked the back of the freezer for some forgotten ice cream. No luck.

"Chris, I'm going out for a walk," I shouted up the stairs. "Maybe ice cream? You want any?"

"What? No? I'm in training. Remember?" A long pause. "Maybe some sorbet? Raspberry? No, lemon. No, I want orange. With chocolate sprinkles?"

"Got it. Back soon."

I walked briskly through the chilly night. The ice cream store would not be crowded this time of year. I debated warming up with hot fudge sauce on mine.

It was exactly what I needed, sugar, cream, and chocolate in perfect proportions. Walking home, Chris' sorbet in hand, I felt much better. I could handle Phyllis in my house at this point in my life. I wasn't the insecure young bride, resentful at the way she rearranged my kitchen and foisted on me family china I didn't want or like.

I stopped to consider buying a doughnut for tomorrow morning. I was standing in front of a small, old-fashioned luncheonette. And there were Joe and his sister at a table in the back, uneaten dinners in front of them.

They were having an intense conversation. I could tell by their body language, even though I could not hear a word.

She talked. He talked. He was serious, making points by counting them off on his fingers. She started to cry. He held her hand. She put her head on his shoulder and he put his arm around her. She took the handkerchief he offered, wiped her face, and gave him a shaky smile. She passed him a piece of paper from her purse and he read it, nodded, made notes. He looked at her and said something and she smiled with relief.

He fed her some fried chicken from her plate and she laughed and they both dug into their dinners.

I didn't need sound. I could tell he was comforting her. I knew. He was saying it would be all right. He was saying I promise. I'm here for you. I always will be.

I felt as if I could cry myself. As if I had forgotten for a little while who he is, and now I was reminded. His troubled sister's support. Chris' designated uncle. My own best friend.

Chris' melting sorbet, dripping through the bag, forced me to tear myself away from the window and hurry home. As I did I thought about my date with Dan Ramos. When I had tried to describe my excitement about work, he didn't get it. Joe always got it. I work in a library, I research, I write. Joe works with his hands, supervises, builds, creates. We work in different worlds. But he always gets it, because he gets me.

My mind raced along with sudden clarity. With everyone else I am a mother, a student, an employee, a daughter. But Joe knows me, knows me not for who I am to him but me, my own self. Better than I know myself sometimes. Do I know him that way? Seeing him with his sister was seeing another part of him.

It felt like a shiny, brand new thought and yet like something so right, I had always known it.

I didn't know how to reach out to him but I was full of the certainty that I had to find a path back to where we were. Or where we wanted to be.

I tossed Chris' melted sorbet into the nearest trashcan and headed home, making up my apology to her as I went. I needed a way to say "sorry" without explaining what happened, and thereby opening myself to a discussion about Joe.

But I took care of something else first. There was a text from Ramos:

> I think we had one of the strangest first dates on record. Try again?

I closed my eyes and saw in my mind a very attractive man. Nice. Smart. A parent, like me, who understood what that meant. A public servant with a challenging job, like Jeff. And I had no interest whatever in going any further. And I knew this time, it wasn't because Jeff still owned so much of my heart.

I took a deep breath and texted:

> Let's be friends. I like you a lot but...there is someone...

He replied:

> No hard feelings. But try to stay out of trouble, ok? No more crime scene witnessing. You know we'll have to bring you in to court if we ever get to trial?

I wrote:

> I know. But I won't be that helpful.

I added a smiling face, then added:

> It's not Jennifer and I am still sure of it.

His answer:

> We'll see about that.

Chris' door was closed, her voice was murmuring away. Not homework. Probably Jared. The light under her door stayed on, but she never came out. In the middle of the night, I thought I heard steps on the stairs, but I didn't get up.

The reckoning came in the morning when she was rummaging in the freezer. "What happened to my sorbet?"

Deep breath. Mine. "It's breakfast time. Sorbet is not breakfast food." Changing the conversation seemed like a good move.

"Well, it's orange. Full of vitamin D. Instead of juice, I thought."

"Nice try."

"I thought it was worth a shot." I saw her reach for her healthy cereal.

"But did you forget it? I looked for it in the night."

"My mind was on other things." Inspiration came to me. "Like Phyllis' visit."

"You worry too much." The doorbell rang. "That's Mel. I'm off."

The cereal was barely touched. I took a taste. Yes, still tasted like hay to me. I wondered, if I followed Chris and Mel, would I catch them at a bakery? But I did not have time for spying today. I had to get ready for a visit.

I cleaned the bathroom. Put out fresh towels, put fresh sheets on the second bed in Chris' room. As thorough a dusting in Chris' room as I could manage, working around her scattered possessions. A thorough cleaning of the kitchen. At least all the visible parts. No way Phyllis would overlook crumbs around the toaster and grease on the stove. Wiped up a spill in the refrigerator.

By the time I was done, I was exhausted and more than ready to tackle my real job for the morning.

Philomena despaired of convincing her family and set aside dreams of the white gown and veil and her nieces scattering flowers. She confided it all to her diary, since she didn't dare tell even her closest friends. They would meet at City Hall. She had a nice suit she could wear and a new hat, carried in a shopping bag to avoid any questions. He would bring a corsage for her, the license, the ring, and his own camera. They thought someone there would be kind enough to take pictures.

She wrote, *"I've saved most of my wages, and I could have paid for it, the gown and veil, a reception and all. But all that matters is HIS ring on MY hand, and I will have a great big smile in those pictures. And in my new Lily Daché hat…me in Lily Daché! I will be as stylish as a movie star."*

The next page told me everything and nothing. *"He never came."* And on the page after, I learned the rest. *"I waited and waited. I found a phone booth but I was terrified to go call in case I'd miss him if he came. I finally called the phone at his boardinghouse and his landlady said she hadn't seen him. I am worried. I am hurt. Should I be scared for him or furious at him? I am so mixed up. And I keep crying."*

And later, *"I forgot to write that when I was leaving the marriage office, Frankie showed up. He had some business downtown, he said, and he took me home in a taxi. He never even mentioned my hat or asked why I was there."*

She didn't see what I did. What I suspected. There were other explanations but my money was on her brothers. How could I find out?

I went out to buy some groceries, so Phyllis could not think I was neglecting her granddaughter. As I walked there and back, I realized there was another way to go on Philomena's mystery. Maybe Phyllis would have some ideas working from the family memory. Maybe I could imitate Lieutenant Ramos and urge her to search her memory.

I came home to an e-mail from my advisor, asking if there would a completed chapter by the end of next week. I recklessly wrote, "Sure" and hit Send. Why not? Maybe I would have it done by then. And if I didn't? I did not have time to think about it now. My visitor would be here any minute and I had groceries to put away.

I'd finished just as my doorbell rang,

They came in with a flurry of hellos and kisses and bags to put down. She had an insulated carrier with contents for me to put away immediately.

"I brought a lemon ricotta pie, and some lasagna for you and Chris, to go in the freezer. I'm sure you don't have time to make it yourself."

I had an impulse to argue with her sneaky criticism but it was true. And her ricotta pie was nothing to turn down. I served coffee and some supermarket cookies.

Phyllis made a face and promised to bake biscotti while she was here. "You will like them better." It was statement, not a question.

"So, honey, how are you doing? Are you and Chris moving ahead on birthday plans?"

I gave Dad a look that said, "Not now." For once he got it and changed the subject.

"How's your dissertation coming along? And that new advisor?"

How did he manage to pick the other topic I did not want to discuss? I answered with a dismissive, dishonest, "Fine." and asked Phyllis how the trip went.

"Very nice, except for the long lines at the airport. Security was interested in the food I was carrying, though." She shook her head and made a little clucking sound. "This world we are in. I finally had to ask the kid in uniform if he didn't have a grandmother who cooked! But the flight was good, only an hour and a half, and the stewardess served up drinks and snacks. Here, for Chris, a bag of animal crackers. I told them I wanted it for my youngest granddaughter." She winked. "Didn't tell them how old she is.

"But here's the funny thing. There were men serving too. And the stewardesses weren't all young and pretty like they used to be."

"How long has it been since you were on a plane, Phyllis?" My dad smiled at her.

"Not since 1982 when we went on Alitalia to Italy. Rome airport, don't ask! Crowded as could be. Flying out of Buffalo is much easier, except for the security line."

Then she fell asleep, suddenly, sitting up, exhausted from her long day.

I motioned my dad into the kitchen where we could talk without waking her.

"I have been too busy to think any more about this birthday party, Dad. I'll get to it. You can be sure Chris won't forget about it."

"That wouldn't be like our Chris. How about we—meaning Chrissie and me—we figure it all out and take it off you?" Before I could even protest, he added, "Remember, I'll be paying for it."

My dad, who knows nothing about restaurants that are not diners or decorating of any kind, planning a party? Partnered by a teenager with ideas we cannot afford? No way.

"I'll get to it, Dad. I will, but not right now."

He looked unconvinced. He stood up then, and muttered, "I've got to be going. Love to my girl."

"She'll be home from school soon. Do you want to stay?"

"I would like to, but I have things to do. Give her a hug for me."

Chapter Twenty-one

When I went downstairs in the morning, I was surprised to find Phyllis up, dressed, and ready to roll. She was smartly dressed in dark pants and a blazer over a ruffled blouse.

"Coffee is made, but seriously, Erica? You got to get a better coffeemaker. And I made you French toast but I couldn't find any maple syrup. We need to get moving."

Grateful for the coffee? Annoyed at the criticism? It was too early to say anything about either.

"Uh, why do we need to get moving?" seemed adequately noncombative.

"We are going to see my Uncle Georgie. I already called the nursing home. They said he is having a good morning, pretty alert, so we should go quick. And my cousin will meet us there."

I gulped some coffee. "I don't understand what you are talking about."

"Erica! We talked about this before I came. You forgot? I have one uncle left, my dad's youngest brother Georgie. I haven't seen him since I moved up to godforsaken Buffalo and he's failing fast now. He lives in the veterans' nursing home way out on Long Island." She gave me a scrap of paper. "Here, I have the address. Is that far? It is far, isn't it? So we have to get going. And you can tell me what you learned about Philomena on the way."

She had never mentioned this uncle or this visit. And whatever happened to my Dad's promise to keep Phyllis entertained?

"And Chrissie's coming too. For her project."

"No. It's a school day."

"She got something, a pass or a note."

"No one ever mentioned any of this to me. No one! Not a word."

"No?" She looked embarrassed, but only for a fleeting second before she recovered. "Maybe it was your dad I talked to. Yes, that's it."

As if summoned by her words, there was my dad, letting himself in with a key I didn't know he had.

"Phyllis, are you ready for our road trip? I've got unhealthy snack food waiting in the car for us." He gave me a kiss and whispered. "Like when you were a kid—potato chips to keep her from complaining."

"So it was you, Len! I told Erica I made this plan with her." She did not apologize.

"Will everybody stop chatting?" I needed more caffeine. A lot more. "And then tell me what exactly is going on? Exactly?"

"You must listen this time. I have one uncle left from the older generation, and he is in a veterans' home out there in the country. His kids have all moved out to there, to Long Island. And he's fading fast. So this is my one chance to see him. He's my last link to them. My parents and all the others. Len, you want coffee before we hit the road? And maybe a piece of French toast?"

While they chatted, I finally had enough coffee to cope, plus sugar on my French toast. True, we did not have maple syrup

I hoped maybe Dad could go instead of me. I had work to do. Then my own ideas about Philomena's mystery came back to ambush me, the thought that we could look at family memories. I had to go.

"Give me ten minutes. I'll throw on some clothes."

In the backseat of the car, fortified with the promised potato chips, I passed Phyllis the notes I'd made about Philomena. She passed them right back.

"I can't read in a moving car. You tell me."

I read from my notes, with Phyllis turned to look at me over the back of the front seat. She was wide-eyed at the story I told.

"So very sad. Poor Aunt Philomena. I never knew any of it. Of course I was a little child then, but not even later. She never talked about it at all." She frowned. "But you haven't found out what happened? And Chrissie? Do you know anything about this, for your project?"

"Yes, Grandma. I read it all too. Her heart must have been broken."

"But there's no end to this story. What happened?"

"I'm working on it. You never told how she died or where. Maybe that could help."

"She had a bad heart, I think. People didn't like to talk about illness back then but it was before all the fancy heart surgery that came along. She died at home, actually."

Chris looked over at me and I guessed what she was thinking. A broken heart for real.

As we drove up to the home, Phyllis was reapplying her lipstick and poking at her bottle-blond hair. She caught me staring at her and explained, "I haven't seen these people since I moved away. I know I look a little older."

We were met as soon as we walked in by a middle-aged, graying cousin.

"Richie! Oh my God. And Louise." Lots of hugging and kissing and "how long has it been?" ensued.

"And you are Erica." Louise folded me into a big hug. "You are the only one of us who hasn't changed so much. I'm married to Phyllis' cousin Richie."

Phyllis introduced my father, who claimed he too hadn't changed a bit. Everyone laughed at that.

"Well, Pop's right over there." Richie pointed into the lounge area. "He's having his before-lunch nap, though." He pointed to a very old man, dozing in his wheelchair.

They led us to a cluster of chairs and launched into an endless conversation about the whereabouts of many relatives, none of whom I knew. Very boring for Dad and Chris, who went out to stretch their legs. Perhaps I should have been taking notes but I kept my eye on the sleeping old man. Phyllis could bond over her family tree with Chris tonight.

As soon as he started to stir, I motioned to the others. Richie sat down close to the wheel chair.

"Hi, Pop. How ya doing?"

The old man squinted, then said with a big smile, "You're my son!"

"Yes. Yes, I am, one of them. You know my name today?"

His father smiled slyly. "My son. You are my son."

"And here's my wife, Louise, Pop. Remember her?"

When she leaned over to kiss him he said, "Lavender scent. Aren't you—are you Louise?"

"And we have a surprise for you. Look who's here! It's been awhile. You might not quite recognize her."

Phyllis approached the wheelchair, unusually tentative, and Richie gave her his seat. She smiled and held her uncle's hand, waiting, as he scrutinized her.

"So why haven't you been to visit in so long? I've missed you. Missed Frankie too. The others not so much."

"I moved far away, dear. I've missed you, too, and all of them. How are you doing today?"

"Not bad, not bad at all. I sleep, eat good meals. On a nice day someone takes me outside." He leaned over and whispered, "But they won't let me smoke. You don't happen to have one on you?"

"You already know you can't do that here, or anywhere."

"Says who?"

"The doctor. And the VA. And the law. Who do you think?"

Phyllis put up her hand to make Richie stop talking, leaned over and whispered, "Later, I'll sneak you one. Shhh."

Chris and Dad came back and the old man stared at Chris for a long time. "Why, it's Philomena, my favorite sister."

She looked stunned. "He thinks…" Phyllis' voice was breaking. "I guess—you're blond, like her, and tall." She grabbed Chris' arm and whispered, "Keep him happy. Go along with it."

"You look prettier now, with your hair, than those old kerchiefs and the boys' clothes." He held her hand. "You remember that time we laughed about both wearing overalls? You were going to work—weren't you? And I was dressed like a little boy."

Chris muttered, "Sure I do."

"And the night you took me out, it was during the war, to see the searchlights in the sky from Prospect Park? That was so exciting." He fidgeted. "Whatever happened to that nice boy you used to bring around? I liked him. He talked to me like I was his friend. You both took me to the movies one time. We saw…we saw… Donald Duck! It had a Spanish name, but Donald was in it too. Remember? We laughed and laughed."

Tears in her eyes, Chris whispered, "Of course I remember."

"And to see Santa…somewhere. I told him I wanted my brothers to come home safe, but the truth?" He leaned over. "I wanted a bike."

"You were only a kid." Chris said. The rest of us stood there, silent, waiting for what he would say next.

"But what happened to him after the war? He never came to see us again."

"I don't…I never knew."

"Was he the one our brothers didn't like? Was that it?"

"Maybe. How did you know that?" She looked up at me, quickly, and I nodded, putting my thumbs up. I was proud of her.

"Oh, I knew. I knew. I listened to everything. They thought I was a dumb kid, our big brothers, so they didn't guess how much I heard."

"What did you hear?"

"I knew someone's wife was fooling around while he was overseas. I knew before he did, 'cause Frankie talked about it to someone." He chuckled. "And I overheard. Not that I understood then. And after he came back, she had a big black eye. That, I understood!"

"But about Philo…I mean, my…my boyfriend. What did you hear?"

"They didn't like him. Didn't want you to marry him. Were you going to?"

"Yes," she whispered.

"You should have! At least I liked him."

"And did you hear more? *Why* didn't they like him?"

"You know. Not Italian, not Catholic. Not one of us. And especially his politics."

Phyllis, upset, broke in. "Georgie, do you know what happened to him?"

"That's what I'm saying! Aren't you listening?" He went back to addressing Chris. "They beat him up good one night. "

"And? And?"

He looked at her with surprise. "What? They talked about it late that night and I was listening through the door. Frankie at least felt bad." His voice faded. "I never knew until then that men could cry." His own cheeks were wet with tears.

Chris was on the point of tears herself. Phyllis looked stunned. She could not even say anything.

The effort of so much talking seemed to have worn George out. He sat back in his chair, head sinking down into his shoulders. His son stepped up and put his hand on his father's shoulder. "Are you tired? Do you want to go back to your room and lie down?"

The old man's head snapped up and his eyes opened. "Hell, no! I want my ice cream. You roll me over to the cafeteria, and this pretty young lady can come too." He was smiling up at Phyllis now, not at Chris or me. "And what's your name, dear?"

Chapter Twenty-two

Only my dad knew what to say. "May I wheel you in, Mr. Palma? It would be an honor, one vet to another."

George Palma scrutinized him. "How'd you know I served? Marines, Korea. Semper fi."

"This is a veterans' hospital, after all."

"Of course it is. See that fella over there? He was in Korea too. We talk about the old days. Bad times, to be honest, but then, we were young, so good times in some ways. I volunteered, dumb cluck I was. But all my brothers were in the big one so I felt like I had to keep up. How about yourself?"

"Vietnam. I would have been drafted, so I signed up for Naval Reserve. You know how they used to say, 'Join the Navy and see the world'? I spent my two years down the road at the Brooklyn Navy Yard!"

The two men laughed, but I wasn't laughing. I was too surprised. He never told me any of this.

We left George in his family's care, saying fond good-byes to a man who had no idea who we were. It was a tense, silent car journey for a while. I finally broke the tension.

"Dad, you never told me you were stationed at the Navy Yard!"

"It was when they were in the process of shutting down. I don't even remember much. Plus I was a young knucklehead back then and you never asked. So I didn't have much to say and you were never curious about it."

I changed the subject.

"Chris, how did it feel to be someone else for while?"

"Omigod. It was so strange. I mean, could it be true? What he seemed to be saying? That something really bad happened?"

"I could try to find out but I'm not hopeful at all."

We all went silent again until Phyllis said, "Not one word could be true. He's lost somewhere, poor Georgie, wandering around in the past now."

"Got nice kids." Dad, sweet-talking again.

"That's my family." She stated it with authority. "The finest people. We would never, never, neglect our old folks. Other families maybe, but not mine!"

Today suggested they weren't quite as perfect as she claimed. My desire to stipulate the facts fought a brief battle with the knowledge that it was not worth the energy to start a fight. This visit was too important to Chris.

"I'm sure you'll tell some great stories at the class visit."

"You bet I will. Chrissie and I are going to rehearse tonight. You promised me no surprise questions, right, hon?"

There was heavy traffic and during the tedious drive home, I drifted off into sleep for a little while, dreaming of Jeff when we were young. When we were young was all we ever had. He was trying to tell me something. About his mother? No. Something else. Young love? Reminding me.

I lost it as soon as Dad wrestled his car into a tight parking space on my block and I opened my eyes.

At home, Chris assured all of us, including my dad, that she would provide supper.

"You will?"

"I know how to make a phone call, just like you do." She stood up to my skepticism with comical dignity.

The ordered spaghetti and meatballs were there at the door in no time. Phyllis was critical of the sauce, but I noticed that she went back for seconds.

Dad cleaned up after dinner. He did it badly but I appreciated it, and then he left. Chris' reactions to our visit finally came pouring out.

"It was so sad. So sad. She obviously loved him. It's right there in her diary, the real thing. And those brothers? They just…they just…tried to break it up, like she had nothing to say about it."

"Honey, they thought they had good reasons." Phyllis spoke tentatively, not at all her usual style. "She was young and she would get over it. They thought…"

"No, Grandma! It wasn't fair! Even young people have feelings and she wasn't so young anyway. She was working and all. My mom and dad were young, too, but they knew what they wanted. How could her brothers take over like that?" Her eyes never left her grandmother's and I held my breath, waiting to see what Phyllis would say next. I had not forgotten all she said when Jeff and I wanted to get married.

"They were good men, Chrissie, they were, my father and his brothers. They must have truly thought it was the right thing to do, protecting the family from trouble and threats, keeping their jobs. Without jobs, how do you feed your children and keep a roof over their heads? Pay a doctor? I'm sure they meant well. Sure of that."

She sounded tentative, though, without her usual certainty. And as her voice dropped, Chris' rose.

"And you said she seemed sad the rest of her life. You said that! It was cruel. They could have been happy."

"You're only a girl, you don't understand."

I could have told Phyllis those were fighting words.

"I'm not a little girl and I do so understand." She punctuated the words with a dramatic stalking out of the room.

Phyllis looked shaken. "I was only trying to show her how it would have seemed to them. Was I wrong?"

Words I had never expected to hear in her voice. I was tempted to tell her that, but she stood up. "She is more important than those old fights. What do I know? I was just a child then."

She walked upstairs and soon I heard teary sounds in Chris' voice and firm ones in Phyllis'. Then there was some shaky laughter from Chris and steady voices, back and forth. Phyllis had accomplished her mission and I went to do some work of my own.

In the morning, they seemed to be the best of friends. Chris waved a handful of index cards. "Here they are, Grandma. All the questions we practiced. Ready?"

"Not before some breakfast, young ladies." They both giggled at me laying down the law. I poured juice for Chris, and coffee for Phyllis, and set out both kinds of cereal, milk, craisins, and banana.

"The breakfast buffet for this morning." They giggled again and ate a few bites. "And how is Grandma getting back after your class?"

"Didn't I say? She is spending the whole day with me!" She quickly added, "The teachers said it was okay. Even in chem."

"Phyllis, you think you'll enjoy chemistry class? I don't think Chris does."

"But we have lab today. Grandma said she'll pass us equipment. Right, Grandma?"

"Anything with my youngest granddaughter is a treat for me. Anything at all."

Chris added, as they walked out the door, "And maybe we'll get to blow something up in lab today. You'd like that, right, Grandma?"

"You betcha!" They giggled again, and again, I was baffled. How had they formed this cozy relationship? Did it matter that it did not include me?

I glanced at the clock and swore. My musing was going to make me late for work. Out the door and caught a downtown bus as it was pulling away from the stop.

I had routine work to do, and a lot of it, so my quiet morning was a welcome respite. A question still roamed around the back of my mind, though. Could I reach all the way back, sixty years or more, and find any records at all for a young man with no family who disappeared one night? I would have a chat with the museum archivist, but, I thought, *Not bloody likely.* I'd have to reconcile myself, and Phyllis and Chris, to the idea that this was the end of Philomena's love story. Not looking forward to that conversation. Chris tended not to accept that there were no answers to some questions.

My thoughts seemed to have magically conjured up Chris and Phyllis, who were standing at my office door. It was already after school and my day had disappeared. I'd even skipped lunch.

"How was it?"

"Mom, it was great. Grandma is a *star!* She had such good stories about the old days."

"What do you mean, old days?"

"You know what I mean." Chris giggled. "And honest, Mom, everyone forgot she was old. In fact, they liked her stories so much, they invited her to come back tomorrow and visit the other history class. Cool, right?"

"But, aren't you going home tomorrow? You have a ticket for tomorrow afternoon."

"Chrissie will take care of it. She is going to call the airline for me."

"What, call? Grandma, I can do it online."

"Chris! You have never made plane reservations in your whole life. What makes you think...?"

"Mom, I can do anything online that I need to. Anything. Don't worry. We will fix it and she can stay an extra day. So we're good, right?"

No, we weren't good. I didn't trust her to wrangle with an airline and I didn't want Phyllis to stay another day, either. She was a distraction for me.

Before I could even collect my thoughts, Chris was kissing me good-bye. "Gotta run. Come on, Grandma, we can go home and do another rehearsal." She took her arm. "Don't want to embarrass me tomorrow, do you?"

Phyllis looked indignant, saw Chris was joking and patted her hand. "Let's stop for a treat. On me!"

As they were walking away I remembered something. "Call Grandpa and tell him Phyllis doesn't need a ride to the airport tomorrow."

Without even turning around, Chris wiggled her hand above her head and called back, "Already done. One step ahead."

I put my head on my desk and contemplated a brownie from the nearby bakery. Or an overpriced latte. Or a glass of wine. Smart aleck daughter plus another day of Phyllis was more than I could stand right now.

I don't think I nodded off but my mind seemed to swirl with young lovers. Philomena and her beloved. Jeff was there, too. I couldn't hear his voice but I felt, somehow, what he was trying to say. It felt like good-bye.

Chapter Twenty-three

I sat up, determined to apply my mind to my work, but I only stared and stared at my computer screen. Almost seeing Jeff's face.

I typed. I shuffled files around. And I thought some more because there was a voice—it sounded strangely like Chris—telling me it was not Jeff on my mind today. Or Ramos. I found myself saying, out loud, "Shut up, Chris," and then saw it was finally the end of the day. I was so glad to be heading home, even if Chris and Phyllis would be there, but someone had decided this day would never end.

As I was walked down the hall, I met Jennifer walking toward me. Her smile was warm. "I'm so glad I caught you." I was not glad. I suppose it showed in my face.

"And you were leaving to go home? I am sorry. Sometimes I forget about office hours. It's been so many years. Do you have a few minutes?"

Reluctantly, in fact resentfully, I led her to my cubicle.

"How did you even get upstairs? Security never called me."

She looked amused. "I may not be a young cookie anymore but I can still charm a man in uniform."

"It's a skill worth having, I imagine."

"You bet. At least, when it comes to speeding tickets." She made a little face. "It has not worked on that Lieutenant Ramos and the other detectives."

"I told him the person I saw definitely was not you."

"Aha. I thought he might come back to you. I came to talk to you about what you'd tell him."

Now it was my turn to be amused. "You do realize that is a crime? Suborning a witness, I think."

"Don't be so harsh. It's nothing of the kind. We are friends. You know the killer wasn't me, and that's what you've been saying. So we're both fine and behaving appropriately."

"Fine? Are you?" That was impressive, I had to admit, a woman who was out on bail for murder and said she was fine.

"My very peculiar legal situation? It is unpleasant, but I know they cannot make the charges against me hold up because I know I didn't do it. That's that. Not that he didn't have it coming."

She laughed at my face. "I don't say that to everyone, of course." Under the chair, one of her stylishly shod feet was persistently tapping. Perhaps she wasn't as fine as she claimed to be.

"I don't understand why they arrested you at all."

"Are you asking about possible motive? Well, the gossip is true." She made a face. "He was getting ready to leave me. I overheard a conversation about him auditioning the next Mrs. Conti. It was even someone I've met. Was I hurt? No. But I was, I am, angry. Sure. Enough to tie him up in court for the rest of his life, short though it turned out to be." She smiled slyly. "I would have liked to have dragged him through the legal system for a lot longer. But put myself in jeopardy over it? No way. The only thing is…" She stopped and seemed to consider what to say next. She considered it a long time. "The only thing is, I was in fact at a bar across the street. They got that right."

What I already knew. She was confirming it.

"No! I've seen that place." Would she tell me more? "What were you doing in a sleazy hangout like that?"

"Not up to something, as they think." The foot was tapping faster. "I followed him." For the first time ever, I saw Jennifer look less than self-confident. "Ooh, don't look at me like that. It's embarrassing but it's not as crazy as it sounds. I thought he was lying about where he was going that night. And then he wasn't, but I wanted to see where he went after the meeting. And who with. If I could catch him in the act, so to speak. I know. I know! It was a dumb idea. I was so angry, I didn't think it through."

I kept quiet and it took a lot of effort.

"Here's the important point." She started to sound confident again. "They cannot ever tie me to that Mary Pat's murder. I knew nothing about her. Not a thing. And that, my dear, is the truth. I can't tell them what I don't know, no matter how many times they ask the question." She shook her head. "Did you know they do that? They ask and ask. A woman could be so exhausted by it she'd say anything."

"And maybe even tell the truth?"

She sat up straight. "I *have* told them the truth. I think it's as likely someone would make up something to get them to stop, but I did not. I didn't know about Mary Pat. Not a thing. And that, my dear, is the whole truth. Now Annabelle did know about her, and never told me. I've had words with her about that! But she thought it ended long ago so there was nothing to tell. She says. Maybe it's the truth. Maybe not."

"I thought you and Annabelle were friends."

"We are, in a strange way. That daughter hates me, though. That never changed, even when her own mother and I stopped being enemies." The tapping started again. "To think she will get half his money! And Annabelle would always protect her before me, I'm sure."

"Annabelle seems very worried about you."

"How like Annabelle. Sweet little thing. So, dear, if you would keep telling them you didn't see me? Because you didn't! That would be so helpful. And I'll let you go now. I apologize for keeping you here when you were ready to leave."

She shrugged herself into her fur coat and was down the hall before I could get over my bafflement. It wasn't clear to me why she had gone to the trouble of this visit. It was not social. To remind me to tell the truth? To make sure my truth was her truth? Perhaps to find out exactly what I was telling the cops? To exert influence, if needed?

I thought about it all the way to the subway station, but then my mind refused to take in anything more challenging than holding my place in the crowded rush-hour car. And all the way home from our subway stop, I thought about dinner, a glass of wine, a night glued to undemanding television. If only I could think of a way to make Phyllis and Chris disappear.

They disappeared themselves. There was a note saying they had gone to the local Chinese restaurant and would bring me dinner. My little house was all mine again. Quiet. No demands, at least for a little while. I scooped up the mail from the foyer floor where it had come through the slot. I dropped my coat on the floor instead of hanging it up; I sprawled on the sofa, and tried to process my day.

When my mind stubbornly refused to process anything, I decided to postpone that effort and do something concrete instead. Clean? File? Aha, finish unpacking Philomena's trunk. The bottom layer was old clothes. We were so absorbed by her diary and photos that we had not looked through them yet. Then I could shake out the trunk, sponge off the dust and return it to Phyllis. An attractively mundane, doable project.

There was a mechanic's coverall on top, neatly washed, pressed, folded away. Philomena's name was stitched above the breast pocket. There was an angora sweater, packed in a bag with mothballs. What had it meant to her, I wondered? A dashing hat with a feather and a tiny veil stuffed with tissue paper and wrapped in a clean cloth. The label said Lily Daché. I had to stop then and pull myself together, because I knew what I held.

I almost overlooked the scraps of paper that were clinging to the last item and had also drifted into corners of the trunk. They were crumbling around the edges. They had been ripped into pieces and then taped together again. I could see the brown marks where tape had dried up and fallen off over the decades. And it was decades. A scrap showed me it was a letter with a date.

Some of the bits must have crumbled all the way to dust but I was able to piece most of it together like a jigsaw puzzle. In some places I guessed at missing words.

It began "Cara Philomena," but the rest was in English. It was from her oldest brother, Vito, the one she didn't like much.

They tell me I will not recover and there is only a little time left for me before I go to God. I cannot face that with a bad conscience so this confession is for you, not a priest.] Telling you the truth will have to be my penance. I pray it heals [...]

Your Commie boyfriend did not desert you. Me and Victor and Frankie took him out one night and told him he had to get lost, leave you alone, disappear. He stood up to us—shouted about love—but we could back up [our words with deeds?]. And there was more of us.

Honest to God, sis, I don't know what happened. Yeah, we were knocking him around pretty good. He wouldn't promise, stupid kid, and we got mad. It got all crazy. Then he like, [...] collapsed and he wasn't breathing. We never meant it. Hon[...]

So we was scared and ran, but first we took off all his ID. And we put his body in the water in a place we [...]. And we made a deal, a vow, never, ever to [...]

We didn't meant it, Phillie. We only wanted to scare him. And then he had to go die on us. So sorry. We didn't want you to ruin your life married to a guy like him. [...] protect you. And we didn't want him to hurt your family with his cra [...]

The ink was badly faded but I had enough to be sure that's what it said. I read it again. And then again. I had trouble believing what I was seeing.

When I did believe it at last, I started to weep. I imagined poor Philomena reading it and then ripping it to pieces in rage, then deciding she needed to keep it and taping it back together. Did she read it again and again, hoping the repetition would dilute the pain? Did she bury it at the bottom of her trunk so she would never have to see it again?

That poor girl. I wanted to reach across the decades and hold her.

And what now? Did I tell Phyllis and Chris? Or let the past bury this secret? Was Chris old enough to read about something so heart-breaking? And so deeply disturbing? Was Phyllis too old to be so disturbed? Just for now, I hid it away, as Philomena once did, under a pile of my own clothes. One day, when she was older, I would share it with Chris at least.

I went down the stairs, still haunted, and stepped back into my present-day life.

A quick look at the mail, mostly catalogues, fun to browse if I could resist buying, but here was a square, high-quality paper envelope—an invitation, certainly. It would be about the museum gala, which I could not afford to attend.

In fact, it was an invitation to a memorial service for Michael Conti.

No way would I go to that. Completely inappropriate and actually quite weird. And who in the world could have sent it?

If Jennifer could interrupt my working day, I could interrupt her evening. She wasn't exactly a widow in mourning. She didn't need to be treated with extra kindness.

"Why, yes," she told me. "I put you on the list. I thought you might want to be there."

"You what? I don't think so. I mean, is it just because I was there when it happened. Is that why?"

"Don't be silly. Because you are writing about him. Don't you think it would be amusing to see some important men tell lies about how great he was? And it's the service he planned himself, some time when he realized he would probably not live forever after all. The big boss to the very end." She had a point. What might I learn if I went?

I put the envelope away, carefully, so I could find it again.

Phyllis and Chris returned from what was, apparently, another rollicking day at school. They were loaded with Chinese leftovers, and Phyllis pointed out it would be meals for the whole week. I knew she was needling me—a good mother cooks every day—but I let it go. I just didn't have the energy.

Phyllis had a lot to say about how nice Chris' friends were. "I thought they might be snobs, these private school girls but they were lovely to me."

"Well, Grandma, some of the girls are definitely bitchy—whoops, I meant to say, mean and snobby—but we're not all alike you know."

"How would I know? Public school was good enough for my children. And they all turned out fine."

"Wait! Didn't most of your kids go to parochial school?"

"That was fine, too, either way, but not all this poshness."

Phyllis soon told Chris, "Go off and do homework. Or talk to that fella. Whatever you do upstairs. Your mother and I want to talk grownup talk."

We did? First I heard about it. Would this be the time to tell her what I had learned? Was I ready?

"Your father is taking me to the airport tomorrow," she told me. "Such a good man. How come no woman has snatched him up?"

"Someone tried. She wasn't a good woman, though. I'm still mad at him for that."

She was silent and I began to get itchy. I had things to do. Just when I was about to get up and leave the room, she finally said, "Chrissie told me about a man in your life."

I felt like I had been punched. There was no way this could end well.

"I think it's about time."

What did she say? Had I heard her correctly?

"When Jeff died, all our hearts broke but good. Life just stopped. Hearts stopped beating. But your life isn't gonna stop. You have a long time to go, if God wants it that way. Why should you be alone? Chris tells me…"

"Chris should not tell you so much. She should not tell you anything. And she doesn't know as much as she thinks, either."

"Then you tell me. Is he a good man, this man?"

"Yes."

"So what's stopping you? You loved my darling son, but he's not coming back. Honestly, I would be glad to see you happy now. We all would, but Chrissie especially. She worries about you. Believe me, I get it, being alone."

In the nick of time, an opportunity to change the subject. Thank you, I said, to Whoever. "You never looked for anyone after Jeff's dad."

"Who says?" She smiled smugly at my shocked expression. "I got a friend up in Buffalo. We go dancing at the church community center." She smiled. "One time we went to a casino in Niagara Falls." She nudged me. "I won more than a few bucks, too. We're talking about going on a cruise in the spring. I've never been on a cruise. See? There's a lesson here. I know how to keep going. I told your father to do the same. He appreciated my advice, too."

My father? Appreciating advice? Anyone's advice? The floor seemed to be crumbling under my feet. And she was still talking.

"Besides? If he's a good man? I don't like Chrissie growing up without a man in the house. It seems like she needs a father."

"I've been doing fine so far," I sputtered. "And she's been fine. No one else can take the place of her own father."

She gave me a long, silent look, and finally said, "Not even you, honey. Give it some thought." She got up and announced she was going to finish packing, leaving me barely breathing. And feeling ambushed.

Before bed, I glanced at the funeral information again, and saw that the actual funeral service and interment would be private, but the memorial would be more public. It was going to take place in a few weeks at the Navy Yard, in the catering space at the movie studio. They did weddings there, I knew, and celebrations of other kinds, but a memorial service? But the invitation read, "In tribute to his career at New York Harbor."

Of course I was going. Change my schedule at work if necessary. Put off my advisor, as needed. I'd tell her it was research, which, come to think of it, it was. More or less.

In the morning, all was forgotten in the rush of breakfast and getting everyone out the door on time. Dad helped Phyllis with her suitcase and her bag full of only-in-Brooklyn groceries and

Chris cadged a ride to school. Then they were gone and I had some time alone with my thoughts, company I did not want.

I needed to figure out what to do with the letter I had found. I needed to think about Phyllis' advice. I needed to throw myself into chapter writing. That lasted about half an hour, as my unwanted thoughts kept intruding.

What I needed was an old-fashioned mental health day. Play hooky. Do something that was not a walk or even a museum, where I would continue to think. Not playing with a friend, because if she asked how I was, I might actually tell her. Plus, my friends were all at their jobs. Not shopping, because I had no money to spend.

A movie. I hadn't been to see one in a theater for, I don't know, a long time. Something exciting, where I could live in someone else's mind for a few hours.

It worked. A neighborhood theater. Discount matinee. Over-buttered, over-salted, overpriced popcorn, and a lot of it, made a great lunch. A long movie that involved spaceships in a world nothing like my own. I came out to late afternoon cold, with long shadows on the streets, but with a clear head. I had a lot to discuss with Chris. What had she said about Joe to Phyllis? How had they become so close?

I came home to find my dishwasher full of dirty water, and my sink full of more dirty water that had somehow backed up. There were dirty dishes stacked up on the counters and my daughter trying hard to pull out the racks.

"What the…?"

"I have no idea." She sounded frantic. "It just stopped working. And now there is all the nasty water to get out, and I spilled some on the floor. Ooh, watch out!" she shouted as I slipped and grabbed the counter just in time.

"I can see that."

"And I didn't know what to do, so I called Joe. Don't look at me like that!"

I was certainly giving her a look.

"It's a mess and I knew he could fix it! And where were you, anyway? While water was overflowing onto the floor and I was all alone here."

She was on the verge of tears. Or a nervous breakdown. Poor Chris. She really isn't old enough to deal with these household crises.

"Uh, okay, okay. Let's not touch anything for now." But Joe? I wasn't, I don't know. Ready. "Is he coming?"

"Soon as he gets done somewhere else. That was a while ago, so, soon."

"Okay. You and me retreat, very carefully, to the living room. Are your shoes all wet?"

She stepped out of them and then it was her feet that were immediately all wet.

"Don't move." I stepped into the hall bath and snatched up all the little hand towels there. "Here. Dry your feet and walk out of the kitchen."

She put her feet on the towels, slid cautiously out of the kitchen without spreading much of the water and left the towels in a pile by the door.

"Mom? It'll be all right. You know Joe is a genius at these things."

"It's not an old dishwasher. I can't believe it's broken already and we for sure don't have enough spare money to get a new one. Or even fix this one."

"Come on. You don't think Joe will charge you? Do you?" She looked hard at me. "You do! It must have been some big fight."

"It wasn't a fight, it was…" Nope. I was not discussing this with a teenager. I didn't want the advice she was sure to give, either. "You've talked to him?" I fought down the desire to ask for details.

"Of course. *We* are friends, whatever you have become." She shook her head in disapproval, then looked at me with something I was sure was curiosity. "Did you know his sister stayed with him for a week? That kind of messy-looking girl he's been hanging around with?"

I nodded, waiting.

"And he bought her all new clothes? And took her to the dentist?"

I shook my head at that.

"She had some serious, like, issues? I think maybe she is mentally...something?"

I nodded.

"And she's going to a...a therapy home."

"Rehab?"

"And he is taking her there himself to get her settled."

I shook my head.

"Well, you would know all about it, if you were still friends."

It was impossible to argue with that.

"And how do you know all this?" Did I want him laying his grown-up problems on my tenth grade child?

She smiled mysteriously. "He listens to my problems, so turnabout."

I didn't have long enough to mull that over before Joe was there, ringing the doorbell. He has a key. It hurt that he was being so formal

"Hello, ladies," He nodded, avoiding locking eyes with me. "What's the problem? Oh, wait, I can see it from here. Okay."

He stepped into the kitchen, opened the dishwasher carefully, tried a few buttons. I tiptoed over to the kitchen entrance to see what was happening, compelled by fear of the financial damage and something else that was more than curiosity.

"Chris! Come tell me exactly what happened."

She did, with a great a deal of drama, while he and I listened. I caught a second of a smile from him, as she told her tale, and less than a second of looking at me to see if I shared his amusement.

"Okay. Got it. Let me try a few things."

He sent us away and got to work, humming. When he called us in, the sink water was gone, the dishwasher water was gone, and he was mopping the floor.

"You had a clogged pipe and a valve all messed up. I got the water out, but there's a small piece missing."

"Ooh, I found something on the floor, when I was trying to stop the flood and I...I put it somewhere...oh, I remember." Chris went to a drawer and pulled out rubber thingy. "Is it this?"

He looked surprised but examined it carefully. "Sure is." He turned, did a little more contractor magic and pushed a few buttons. And there it was, the reassuring sound of water swishing around just as it was supposed to.

While he dried his hands, he gave Chris a peculiar look, but she stopped that with hug.

"You are the hero! You saved the day."

He and I did share a smile then.

"Yes, Miss Drama Queen, I did. As any slightly experienced workman could have."

"But you are the best. You came when I called. Thank you a million times." Another hug. "I hear my phone. Must run."

She disappeared instantly and Joe and I were left to look at each other awkwardly, say thanks awkwardly, respond "It was nothing" awkwardly. Then he was packing up his tools and walking out the door. I was paralyzed, not knowing what to say or do. Before I could go out and stand on my steps to say, loudly, "Please come back," he was opening the door and walking back inside.

No greeting. No preamble.

"Has it occurred to you we were just played?"

"What?"

"There is no way that part she had could have ended up on the floor by itself."

I was beginning to see the light.

"Chris? Set this up?" I sat down with a thump, too stunned to know what to say next.

He finally crossed the living room and sat down across from me.

"I don't see any other explanation. Would you put it past her?"

"No. No, I can't. Except for the part about messing with an appliance and messing up her manicure. And the knowledge that I will kill her. Or at least ground her for life."

He finally smiled.

"She's pretty smart, your kid."

I started to laugh. I may have sounded slightly hysterical. It had been a very long and crowded day.

"What now?" He was not looking at me. "Do we try to talk? Or say good night and good-bye and have all her work wasted?"

"No good-byes and no talking." I was having a rare moment of something like wisdom. "Can I make you some supper, in my kitchen you saved?"

"I'll cook. You have eggs?" I nodded. "Any cheese?"

In no time, we were having a light meal, eggs and toast. It was cozy, sitting across from each other at my table again. It felt right. I searched my mind for safe conversation. I told him funny stories about Phyllis' visit. We mused about Chris' deviousness.

"Did it work out with your sister?" Perhaps not a safe topic, but safer than the others that came to mind.

"She's still with me, and she swears she is ready now to clean up her act. I found a treatment center in Connecticut and I'm taking her next weekend." He shook his head. "It's been tough, but there's a little hope out there now."

"You are doing it all for her."

"No. No, she's doing the hard part. I admire her."

I looked as his exhausted face. "She's not the only one to be admired."

He smiled sheepishly. "Well, she's my kid sister, you know? I have to protect her if I can." Where had I heard that before? Recently? I didn't remember until the next day.

"Erica, I was stretched so thin there for awhile. I said things…"

"Shhh. They were justified. I was…" I got up and put my arms around him, and he stood and held me tight, and then tighter. "I wasn't fair to you. Or kind. I was being scared."

"Shhh yourself."

I thought I heard footsteps on the stairs. They stopped and then went back up. We ignored them.

Chapter Twenty-four

I'd been to a few funerals in my life. My young husband, killed by a drunk driver when we were just getting started. My mother who died of cancer in middle age. My dad's best friend who planned his own wild memorial, with jazz music and whiskey flowing freely.

This was my first memorial service in a dramatic space usually used for weddings and other joyful parties. Milestone anniversaries, perhaps. Didn't this kind of event belong in a funeral home or a place of worship or an organization that was meaningful to the deceased?

I had no idea what to expect and was still unsure about why I had been invited.

I presented my invitation to be admitted through the studio's large gate. It was a vast modern building, the largest film studio outside of California. I would have loved to look around but I was directed to an elevator and whisked up to a rooftop set of rooms and an open terrace with a mind-blowing view of the harbor and the Manhattan skyline. Even my blasé, native Brooklyn mind was blown. On a bright sunny day or breezy moonlit night, this would be magical.

Today was not that day. It was late fall, chilly and overcast. Those gentle breezes off the water were biting through my wool jacket.

Simple white folding chairs had been set up in rows in a large, simple space. I slipped into a seat in the back and watched the rows fill up. Lots of older white men, some very old, in suits. A flock of stylish younger women were there, hugging and kissing Nicole as she greeted them. Some middle-aged couples, the men also in dark suits, the women in what even I knew were expensive dresses and fur coats, hugging and kissing Jennifer, chatting in subdued fashion and holding her hands with theirs. The men kissed her sedately and stood to the side.

And when they turned away, some had a sly grin, and there was some excited conversation behind her back. A few furtive looks toward the cops. They all knew.

Against the back wall, I spotted several men in less elegant suits. Cops, for sure. Lieutenant Ramos quietly directing them. None of this surprised me.

I jumped when someone put a hand on my shoulder. It was Jennifer, leaning over and whispering "Thank you." She shot a nervous glance to the cops. She looked haggard, under her expert makeup. "You're one of the few people here I don't have to play the grieving widow to. Boo-hoo."

"Why is it here, instead of a church?"

"Mike swore he'd never set foot in one again when he couldn't get a divorce. He wrote it into his funeral plans." She pointed across the room. "And there's another one who isn't mourning."

It was Mrs. Pastore, alone, and walking slowly toward me. She wore a black wool coat and a matching hat, over a black dress. She did look strangely like a mourner. Jennifer's attention was taken by another perfectly dressed, perfectly blond middle-aged woman. Mrs. Pastore was closing in on me.

I whispered, "Are you here alone?"

"Sal's not so good. I made him stay home and rest." She shook her head. "I took a car service."

"Why didn't you call me? I'll drive you home."

"To tell the truth I never thought of you being here."

"And I didn't call you for the same reason." I looked right at her. "I see you dressed like a mourner, but I know how you really feel."

"I got to be appropriate for the occasion, but..." She leaned over and lowered her voice a little more, "I came to make sure the s.o.b. is dead." She winked. "Not that there's a coffin here but this makes it for real. Ya know what I mean?"

And I did.

"And maybe Annabelle would like a friend today. We'll see. There she is for now."

The long divorced-wife sat in the front row between her daughter and the current wife. They held hands. None of them were crying.

They had meant what they said about sitting together.

A couple of official-looking men were standing at the front, and the softly humming room went silent.

I could not be rude enough to take notes, but I wanted to, and I was able to stealthily turn on the recorder in my phone.

The first speaker talked about Conti's long career serving the Port of New York. He actually was a Port of New York official at some time. Then another, older man talked about Conti's early years at the Navy Yard. And there was a third.

Funny. No one said they would miss him. They talked about his skills, his energy, his intelligence. Not one person said he would be missed. It was not funny, of course.

As the last speaker assured us he was concluding his remarks, a shout cut through the room.

"This is all bullshit! The guy was a complete son of a bitch, a crook, and a liar. He was a destroyer, not a public servant. He destroyed whatever he touched. Jobs. Marriages. Lives."

As the voice ripped through the sedate crowd, most of the startled audience turned to see who it was. I did myself, thinking, *How did he get in, whoever it is?*

The cops were in motion, unruffled but very fast, moving toward the man as the rest of the room seemed to move away from him.

I got a quick look at him, the only person in the room dressed in rumpled working clothes. Gray hair and a dark knitted cap. And, dear Lord, a gun.

I grabbed Mrs. Pastore and pulled her to the floor as everyone near us did the same.

He was still shouting, cursing Michael Conti. I popped up and saw him now holding the gun in a shooter's stance, as the policemen stopped and regrouped.

"I will shoot," he shouted. "Nothing left to lose but I can take a few damn hypocrites with me. Which one of you…which one doesn't know who he really was?"

He swung the gun from side to side. I heard sobbing behind me, and a whispered muffling.

I peeked again and got a look at his face this time. I knew him. Dear Lord. He was the man who begged in front of the coffee shop. And he was the man who had loitered on our block. Sure he was. And even in the fear of the moment, I thought he had told the truth that night. He wasn't looking for Chris. He had other people on his mind.

Did Ramos know? I tried to see him and, yes, he was there, cool as ice, directing his men. They all had guns. I didn't know if that made this less frightening or more.

"He made promises. He promised and promised and then he sold out his union brothers. He lied and helped shut down the Yard. More than our jobs. Lives. *Lives*, you stupid fat cats. Destroyed lives." He sounded weepy, but he still had the gun up and pointing.

"Mom!" Nicole screamed it out as her mother stood up.

Annabelle stood, listening, looking at the man.

"I know you, don't I? From the old days. I know you." She stood still, talking softly. "Is it…Tom? And you are right about Michael. Of course you are, but it's not right to say things like that about the dead. Isn't that what we learned in the old days?" She shook her head. "You're Tom Doyle, aren't you?"

"And you're Annabelle. You're as much of a hypocrite as any of them. You married him and put up with him."

"Yes, I did. Remember 'til death do us part? But I made a life without him, maybe the only brave thing I ever did."

He looked at her, hard. "I been trying to find you for a long time. I saw you on the street a few times, and hung around, trying to make out where you lived."

"So how have you been, Tommy? It's been a long time."

"Rotten." He muttered it and then his voice rose. "You know. He took my job away and then my life went down the sewer. Maybe he would have left my wife alone if you'd have been a better one. She despised me 'cause I was broke and he was going up and up. But you? You still have a nice life but I squat in one of the old houses at the Yard.'

"Oh, Tommy." She said it softly

"Last place I was ever happy, so why not go back? But it's getting cold to be out there."

He waved the gun around.

"I'll dance on his grave, I will, happy and proud to know that I put him there. Yes, dumb pathetic Tommy won in the end. I got to tell that to Mary Pat too. Before…before…" He started to sob.

I leaned back in shock, Mrs. Pastore still clutching my hand. Yes, he was the right size, right shape, right hair. He was the man that night.

I heard a sob from Nicole's direction.

"Probably you don't seriously want to hurt anyone else, do you?"

"If you'd have been a better wife, he would have left mine alone."

"Maybe. Maybe. You want me? Well, I'm right here, but think about it. I get that you hated Michael, and you have reason to, but more death won't fix anything now, will it?"

Through the chair legs, I had an odd angle but perfect view of what was happening. His gun was shaking in his hand, and behind him, some cops were moving in.

"Come on, Tom." She moved toward him, hand out. I was holding my breath. Living without Michael was the only brave thing she ever did? Not true now. "Let's go find a quiet spot, you and me, and talk about how much we hated him. Wouldn't that be better? Remember what the priests taught us all those years ago? You wouldn't get off with ten Hail Marys for this."

The gun shook. He let out a strangled sob and a shot rang out before the cops wrestled him to the floor. Annabelle had already fallen, bleeding.

Then it was all noise and confusion. People stood up, there was shouting and screaming and sobbing. Cops and men in suits were trying to calm everyone, contain the hysteria, make sure the hysterical group of people did not make the situation worse. Help Annabelle. Mrs. Pastore finally let go of my hand, where her tight grip had left red nail shapes in a row across my palm.

I stood, pulling her with me, and watched a whole team of men pull Tom Doyle across the floor and out, and Nicole rush to her collapsed mother. I could feel Mrs. Pastore shaking as she leaned on my arm, but she looked across the room and muttered, "Who knew? Sweet little Annabelle finally grew a steel backbone." She looked up at me. "Should we go shake her hand?" Then she answered her own question. "She's hurt. We should leave her to her daughter." She shook her head. "Could we go home now?"

I put an arm around her and then helped her out of her chair. "Soon. Very soon. I don't think they're letting us leave yet." And I didn't want to. I wanted to know how this would end. "Can you wait here for a couple of minutes? Would you like some water?"

"I would like a shot of grappa. And I do think there was a bar set up over there."

It was out in the reception area, and already full of people. There were refreshments too. I wove my way through the crowd, one of the rare instances when being small is a plus, and came back with a plate of snacks and two full shot glasses.

"No grappa. I got you rye."

The plate went on Mrs. Pastore's lap and she lifted her glass to mine.

"*Salut*, Annabelle." I was happy to drink to that.

Annabelle was gone, whisked away by an ambulance crew and some cops. They made a group along with Nicole and—yes—Jennifer, too, supporting each other.

Ramos was everywhere, the man in charge. I would have loved to talk to him, but this was obviously not the time. Maybe someday, in broad daylight, in his office with colleagues all around. Not over dinner. For now, I watched and drew my own conclusions.

He conferred with a man in stylish clothes and spiky gelled hair, who handed him a clipboard. Ramos spoke to an underling. Next thing I knew, the crowd was being organized and an announcement was made by the man with the hair. Apologies for the incident, invitations to help themselves to the buffet table and bar, apologies again. Ramos stepped up and said he had the names of all attendees; everyone was free to go, and be aware they might be contacted as witnesses.

How many phones were out, recording it all? A lot. There was a camera, too, manned by someone who had also been taking notes. Was a paper or local television news covering this funeral? Yes, there was Lisa looking serious and extremely psyched. She had somehow fallen into her best story of the year.

The crowd was thinning out, some with a glass of wine or whiskey still in hand. Lots of pale, shocked faces.

Mrs. Pastore, red in the cheeks after her whiskey, stood up. "I have to get back to Sal. I don't like to leave him too long."

She'd said that before but this time I listened. "Is he all right?"

"Not so good. Silly old man, doesn't like to see doctors. But I'm taking good care of him."

I took her out. There was nothing to see now. As we passed Ramos, he gave me a little salute, finger to forehead. I waved back.

My mind was so stuck on the scene we had just lived through I almost caused an accident on the drive home. Twice.

The fact was, the amazing fact was, the murder of Michael Conti had been solved. The murder of Mary Pat as well. He must have been keeping tabs on his ex-wife through the years. And he'd been there all along, hiding in plain sight. It wasn't Jennifer. It wasn't Annabelle. It wasn't any of Conti's many political enemies.

It was, after all, his past catching up with him. I glued myself to my desk that night, reading everything I had collected about the closing of the Navy Yard. I still didn't quite understand Conti's role in that but he somehow went from leading one of the big unions there to having an administrative job with the Navy after it closed. And his career went on and on, ever upward, with more money with each jump, while his former friends struggled. Some of their lives spiraled down and further down with no relief.

I went to bed very late. I knew I could finish my chapter on Michael Conti now. The end would be more dramatic than I had expected.

Chapter Twenty-five

In the aftermath of that shocking day, I astonished both myself and Dr. Adams. I finished the Navy Yard chapter in one intense day of work. Chris tiptoed in to my office and left without a word. The phone rang many times. Chris grabbed them all and gave me the messages the next morning. Joe's said, "Bravo. Call me when you emerge." Sometime deep in the night, I hit Save, and then Send. I was done with this story.

Then I rashly promised Dr. Adams she would have the first draft of my conclusion chapter before her deadline. Conclusion chapters have to be totally excellent. Strong. Thoroughly supported. Logical. Conclusive. Definitely conclusive. Having said it, I had to follow through.

Was I escaping my frightening experiences by immersing myself into work? No doubt, but there was more.

The universe seemed to be sending me a message. Normally I would have mocked without mercy anyone who said such a ridiculous thing. Normally I don't believe in the universe or its messages or any part of the whole meditative/crystals/ third eye nonsense. I am a scholar. Give me the damn facts.

Nevertheless. There was a message coming at me from all directions. It said "Wake up. Time to break out of that cozy trap. You can't stay in a cocoon forever." Dr. Adams said it despotically. My dad said it, nagging. Darcy and Joe had both said it, gently, as friends. Even Phyllis, of all people. My old job was ending. My academic department was pushing me out.

Yet somehow I couldn't hear it until I became entangled with Michael Conti's life.

Sweet Mrs. Conti had stayed in a bad marriage for too long, because she lacked the courage to leave. Jennifer Conti, with far more choices available in her life, had stayed too. Tom Doyle wanted nothing more than to crawl back into his old cocoon, the only job he'd ever had, and the wife who didn't love him.

I will always maintain I would never have become the graduate student who stays forever. Hear that, Dr. Adams? Or a low-level museum employee, either. I did have goals, fuzzy though they might be. But it was true that I was not at all eager to stretch one more time into yet another new life.

But there was the universe, shouting, "If not now, when? "

When I got my date for the dissertation defense, my heart stopped beating, just for a second or two. That meant Dr. Adams and the rest of the committee had signed off on my final version.

On the day, I dressed in my best, all armored up with lipstick and hose. I reminded myself I knew my subject cold, right down to my bones. There was no reason whatever, I told myself, for the butterflies in my stomach. I ordered them to fly in formation or get lost. All I had to do that day was answer questions and sound smart. At the end, the defense panel asked me to step out for a moment. I stood in the hall, invisibly shaking, until the chair opened the door and said, "Come on in, Dr. Donato."

Joe took me out for an uproarious meal with much drinking. Chris had declined to join us, giggling, and I was so excited I didn't wonder what she was up to. I returned to a large box of fancy chocolates with a card signed, "Chris and Jared." I celebrated for a week, at work, at home, with friends. Even Dr. Adams sent a congratulatory message.

When the week ended, I had to return to real life and that pesky ongoing problem of making a living. That whole spring would stay forever in my memory as a blur of late nights. After dissertation work, museum work, housework, at midnight I would be scanning the journals and websites, sending out letters, re-creating my resumé for each application. Some nights it left me so wired I could not fall asleep, no matter how exhausted I was.

I got a nibble from one of New York's lesser universities, but in the end they were too disorganized to actually get the position funded. I applied for a terrific job that would have meant two hours commuting each way, four days a week. I was desperate enough to take that on but it went to one of their own employees. I suspected that was their plan all along.

I sent many unanswered letters. I met some interesting people at places that had no openings at all. "It's all networking," Darcy said, and more than once. I didn't believe her.

Just at the point where I was calculating how Chris and I could afford to eat on unemployment benefits, looking into good public high schools, and wondering if I could pick up a few extra dollars doing child care, the phone rang.

It was Lisa, writing a series about changing cultural institutions. Or something like that. She started with, "Grab your phone this second! You need to record this number."

She was at the Brooklyn Museum, covering an exhibit. She was not more than a ten-minute walk from my house. She overheard a conversation. A key employee there had just been poached by the National Gallery.

"Call," she ordered. "Right now. Bye."

Unnerved though I was by then about job-hunting, I made the call. Just like that, I was scheduled for an interview the day after next.

My boss, Matt, sat me down to role-play an interview. He edited my resumé, too. Curators I'd worked with sent an animated good luck card. One of them made a call to a friend who worked there, scoping out the inside story on the job.

I dressed up again in my one good suit. I carried copies of my resumé. The letter confirming that my degree would be awarded in May. A list of references. Copies of my curriculum vitae, too, the academic version of a resumé. And just for a little extra luck, I carried a note from Joe folded into a tiny square and tucked under my watch band over my beating pulse.

I was glad to have it there as I walked into the museum. The building alone is kind of scary, a massive white stone monument to turn-of-the-last century civic prestige. It is meant to impress. It succeeds.

I was walking into a major institution that would be the star of the cultural firmament in any city that did not also have the Metropolitan Museum, the Cooper-Hewitt, the Museum of Modern Art, the Frick, and a dozen others.

All I could see in the interview room was a committee of suits, serious people looking like serious executives. I reminded myself that I was not an imposter. I could do this job. In fact I was the perfect person for it. I touched Joe's note and squared my shoulders.

They asked me if I was familiar with the museum, especially the significant American art collection and the historic rooms. Thank goodness I could say yes. They asked me about my dissertation and how it fit with their mission to serve all of Brooklyn. They asked me for my ideas. Thank goodness I had some.

Over the next month, there were many more such interviews, each one with scarier people further up the food chain.

To my astonishment, I ended up with an offer to start the first week of June. Two years, working as the history expert as they redesigned a whole floor. Health insurance. A paycheck. Paid vacation. And a job title, an important step forward and upward in my career. Dad said, "Congratulations! You have finally joined the grownup world."

I won't lie. That's exactly how I felt.

Chapter Twenty-six

One night in early May I stood with Joe on the roof deck of the Navy Yard movie studio, admiring the lit-up Manhattan skyline across the river. It was breathtaking as always.

It was nothing like the last time I was here, for Michael Conti's memorial service. Tonight the music was loud enough to destroy brain cells. It was a party from the metallic balloons to the colored lights turning the dance floor pink, then purple, then orange. Young people were dressed in their sparkly, neon-toned best, trying to behave like very cool adults. There were enough actual adults attending to make sure it didn't slip over into misbehavior.

This all happened because the management offered an apology to the attendees at Conti's service. It took the form of a substantial gift card. Did I jump on that? Of course. My sixteen-year-old was all smiles tonight at her birthday party.

The DJ's patter got everyone up and dancing. I noticed that the boys were finally catching up with the girls in height but the girls were still far ahead on the style meter. A few of them were already far ahead of anyone I knew. How did they dance in those platform sandals?

There was the usual drama in the ladies room with weeping girls and comforting friends. There was the usual slow dancing in the dark corners. There were some balloon stomping contests, too.

Any lingering evil from Michael Conti's life and death was blown right out the floor-to-ceiling windows.

Of course the most special guest was Jared, the boyfriend from Riverdale. I watched Chris dance with him, and suddenly wondered how deep this puppy love went. I had tolerated it with well-concealed amusement, and so had his parents. Now, tonight, whenever the music went all soft and yearning, Chris and Jared were very entwined. Was this something to worry about? What did I need to say to her? He was a nice boy, truly. But still a boy, as Chris was still a girl.

There would be other nights to worry about Chris. For now, Joe had whisked me on to the quiet roof, keeping me warm in the river breeze. We were together and we were happy. I was slowly getting reacquainted with that emotion.

I just enjoyed his arms around me, and looking over the party scene.

Darcy and her husband were dancing and sizing up the location for some future wedding. Leary, his presence a surprise, was deep in conversation with Lisa. I'd done a good day's work when I brought her to meet him. She thought he was a hoot and he was happy to show off his journalistic wisdom.

I thought briefly of Mrs. Pastore. She was touched by her invitation, and knit Chris a scarf, but she politely declined. Sal had died that spring, and she was not ready for a party. Her heartfelt mourning was the equator to the North Pole of Michael Conti's ungrieving women.

Of course my dad was there. I had told him sternly that he was not to embarrass Chris by dancing, so he settled for tending bar. The kids actually seemed to enjoy his elaborate no-alcohol concoctions and corny jokes. And Chris pulled him out on the floor for a birthday dance after all.

I would be graduating next week. Joe had bought me the whole elaborate regalia as a graduation gift. Dignified navy and gold. Velvet bands on the sleeves of the robe. Elaborate hood. I hadn't yet figured out how to wear it. I felt ridiculous.

I felt proud.

A week after that, the new job would start. I was still deeply intimidated by this leap to the big-time, but I had a bound copy of my dissertation on my desk, reminding me every day that I was prepared.

Something else had happened, too. In the aftermath of Michael Conti's murder, I had a chance to write a small article about the Navy Yard for a small local paper. I dashed it off and forgot about it.

Two months later, an astonishing message from a book editor popped up in my mail. He had read the article. Would I be interested in discussing a book?

I read the message twice, and then read it again. It didn't make sense. I explained I would eventually try to turn the dissertation into a scholarly book but not right away.

He wrote, "Call me."

Brooklyn is a red-hot topic, he said. Neighborhood change is hot. Everyone is talking about it. Not your dissertation. A general audience book. You have a relatable writing style.

I had no idea what that meant, but we met and he convinced me to write a few sample chapters. All you have to do is be yourself, he said. And get it done pronto. The moment for this is right now. Yesterday.

It would be a new set of pressures, but I agreed that I'd give it a shot. That famous adopted New Yorker, Yogi Berra, once said, "When you come to a fork in the road, take it." And that's just what I was trying to do.

I looked out at the lights blazing away against the night sky. I looked at Joe. I thought about all that would be waiting for me tomorrow. Tonight? I drank up the last of my wine and led Joe onto the dance floor.

Afterword

Since all my books combine history with fiction, I like to include an explanation of which is which.

Brooklyn Wars is easy. All the characters and the family history are entirely fictional, but Philomena's diary was partly inspired by real accounts.

Everything about the Brooklyn Navy Yard history is as factual as I could make it. I had the great luck to find a doctoral dissertation on the closing of the Yard, a terrific source for the politics and conflicts of the time.

The property that used to be the Navy Yard is changing so rapidly, like much of Brooklyn, that the description of it "now" is already somewhat outdated. I've done my best to capture some of the issues and atmosphere, compressed for storytelling purposes. There is a real movie studio there. I haven't named it, because I described it for story purposes rather than for accuracy.

The building at the gates in the first chapter is real (Building 92), has terrific exhibits, and is the meeting place for tours of the Yard. I recommend a visit and a tour.

Some of the books I found most helpful were Lorraine Diehl's *Over Here!*, Kenneth Jackson's *WWII & NYC*, Thomas F. Berner's *The Brooklyn Navy Yard* (Images of America series) and the chapter "Torch Songs" in *Brooklyn: A State of Mind*, edited by Michael W. Robbins. John Bartlestone's beautiful photographs in his book, *The Brooklyn Navy Yard*, were inspiring.

To see more Poisoned Pen Press titles: